MW01616167

DRAVEN (SPECIAL FORCES: OPERATON ALPHA)

NEMESIS INC: BRAVO TEAM

BOOK THREE

BELLA STONE

ANNABELLA STONE

Cover Design: Golden Czermak
Editing: Crowden Editing
Proofreading: Julie Deaton

Dear Readers,

Welcome to the Special Forces: Operation Alpha Fan-Fiction world!

If you are new to this amazing world, in a nutshell the author wrote a story using one or more of my characters in it. Sometimes that character has a major role in the story, and other times they are only mentioned briefly. This is perfectly legal and allowable because they are going through Aces Press to publish the story.

This book is entirely the work of the author who wrote it. While I might have assisted with brainstorming and other ideas about which of my characters to use, I didn't have any part in the process or writing or editing the story.

I'm proud and excited that so many authors loved my characters enough that they wanted to write them into their own story. Thank you for supporting them, and me!

READ ON!
Xoxo
Susan Stoker

ACKNOWLEDGMENTS

Thank you to my Sailor for always having my back. You have owned my heart for almost three decades, and you will always be my hero—even when you make me insane, and I find pens and other crap from your pockets in the dryer. You and our amazing kiddos, Potterhead and Pottermonkey— you make this crazy life worth it.

Thank you, the family of my heart, who not only claimed me as theirs, (in public I might add…) who read this story as it was written, answering all my military questions, and helping ensure my information is as factual as possible. Any mistakes I have made are mine. Thank you for the middle of the night conversations and virtual smacks upside the head that were needed to keep me on track.

Thank you to my Operators. All y'all put up with my crazy, without a second thought. You laugh at my silly memes, and you love the stories and characters in my head as much as I do. I am forever grateful to have y'all in my life. #Lovelikeanoperator

I'd also like to take this opportunity to thank the god who discovered that Coffee is an amazing way keeping my eyelids propped open when the characters in my head are yelling out their stories at 3 AM… Without the aid of the coffee gods, these stories would never be written.

#Neverforgotten

For the 31 heroes of Extortion 17.

Brothers don't always have the same mother.
Until we meet again to feast in the halls of Valhalla.

Special Warfare Operator
Petty Officer 1st Class (SEAL)
Aaron C. Vaughn

A NOTE FROM THE AUTHOR

I have been a Susan Stoker fan since I first read *Beyond Reality* when it first came out. When *Protecting Caroline* hit my kindle, I became a huge fan, and I landed firmly on the Stalker Posse. It's an honor to be allowed to borrow The SEALs of Protection Heroes and to write them into my world. Susan, thank so you very much for allowing me to play in your sandbox. Being allowed to borrow your characters is a dream come true. I can never thank you enough for the opportunity you so graciously gave me. I really hope I did Wolf, Caroline, and the rest of the SEALs of Protection family, the justice they deserve.

Stalkers and Operators, magic happens when you trust your gut and follow your dreams.

#LoveLikeAnOperator
XO
Bella

CHAPTER ONE

Nemesis Inc. Headquarters, Montana

"Fucking torture devices."

Draven pulled at the bow tie and tugged it free of his neck. He'd never understand why weddings required bow ties and monkey suits.

He flopped into one of the chairs surrounding the firepit. Kentucky Smith and Becky Jones were married. The speeches were done. The food eaten. The first dance done. Momma Smith had cried, smiled, and insisted Kentucky's father would have been so proud of him and delighted to have Becky in the family.

Who the hell knew Tex Keegan would scrub up so well? Although, if Draven was to hazard a guess, the bridesmaids— aka Caroline Steel and her posse from California—had a little something to do with that. He snorted a laugh when he remembered how tiny Willow Ford had squared up to Kentucky and warned him he better not make Becky cry, or she'd be whipping out some of her daddy's old tricks and making his life hell for at least a decade.

Nope, weddings and shit weren't for him. Draven was happy for his friends. But that happily-ever-after shit wasn't in his wheelhouse.

As if fate had been waiting for him to toss her a challenge, his phone buzzed and beeped in his ass pocket.

This better not be someone wanting me to do anything.

Draven had exactly zero plans for the next month but to sleep, eat, maybe drink some beers, before repeating everything all over again. He pulled out the phone and scowled at it. The notification had already disappeared from the screen. Of course, it had; why wouldn't it disappear, forcing him to remember his password?

He was down to last chance saloon on the password front when he finally got it right and his phone unlocked.

IF: 4°30'17.99"S - 21°42'52.89"E

Draven stared at the coordinates for a heartbeat until his brain figured out what they were and who had sent them.

"Shit."

DK: On my way.

If there was ever going to be a person besides the ones on this ranch tonight for whom he'd come on the run with no questions asked, it was this woman. His childhood friend.

"What kind of shit have you gotten yourself into now, brat?"

Draven drained the glass of brandy and turned in time to see Kentucky kissing his bride as he carried her over the threshold of their newly built cabin.

"Have the best life," Draven whispered softly. "You both earned it."

He waited until the door had closed behind them before he went looking for Trev. If he put those coordinates into Google Maps, he'd probably end up in the fucking Congo or somewhere, and that wouldn't help the little troublemaker who loved to make him batshit.

He made his way through everyone, sidestepping to avoid stepping on Mozart's woman's toes as he made his way to where Trev was propping up the bar with a dark scowl on his face. Draven hadn't even known Mozart had a woman, but Summer Pack was one hell of a strong lady. That she'd been through a similar situation to Becky and Willow made her an ideal match for Sam Reed.

He tapped Trev on the shoulder. "What's wrong, bro? This is a happy day. What have you got to look like you want to punch someone for?"

"I think I have hives." Trev tipped his beer bottle toward the dance floor and shuddered. "Kentucky's momma made me dance."

"What's wrong with that?"

"I don't dance."

Draven wasn't above needling him a little bit. "Apparently, Ma Smith thinks you do." When Trev's face darkened, he remembered he needed him on his side. "Wanna get out of here and classify it as work?"

"Hell yes." Trev placed his beer bottle on the bar. "What did you do?"

"Nope." He shook his head. "It's not me this time. It's a friend of mine. She sent me coordinates, and I need to be sure I head in the right direction."

"She?"

Draven could hear the curiosity in Trev's voice, but figured he didn't need to tell him everything. Especially the bits which were none of his business.

"My little sister's friend from when we were kids."

"Bro." Trev walked beside him as they made it to the door which led to the main offices. He punched in the code to open it for them. "Have you not watched the Hallmark movies? Sister's best friend is in trouble and you run in to save the day. Do I say congratulations now, or should I wait until you figure it out?"

"Are you drunk?" Trev better not be so drunk he couldn't figure out how to switch on his computers. "I'm just going to save her butt and drop her home. It's not anything weird or wonderful."

"If you say so…"

"She is a child, Trev. A kid! What the hell do you think I am?"

"How old is your 'little' sister, bro?" Trev pulled back his chair, sat in it, and scooted forward until he was in front of his keyboard.

"What's that got to do with anything?"

"You said the person who sent you the message is a child. Is your sister also a child?"

Oh, he could just go fuck himself sideways with a dry cactus, preferably in the ass. "Man, you aren't even barking in the same forest, never mind at the same fucking tree." He pulled out his phone and handed it to him. "It's the last message."

Trev sighed and unlocked his computer. "So you haven't been bitten by the love bug then?"

"Hell no. I just need to go grab India and make sure my sister isn't right there beside her causing chaos or my mom's going to lose her shit. Where am I going?"

"Um. Gimme a sec." Trev tapped the coordinates into his program and they both watched as it zoomed in on a location. "You, bro, are heading to the DRC."

4

CHAPTER TWO

India Fox stared at the darkened screen, waiting for a response to her text message. There were very few people she would call when shit hit the fan... Draven Kilkenny was one of them.

Her daddy was getting an earful when she got home, and she didn't care if her father thought she was being rude. It wasn't as if she was going to yell at him in the office... oh no, she would save that for the next time he summoned her to dinner at the main house.

It will be an easy in and out. Pick up the intel packet and come straight home.

She could hear her father's voice in her head and snorted silently. She'd been a field agent at the Central Intelligence Agency for long enough to know *easy* was rarely part of the job, no matter what the deputy director, aka her father, promised her.

The last time he promised you easy, you got shot.

She didn't need to remind herself of that either; she had the scars to prove it. And she especially didn't need to remember it right now when she was trying to avoid bumping into one of the Lord's Resistance Army, who were crawling all over this freaking little piece of hell tonight. Even on the lowest setting, the back light on her satellite phone lit up the cave she'd stumbled across and was using as a hiding spot. She immediately cupped her hand around it and read the message.

DK: On my way.

Thank you, sweet suffering baby Jesus on a bicycle.

If there was anyone she wanted to come pull her out of here, it was her best friend Lizz's big brother. The former SEAL now worked with Nemesis Inc. Black Ops contractors with bases in multiple countries across the globe. It was probably too much to hope for that he was in Djibouti or at least somewhere in Africa and could get here in hours, but she'd take the help no matter how long it took for him to get here.

The sound of yelling from the jungle outside sent her into the deepest recesses of the cave. Bats, rats, snakes, or any other creature didn't matter at this point. She had to remain hidden.

Stay alive until Draven gets here. That was all she had to do. She hoped that would be as easy as it sounded. But the way her luck was running... things weren't likely to pan out that way. She didn't dare turn on a light, but still had to figure out a way to hide the dispatch papers she'd picked up. She steeled herself to stand up and run her hands along the walls of the cave.

Yes, you will do.

Her fingers traced the small opening. Hopefully it wasn't one which gushed water when the rains fell and was a fissure which had developed for some other reason. Either way, she figured it was big enough to hold the envelope she carried in her backpack. She shrugged off the bag and placed it carefully on the ground.

More yelling and the sound of boots hitting the ground told her the LRA had discovered the drop-down she'd fallen over earlier, before her hand had come through the branches and foliage which covered the cave entrance.

Stupid. Silly girl, you should have kept running.

Now you're going to get caught and then you're screwed.

She patted the backpack, using her hands to make sure her Velcro patch, declaring her a member of the press, was still in place, and then moved to the zipper. If she was hoping for it to open quietly, she wasn't rewarded, as it sounded so freaking loud in the cave. India held her breath and hoped they didn't hear it. But of course, she heard one of them asking for silence. She paused with her hand on the half-open zipper. Maybe if she didn't move, they wouldn't hear her.

When a couple of minutes had passed, she figured she was safe to pull the envelope out of the bag and hide it.

This is worse than trying to keep my hand steady for that stupid buzzing game.

The mind does funny things when you are in dangerous situations. Throwing India back to a childhood memory of weekends at her friend's house trying to move a loop along a twisty wire was apparently one of them. She understood the logic behind it, though waiting for the freaking buzzer to make you jump was similar to how she felt right now.

She got the papers out, and somehow finding the fissure on the wall was more difficult this time around. But she did it, even if she had to bite down so hard on the inside of her cheek she tasted blood to prevent herself from screaming when she brushed a cobweb, and again when something ran over her hand. Those documents were now safe... she hoped.

* * *

INDIA COCKED her head to one side, listening, hoping the people outside had moved on, but was disappointed when she could still hear the snoring from whichever one really should see an ear, nose, and throat specialist. From the way his breathing paused and then restarted on a snore loud enough to wake the dead, he had sleep apnea or something.

She turned away from the direction of the entrance and turned the watch she wore inside out to prevent the luminous face from giving any hint of her presence. Damn, she was almost up to twenty-four hours. She needed to check in. But she didn't dare turn on her phone. It would beep or vibrate, and with the lack of animal sounds, it would echo out of the cave. Then she was screwed. She couldn't even switch on a flashlight to see if there was any water source in here.

Don't think of water.

Damn it, why did you think of water?

She silently berated herself for it. Because now the thirst she'd been working so hard to ignore was all she could think about. She stuck her hand into her pocket for the Tic Tacs she kept there. Draven had been the one to tell her to take them out of the box and stash them in a cloth handkerchief, as it would make less noise should she need to keep silent. She felt through the folded material and popped one into her mouth. Sucking on it would hopefully produce some saliva and help with her thirst.

I'm going to kiss Draven on the lips the second he arrives for teaching me this one, and I don't even care that he thinks I have cooties or something.

She grinned. He'd wipe his mouth off and grumble at her that she was infecting him with germ-itis just like he used to when they were teenagers.

Ha, you had such a crush on him. Germs were the last thing you thought he had.

8

She understood now why he'd pushed her away back then. The six-year age gap between them would have landed him in jail if he'd taken her up on her brazen hussylike offer on her sixteenth birthday. She'd been wrong to refuse to speak to him for so long afterward.

Amazing how being stuck in a cave in a jungle with terrorists sleeping outside the door makes you forget all about your embarrassment of his rejection, isn't it?

Shut up.

And now you are talking to yourself.

No, I'm not.

Yes, you are.

Oh, crap, she was.

In her defense, it was that or lose her mind. This was probably one of the many stages of exhaustion and dehydration setting in. But she couldn't remember which, and she figured it didn't really matter. As long as she kept the conversations confined to silent ones in her head... then nobody could hear and nobody had to know.

She leaned her head back against the rocks and closed her eyes. She needed another cat nap. Ten minutes, that was all she could allow herself. Anything longer, and she'd drop into a deep sleep. Then it would take a tornado warning going off to wake her. That wouldn't be a good thing. Not today or tonight, whatever it was now.

He'll come. He said he was coming. Now I just have to wait.

She thought it was a damn shame she'd never really learned the art of patience. But she'd better figure it out fast... because getting caught meant certain death.

CHAPTER THREE

"Bro, who the hell is IK?" Trev tapped on the screen of Draven's phone. He searched his desk for a pen, then changed his mind and connected the phone to his computer with a cable. "And what the fuck is she doing in the Democratic Republic of the Congo?"

"IK is India Fox." Now that he knew where he had to go, there was no point in trying to hide any of the information from Trev. The nosey fucker would probably just tap into his phone and find it anyway. "And I told you, she's my sister's friend from when we were kids."

"India Fox?" Trev's hands stilled. "You mean the deputy director of the CIA's daughter? That India Fox?"

"Yeah. Why do you know her?" If he had to punch Trev for sleeping with her, then Nemesis better get ready to pay out the big bucks for a new fucking war room.

"We pulled her out of Eastern Europe a while back," Trev said. "On the mission where Dalton saw Lina again for the first time."

Reality slammed into him. India wasn't just his little sister's friend. There was only one reason she could have been in Eastern Europe and only one which made perfect sense for why she was in the Congo. "She's CIA?"

He already knew the answer before Trev answered. "I can neither confirm nor deny…"

"Cut the crap and give me a straight answer."

"Bro, you know the rules."

He did fucking know the rules. The only intel they received was on a need-to-know basis. He didn't give a rat's ass if he wasn't supposed to know. She'd called him for help… ergo, he needed to know.

"Give me that." He snatched his phone off the desk.

"Hey…"

"Shut it." His finger hovered over the text message, and he tapped it to pull up her number, but changed his mind at the last second. He went to his dial pad and tapped out a number from memory and put it to his ear. On ring number three the call was answered. He heaved a sigh of relief when he recognized the voice on the other end.

"Fox residence, how may I help you?"

"Hi, Mrs. Mac. It's Draven Kilkenny, do you remember me?"

"Why yes, I do. How can I help you, Draven? Your sister isn't here if you are looking for her."

He figured this time Mrs. Mac wasn't covering for India and Lizz and attempted to keep the urgency out of his voice. "They aren't the ones I'm looking for this time, Mrs. Mac. Is the DD around, and if so, will he take a call from me?"

"Why, he's been in his office since last night. Stomping and hollering like a bull," Mrs. Mac said. "Give me a moment and I'll put your call through to him."

"Thanks, and, Mrs. Mac?"

"Yes?"

"It's good to hear your voice again."

"And it's good to hear yours, too. Just a moment, Draven, and the DD will be right with you."

When the housekeeper called her boss the DD, that was how you knew you were accepted in India's house. "Thanks."

"You have the deputy director of the CIA's home number and you can dial it from memory, and you didn't think to tell me?" Trev muttered.

The door of the war room pushed open, revealing Dalton with his sleeping son strapped to his chest. "Who does?"

"Me," Draven replied just as the deputy director picked up the phone in his office.

"What can I do for you, Draven?"

"Hi, Sir." Draven wasn't in the mood to play games and figured ripping off the Band-Aid was probably the quickest way to get answers. "Want to tell me why India is in the DRC and what the hell went wrong over there?"

"You know about that, huh?"

"I know she's in the Congo when she's meant to be working at a store in Riverton with my sister." Draven's words were bordering on rude, but he was past caring. "Why the hell didn't I know you had dragged her into the Farm after you? Have you lost your damn mind… Sir?" Given the way Nemesis was scowling at him, he figured he better tag on the 'Sir' at the end.

"If you wake…" Dalton didn't get to finish the sentence as his son started crying before he had a chance to. Dalton pointed a finger at Draven. "Asshole. I just got him to sleep."

He made an apologetic face toward Dalton. He hadn't planned on waking the baby, and mouthed *sorry,* then went back to the phone.

"Sir, I need you to explain what the hell is going on and I need you to do it before my ass is on a plane to go get her."

He could picture India's father pacing around his dark-paneled office. While most people would be concerned about pissing the deputy director of the CIA off, Draven wasn't. He'd known the man since he was ten and had to go haul his sister out of the house and down the street for dinner.

"I don't know what to tell you," the deputy director said. The sound of a chair creaking filtered through the phone, letting Draven know he'd probably sat down. "She went to pick up some documents. She hasn't come back."

"How long?" he demanded.

"Two weeks."

"That's not what I mean, and you know it. How long has she been at the Farm?"

"Since high school."

"You, Sir, are an idiot and an asshole. Why the hell would you want that life for your child? Your. Only. Child?"

"That doesn't matter now," the deputy director replied. "What's done is done."

He's such a fucking dick!

"Yes, Sir, it does matter." He would not let India's father get away with being an idiot, not when it might cost them all more than they bargained for, especially India.

"He sent us in to pull her out of a situation before." Nemesis swayed side to side, rocking the baby in his arms. "Why the hell didn't he call us in now?"

Draven started to ask, but the deputy director must have been able to hear what his boss said, because he spoke before Draven could. Halfway through what he was saying, Draven hit speaker as he figured it was better the other two men in the war room heard what he had to say.

"Because this time she's in the DRC on a non-sanctioned mission."

"And her team?"

"I—I don't…"

"The bodies of three Americans were found in Kinshasa." Trev's fingers flew over the keyboards. "I'm just checking…"

He glanced at the phone in Draven's hand and snapped his mouth shut. Draven understood that to mean Trev was going to search any database the deaths may be logged in to see if he could find any identities for the men. "I'm assuming there are no visas and no entry logs for any of them crossing the border into the DRC?"

"No, I would suppose not," the deputy director confirmed.

"Then these probably aren't their real names." Trev pulled photos of three men up on his screen, each of them was clearly deceased at the time the pictures were taken. "I'll send them to your email."

"Okay." The deputy director rattled off a proton email, which they all knew was a throwaway account.

"DD?" An idea teased at the edge of Draven's mind, and he was probably an idiot for asking, but now that it had occurred to him, he needed to know the answer.

"Yes, son?"

"You know how my dad was your best friend. Is this a similar situation?"

The deputy director's inhale was audible, and it took him a couple of heartbeats to reply. "Yes, I suppose you could call it similar. Your father is a good man. You should call him more often."

"Okay, I'll call my dad…"

When he saw the other two look all kinds of confused, he cut off anything they may have said with a hand signal for silence. "I'll let you know what I find out. When India gets back, will you call me and let me know she's okay?"

"Talk to you soon, son. Don't be a stranger."

"Good to talk to you, too." It was way obvious, at least to him, that the whole direction of the conversation about his dad had changed the tone and outcome of the phone call. But he didn't have time to worry about that shit now. India needed his help, and her father wasn't going to give him anything. He hit end on the call.

"Did you send that email?" He crossed the room to see the computer screen.

"No." Trev turned the screen so Draven could see it better. "I was just about to hit send when you went all cryptic and shit. So…"

"What's going on, Kilkenny?" Dalton asked softly. "And be quiet as he's asleep again."

"The deputy director is compromised somehow. First, there is zero chance he'd call my father a good man, considering he swindled the DD out of a fortune a while back." The more he thought about it, the more he knew it to be true. "Second, I don't think he's enough of an asshole to leave India out in the cold with no backup." He glanced at Dalton. "I'm either going to need a team or some backup."

"Charlie Team is in Afghanistan pulling out some tourists who got caught up in that earthquake last week," Dalton said. "Trev, book him a flight to somewhere that gets him close to Istanbul. That's the drop-off point for the tourists."

"Roger." Trev already had the airline website open. "Do you still want me to send him images?"

"Yeah, find some random John Does and send him those," Dalton ordered. "They can't tell from photos where they were taken, right?"

"I'll scrape the metadata and make sure they aren't available to the public before I reset the data as DRC."

"Trev… that's tech speak; plain English will do."

"Yes, Boss, I can give him images which look like they came from there."

"Good." Dalton turned toward the door. "I'm going to put my boy down to sleep and get back to the wedding. I want to dance with my wife at least once more before we're done for the night. Call if you need me." He glanced at Draven. "Is Charlie enough, or do you want me to round you up a team?"

"They are over there," Draven said. "There's no point in pulling all the guys outta here. It's been a shit few months. Let them have the down time."

"Good luck with telling Caleb that," Dalton snorted softly. "If he wants to chase your ass all the way to the Congo, well, I'm not going to stop him."

"You mean you don't want him here, bored out of his brain for the next month, causing trouble?"

"That, too." Dalton shut the door behind him.

"You know, weird as it is to see him with a baby on his hip," Trev whispered in case their boss overheard, "it also suits him more than it should."

"Right? I've been trying to picture it, but now I've see it, anything I had in my head doesn't even come close."

"Truth." Trev pointed to the screen, bringing them back on task. "I have a flight out of Billings which can connect you to DC and from there on to Istanbul. Will that work?"

He fished in his back pocket for his wallet and pulled out his credit card. "Here, put it on this one."

"No need, bro." Trev was already filling in details. "We owe you personal flights, so I'll book it for Nemesis Inc. If the boss or the accountants disagree, we can bill you for it later."

He rarely used the personal flights perk which came with being employed by Dalton. Very few of them did, preferring to gift them to family members who needed them more. "That works. Thanks, bro."

"Go get your shit. You need to be at the airport in two hours if you want to make that flight," Trev said. "I'll figure out what I can from here and send updates to Kristof. He'll have it by the time you have boots on the ground in Istanbul."

"Appreciate it." It wouldn't take him long to gather his

stuff. His go bag was already in the cage below here, and he had a couple of changes of clothes stashed in there, which would do. "Hey, will you feed my cat?"

"Sure, me and Check are buddies." Trev waved over his shoulder. "He likes me because I bring the good food and not just kibble."

"Do not steal my cat," Draven warned as he headed to the door. "You only get to borrow him when I'm working, and don't you forget it."

Trev's laughter followed him down the corridor, but he knew the asshole was just messing with him. *I'll deal with him when I get back if he isn't.* He scanned his hand and waited for the elevator to arrive.

Game time.

Unpack my weapons.

Check my other gear.

Grab my tickets.

Get my ass to the DRC.

Draven made a mental list and by the time he stepped into the elevator, he was already in mission mode. Now he just had to hope he found India before whoever was hunting her got to her.

* * *

"Hey, man, good to have you here."

Draven took the hand Kristof Hunter offered, then did the same with Braddock Keane. "I appreciate the assistance on this one."

"No worries." Kristof led the way into the safe house. "I dropped our guests off this morning, or I'd have waited to give you a lift here. But sitting around in an airport isn't my idea of fun."

"Same." He dropped his go bag where a bunch of others

lay on the floor. "Do we have a plan for getting into the DRC?"

"Yup." Braddock tapped the keyboard on a hardbacked laptop. "We have a supply flight into Somalia. From there, we're trucking it across a nonexistent border. That work?"

"Yeah." It definitely did work. The fewer people who knew they were on the ground, the better. "And getting out?"

"It's not difficult to find a team floating around in that area." Kristof handed him a mug. "We'll hitch a ride once we know which way the wind blows."

Jeez, he could not work like that all the time. Which was why he was Bravo Team and not Charlie Team. Bravo specialized in working the black jobs where the government required plausible deniability. Charlie team worked on rescuing American citizens who'd purchased Nemesis travel insurance. If there was a natural disaster—earthquakes, hurricanes, tsunamis, etc. —an act of terror, or even if war broke out while an insured family was on vacation, then Charlie Team would ensure their clients were returned home safely. It was rare the insurance was offered to non-Americans; Draven was only aware of two instances. One, a prince of Jordan, and another a former Mossad agent who had helped Alpha team out of a sticky spot a few years back. Dalton had issued the phone number on the spot. Draven knew both of those offers would be upheld should the need arise.

"Are there weapons for me? Because I feel naked without them."

"Yeah." Kristof led him deeper into the house and into a bedroom. In the closet on the far wall was a massive safe. "We do our best to hide them, as this isn't the safest part of the world. But take your pick." He stepped out of the way, revealing a full set of the typical weaponry they used. From handguns to M-16s, to RPG launchers, flash-bangs, and grenades. If he needed it, it was here.

"Awesome."

"Vests and armor are in the other room." Kristof locked the safe again once he'd gathered what he needed. "Maybe double up on plates considering where we're going."

"Yeah, good idea." He glanced over his shoulder. "Mind if I bring one for India?"

"Hell no, take what you need. I can order more from HQ if I need them. The smaller sizes are in the back. We carry them for clients and shit."

"Appreciate it."

"She's important, huh?"

"I've known her since she was a kid. She's my sister Lizz's best friend."

"And that's all?"

He figured there was no reason not to tell Kristof. "And her father is the deputy director of the CIA."

"Whoa, you run in circles which are too high for my blood. I'm just a good ole farm boy whose only connection is the old dudes running moonshine."

"When do we leave?" It grated on him to not know the details as of yet. But this wasn't his team. He wouldn't think twice about giving Kentucky shit about being close-mouthed... Kristof, not so much.

"Depends on if you need to sleep off the jet lag..."

"Hell no. I'm ready to roll when you guys are. I slept on the plane." He figured Kristof would know all the sleeping he'd done on the trans-Atlantic flight had been cat naps at best. But it didn't matter. Sleep was the last of his worries. The longer it took for him to get to India, the bigger the chance that she wasn't going to be where her coordinates said she was. "A lot can go wrong in that part of the world, and from what I know, she's running solo."

"That's not good," Kristof agreed. "The DRC is no place for any American, never mind a woman."

"Agreed. That's why I'm on the way. I'm going to pull her pretty butt out of there and send her home where it's safe."

"You say that like you think she's gonna stay there." Kristof locked up the safe again. "Good luck with that, bro."

Draven winced internally because he had a gut feeling that Kristof was correct. There wasn't a chance in hell India Fox was going to do a damn thing she was told.

CHAPTER FOUR

India jerked as a noise from outside the cave alerted her to a problem. She cocked her head to one side and listened carefully. There it was again, scuffling and the sound of boots scraping off rock.

Shit!

Please don't come in here.

She didn't know if this cave was known to the locals, but she hoped it wasn't. Not that all of the men in the LRA were always locals. The Christian extremist organization was known to have reach across northern Uganda, South Sudan, the Central African Republic, along with here in the Democratic Republic of the Congo.

She lowered herself silently into a ball in the darkest corner, curling over herself. If she was small enough, maybe they wouldn't notice her. If Draven could hurry his butt up and get here any time right about now, that would be fricking wonderful.

What's that saying about wishes and horses?

That's you today, chick, and you are going to be in a whole lot of trouble in about two minutes flat.

Trapping herself in an enclosed place like this cave had been the wrong move. She knew that now. She just couldn't do anything about it. She didn't even have a weapon, for heaven's sake. Her handlers had decided the team with her would be armed, but it wasn't realistic for her cover story for her to have a weapon. She'd been ridiculously naive to agree with them during the planning stages of her mission.

I'd like it noted for the record that I no longer agree with me not being armed.

She could hear the footsteps getting closer and closer. Finally resigned to her fate, she patted the cave floor looking for a rock or stone. Anything she could use as a weapon was fair game. With a collection of hand-sized rocks in her grasp, she got silently to her feet. She would not make it easy for them—if they wanted to take her captive, then she was determined to leave a hell of a lot of bruises in her wake as they did so.

She tried to gauge where the people approaching were by the sounds of their footsteps, but everything echoed weirdly in here. Sounds bounced off the rock walls, making it almost impossible to figure out their position.

Just when she thought they would enter the lower portion of the cave where she was hiding, yelling started from outside, followed by bursts of gunfire. She could picture the LRA with their weapons in the air as they fired off rounds. She thought it was a ridiculous waste of ammo to just fire into the sky, but all reports she had read and everything she'd seen over the years said terrorists thought it made them look intimidating.

One man yelled something in a language she'd heard before but couldn't place, his voice so close she almost jumped in spite of her resolve to keep silent. A second voice yelled from farther away, as if he were outside the cave.

"Get down, drop your..." The voice was shut off by the

sound of shots, and immediately followed by what sounded like return gunfire.

She once again made herself as small as possible in her little cubby hole at the back of the cave. She'd just heard someone yelling in English. She was not getting shot… if that was Draven out there on his own, then her odds of getting out of here with the papers she'd been tasked with carrying back to the US had just risen by almost eight percent since last night. If he'd brought a team, then she was close to ninety percent. She'd take those odds.

"She's fucking here somewhere, Charlie One. Keep fucking looking."

There it was—the voice she heard in her dreams when her nightmares threatened to pull her under their cloud of darkness.

"Draven."

She slapped her hands over her mouth, but it was too late. The bad guy in the cave was on her before she had time to regret her life choices.

A hand fisted painfully into the hair at the back of her head and she was dragged to her feet.

"Press. I'm press!" she yelled, knowing if she'd been able to hear Draven, he'd be able to hear her too. "Don't…" She stopped midsentence when the cold steel of what felt like a machete was put to her throat.

"Shut up," the man hissed in heavily broken English. "You will be quiet, or I…" He dug the blade into her skin.

Oh, god. This was how she was going to die. In a hot jungle cave filled with creepy crawlies and a terrorist with no appreciation for human life. She didn't dare struggle as he pulled her out of her hiding spot and pulled her against his chest, then replaced the knife at her throat.

"If they come in here, I will keeeel you."

Yes, this was how she would die for sure. While she'd

never seen Draven in action, at Langley, she'd seen some of the Ground Branch operators, most of whom had been recruited from Special Forces, in action. The silence outside told her what was coming. If they had prevailed in the firefight which had raged, then Draven was coming in through the cave opening as soon as he located it. She refused to close her eyes. If she was going to bleed out right here then she wanted the last view she had to be of Draven Kilkenny's beautiful blue eyes.

How the hell am I so calm?

Why am I not screaming, shaking, or peeing my pants?

"They do not see the cave." The terrorist chortled in her ear. "I will take you with me when they leave."

She could feel the warm trickle of blood down her neck. Despite his bravado, this man was shaking so much he kept nicking her with the blade every time he spoke.

"Do you trust me, Indy?"

Draven's question out of nowhere made both her and the terrorist jump, resulting in yet another cut to her throat. This one deeper than the rest.

"Yes." She wasn't proud of the fact her voice wobbled more than Mrs. Mac's Jello salad. At least her reply had been clear enough that he could understand, she hoped…

CHAPTER FIVE

"She's here somewhere, Charlie One." Draven rolled over another body and snapped a photo. Trev would download the images from the cloud attached to his device, and cross reference them with any known terrorists on most wanted lists across the globe.

If there was a reward for any of them, that money would be funneled into orphanages and schools in the region. Nemesis Inc. was funded by Knight Oil money, along with contracts from the United States Government. It was well known in the community that Nemesis didn't want reward money; their goal was justice.

Draven double-checked the GPS device strapped to his wrist. "We're almost right on top of her, damn it. Where is she?" He refused to consider the fact that right on top of her could also mean she was buried under their feet. He tabbed on the extras on the GPS device to see if any of the teams they'd worked with previously had marked any hiding spots in the area on previous missions. Tabbing through the screens, his heart sank until he got to the last page. It could not be this simple, could it? "I got something."

"Whatcha find?"

"Cave system." He turned his arm to show Kristof. "Marked here by a task force during a mission a couple of years ago. They used a cave in this area for their Mobile TOC."

Braddock grabbed his wrist and tilted the GPS toward himself, then glanced around them. "Damn jungle has taken over since then." He thumbed on his comms. "Charlie Four to TOC, can you get in touch with Castello Moran over at Lynx? We need intel on a cave system they used for their TOC in this location a while back."

"TOC, copy, Charlie Four," Trev replied.

Draven agreed with Braddock, the jungle had claimed back whatever cave system Team Lynx had used previously. "Fan out. Keep searching." She had to be in that cave. It was the only allowable reason for them not to be able to see her, the alternative of her being dead and buried under their feet was never going to be an acceptable option for him. "According to the notes, it's on the left."

"Stay frosty," Kristof warned. "We don't know if she's on her own, or if she's being held captive."

Fear slid down the back of his neck and snaked down his spine. He knew the Charlie Team leader was only saying what made logical sense. But damn, this was not a fate he wanted for Indy. He walked slowly along the embankment, using the muzzle of his weapon to probe at the foliage.

"Charlie, All Stations, TOC," Trev hailed them all. "There's a tree with a broken off limb that looks like the letter L. As the broken branch probably kept growing, it might look different now though."

"An L-shaped branch. I don't see any L-shaped branches, TOC."

"Keep looking," Trev replied. "It has to be there somewhere."

Finally, he glimpsed a change in color from the clay to stone and held up his hand, making a sign for silence. He scanned the trees looking for the branch Trev had mentioned, but couldn't see it. He clicked on his comms once to let Trev know he'd found something, but didn't want to say it out loud yet, and gestured toward the vegetation and mouthed silently to Braddock who stood to his right. "I think I found it."

Braddock nodded, and both crouched lower, hopefully taking their heads and torsos out of the line of fire if someone took a pot shot at them from inside.

Draven dropped his night vision goggles down over his helmet, hopefully with those on he could at least see into the cave a little. He carefully shifted the long vines enough to peer through and into the cave.

Fuck!

Once I've saved her pretty butt, I get to yell at her for five minutes straight... right?

As if the fact he was running around the fucking Congo chasing her ass wasn't indication enough that shit hadn't changed much since they were kids, the machete he could see drawing blood from her neck did. If there was trouble to be found, you could guarantee Indy Fox was stuck right in the middle of it. Locking her up and throwing away the key was looking better and better by the second. Thankfully this time, Lizz wasn't right there beside her. He glanced at the asshole, but he couldn't tell if the dude spoke English or not just by looking at him.

I'm issuing every fucking terrorist with a name tag which says if they speak English or not from here on out.

Bitching, even if it was in his head, kept him from losing his shit, and he needed extra help in that department today. Speaking was risky. Not speaking and having her move while he took the shot, even more so. "Do you trust me, Indy?"

"Yes."

The wobble in her voice straight up pissed him off. Even if she was a brat and she found more trouble than the cartoon cat and mouse, she didn't deserve this. Didn't deserve to be stuck in a damn hole in the ground with a machete to her throat, and death hovering on the horizon.

You should have been quicker. Should have...

He clamped down the internal berating thing he had going on and shut it down hard. Indy didn't have the luxury of him losing his ever-loving mind right now. At least her reply had been clear enough that he could understand it. He leveled his weapon and peered through the sight.

Jesus, there isn't much room for error.

The tango behind Indy wasn't much taller than her. But as long as she didn't move, he could take him. There was one thing guaranteed to happen in the next five seconds or so. The asshole in there had targeted Indy. To Draven that was unforgivable. That bastard holding a fucking machete to her throat better have his affairs in order because from now on, he was going to need someone else to raise his children, if he had any.

"Go right," Draven ordered Indy softly, then inhaled and squeezed the trigger gently as he released the breath. Indy moved on his command and the tango lost the top of his head. Draven was already moving before the retort of his weapon firing had completely sounded. "Cover me." He didn't care who was on his ass, he needed to be sure he hadn't hit her too. Fear raced down his neck, through his chest, and all the way into his soul. "Indy? Did I get you?" A glance at the open staring eyes of the tango told him that asshole was no longer a problem. He crouched next to where she curled on the floor and reached for her.

"Shit. Damn it. Fuck."

Relief slammed into him, if she was swearing up a storm, she was fine. "Come here, brat. Did I hurt you?" He automatically fell into using the nickname he'd given her as a child.

"You deafened me, you asshole."

Thank fuck.

He scooped her off the floor and into his lap. "What the hell kind of mess have you gotten yourself into now?"

"Don't be a dick and just let me hug you," she muttered against his chest. "And you better have wet wipes, because I have his icky blood all over me."

He was so relieved she was okay he wasn't even going to complain about her getting that same blood all over his vest. "Jeez, Indy." He wrapped his arms around her and dropped his chin onto the top of her head. "Don't scare the shit out of me like that again. My heart can't take it."

"I'm sorry," she whispered, her breath hot on his throat. "I didn't know who else to call."

"Your dad? He sent you in here. Why not call him to get you out?" He refused to tell her outright what he thought of her father right now. But the second he delivered Indy safe and sound back home... then the gloves could come off.

"Am I doing the usual with this one?" Braddock asked. "Or does the CIA need him?" He nodded in response, silently telling Braddock to follow the usual protocol for a dead tango. Photos, fingerprints, DNA, the whole freaking shebang.

In his lap, Indy stiffened. "You know?"

Oh, yeah, baby, I fucking know.

"My boss pulled you out of Eastern Europe a while back. Did you really think I wouldn't find out eventually?" There wasn't a chance in hell he was going to tell her that he'd only found out as a result of her text message. He reached into

31

one of the pouches on his belt for an individually wrapped wet wipe and ripped it open with his teeth.

"I can do it." She took the wipe from him and washed her face with it. It took four of them. "Is it in my hair too?"

"Yeah, we'll find you somewhere to clean it off." It wasn't lost on him that she'd completely ignored his probing on why he had to find out from Nemesis that she was not only a CIA agent, but a field agent. "But right now, we need to move in case the gunfire caught someone's attention. We don't want to have to fight our way to the extraction zone."

"Yes, please, let's not do that." She sucked in a noisy breath and he was impressed at how she locked her shit down and got herself back in the game. She scrambled off his lap and he stood too.

He frowned when she took two steps toward the back of the cave. "Where are you going?"

"I have to get my gear," she called over her shoulder. "I stashed it back here. I didn't know they would show up outside. I was just looking for a bolt holt to catch my breath."

"They weren't chasing you?"

"Not unless there are CIA assholes dead out there too, no they weren't. I think."

"Those dudes were killed on the streets of the capital," Draven told her. "At least that's where their bodies showed up."

"I didn't kill them…"

"I know you didn't, brat." Draven clenched his jaw. She couldn't seriously think he'd think she'd have killed them… right? "Unless they gave you reason to do it. Then I could see you taking them down."

"You don't have to kill a man to take him down. A sharp knee to the balls will do it, every single time."

He winced and ignored the snort from behind them. Braddock could wince all he wanted. It didn't change the fact

32

what Indy said was true. A knee to the balls as a simple way to drop a man to the ground… if you could get close enough. Smarter would be putting a bullet through their brain stems. He just wasn't entirely sure which Indy would do if she was pushed far enough. But he didn't get a chance to ask anything further as she disappeared into the shadows at the back of the cave.

CHAPTER SIX

"Can I borrow a light?" Now that the danger had passed, there wasn't enough money on the planet to pay her to hand-feel her way back into the cubby hole she'd been hiding in.

"Still afraid of spiders, huh?"

She nodded. He better not start teasing her about it, or she might lose the tiny fingernail grip she had on her sanity. "Something like that." She gratefully took the penlight he handed her and switched it on. Once she caught an eyeful of all the spiderwebs, she swallowed hard against the lump in her throat.

Shit.

They are all in my hair. I just know it.

But she refused to look like a wimp in front of Draven and resisted the urge to shudder because he'd tease her about it for sure. Indy forced herself to keep moving forward, as if those spider houses didn't exist.

Close your eyes and pretend you are about two hours back in time.

That's not going to work.

She dug deep into the reserves inside her, just as she had

when she was in training at Langley and the instructors gave her a hard time. She would not allow herself to be beaten by a freaking spider. Nope, that was what hours under a hot shower were for. To scrub every inch of her skin until she couldn't feel them crawling all over her anymore.

"What's wrong?"

"I—" Crap, so much for not letting Draven see she was hesitating, "I forgot where I stashed something. Give me a minute." She scanned the wall, looking for the fissure she had stuffed the papers into. "They all look the same."

"What does?"

"The holes in the wall," she explained. "I put the important stuff in one." He huffed in what she was going to assume was annoyance. But he would just have to deal. She was not leaving without those papers. They were the reason she'd ended up in this pickle in the first place.

"Gimme the light." He held out his hand. "And come back here and start at the beginning with your eyes closed. Just like you had the first time you came in here. Maybe it will jog something loose."

She'd been afraid he was going to suggest that. It was what she would have suggested too. But it didn't mean she liked the idea any better. "Okay." She squeezed her eyes shut when he positioned her in front of him, facing into the back of the cave.

"I'll keep the webs off you."

His husky whisper in her ear did what she'd refused to let the spider webs do, and she had a full body shudder wracked through her. "Thanks." She placed her hand on the wall next to her, trying to remember the nuances of the rock wall as she'd felt them before. "It's further down where we were a minute ago."

He stood close enough to her back that he was almost

stepping on her heels as they moved. "Trust the process. Concentrate on the memory of coming in here earlier."

"I was concentrating on not giving my presence away," she whispered back. "I knew there was someone outside, I just didn't know who and I didn't want to risk that it was someone who knew who I was."

"Letting people know you work for a three-letter agency is never advisable," he agreed. "How long were you in here?"

"About two days, I think. Maybe it was three." She ran her fingers along the cool rocks, wincing every time she skimmed over an opening. Now she knew for sure the spiders were here, she couldn't get them out of her mind. The knowledge screwed with her ability to remember. "I don't know. I just don't know…"

"Shh," he cut her off. "You can do this."

She wasn't as confident about that as he was. But having him here helped push the urge to bat at everything and anything which touched off her. She inhaled and blew out a long slow breath, striving for a calm she didn't feel.

Those papers are in here. They couldn't have walked out of here as you were right in the way.

She jumped when Draven wrapped one arm around her waist and pressed against her diaphragm, his fingers tapping out a slow, steady beat. "Wha—?"

"Breathe with me.

"Stay calm.

"You can do this."

His order cut off her protest. At this point she had nothing left to lose. She already trusted him. They both knew it. She gave in and followed the slow beat of his fingers on her stomach, breathing in time with them until her panic receded enough that she could try to focus. "Okay, I'm ready to try again."

"Then, let's do it, brat. I'll stay right here with you every step of the way."

And you expect me to concentrate with you all pressed up against me like THAT?

Is he insane?

Yes. Yes, he is. Remember Lizz has been telling you that for years.

"Ready?"

"Yeah." She ignored his chuckle in her ear. Maybe she'd even remember to kick him in the shins or the balls for laughing at her later. Or maybe she wouldn't because he'd come running to save her the minute she'd asked him to. She took one step and then another, and just like he'd promised, he kept one hand wrapped around her waist as he moved in time with her. Her fingers ran over the stone, brushing over lumps and bumps. She kept probing just as she had the first time she'd come in here. When the tips of her fingers dipped into an opening big enough to fit her hand in, she paused. "I think I found it."

"Let's see." He removed his hand and flipped on the light again. Both of them blinked against the brightness. He ran the beam down over the opening. "That looks like it would fit something as long as it wasn't bulky."

"It's papers," she admitted.

"Then let's see." He nudged her to one side and peered into the opening. "I don't think my hand is gonna fit in there."

"It was tight for me and I don't have your muscles." She slipped under his arm and peered into the opening and reared back as soon as she saw what was in there with her papers. "Uh, Draven, that's a snake…"

"Yeah, I saw that." He thumbed on his comms. "Bravo Three to TOC."

She wouldn't be able to hear the other side of the conversation, but it sucked not to have both sides of it.

"TOC, if I send you a picture of a snake, can you tell me if it's venomous or not?

"Yeah. It's gonna take me a hot minute, I need to take off the wrist-held." As he spoke, he pulled on the tabs of the device she knew was used for everything from intel to GPS to taking photos. "Yeah, I got her. She's good."

She wondered if the TOC he was talking to was the same person who'd been on the other end of the comms unit when she'd been rescued in Eastern Europe.

He's going to think I can't do anything but land myself in trouble and need rescuing like some damsel in distress. Dang it.

Draven angled the rectangular device into the opening of the crevice and pressed a button. "Did you get that, TOC?

"Shit. Hell no, I'm not getting closer. That fucker is hissing at me."

"What's happening?"

"The photo isn't clear enough as my wrist-held doesn't have a flash."

"Will a phone work?" She remembered she'd switched it off and stuffed it into the bottom of her rucksack. "I have one."

"Yes, please."

She checked over the bag before grabbing it and digging inside to search for the phone. Where there was one snake there were often more, and she didn't want to add losing a limb or her life because she wasn't careful enough. "Just give me a second to turn it on."

"No worries," he replied to her. "TOC, how do you want me to send the number to you? Does email work?

"Okay."

She breathed a sigh of relief when the phone turned on

then glared at the screen. "It's only got twelve percent battery, once it hits ten the flash won't work." She placed the phone in his hand. "It's open on camera, just point and hit the button."

He nodded in response and pointed the phone at the snake, taking a shot. "I need you to email that to this address if you can do it."

"Okay, let me try. It allowed a text to get out, so email might too." She opened the app for her throwaway personal account and attached the image to it, filled in the address he rattled off to her, and hit send. She watched the circle in the center of the screen and then the phone died.

"It died."

"Fuck." Draven pinched the fingers of one hand into his eyes as if his head was going to explode. "Repeat that?"

"It die—"

"Not you."

He could growl at her any day of the week he wanted to, as long as he wasn't mad at her. The growl... that was sexy... the mad... not so much. "Sorry."

"What's your login and password?" he asked her. "TOC is gonna log in from his side and see if the message is in your drafts folder."

Shit.

She chewed on the corner of her lip. Now what was she meant to do? She didn't give logins and or passwords to anyone. Not even a tactical operations center.

"Now, Indy! Unless you want to stick your hand in there with the fucking snake before we know if it can kill you or not."

It's a throwaway, never use it for anything again.

She huffed in annoyance but gave him the information he wanted, and he passed it on to his tactical operations center. She kept one eye on the opening and one eye on Draven. It would be just her luck that the snake would decide it no longer liked hiding in there and slithered out on top of them.

"Okay," Draven replied to whatever TOC said to him then turned to her. "It's not poisonous, but it has a nasty bite, so we're gonna have to move it."

"Ugh—just ugh."

"Thanks, TOC. I'm leaving you live until we get this thing out of here."

She wasn't sure which of them he was warning that the comms was open. Probably both. Either way, she appreciated it. It was one thing to be all kinds of familiar with Draven, and a whole different one to do it when there was someone on the other either of a comms unit, especially when she didn't know if it was being recorded or not. She watched him move his weapon up and poke it into the hole. "What are you doing? You can't shoot…"

"I'm not going to shoot it." The *you idiot* was implied in his tone. "I don't have a stick and I figured if I can get it to wrap around the muzzle, it will work. If not, then I can shoot it."

"As long as it's in a place where you can shoot it and not snapping on your nose and chomping it off."

"Seriously?" He turned toward her with the muzzle of his weapon in the hole. "You are going to make me nuts by the time we get back home, aren't you?"

"Of course," she quipped. "Why change a good thing now?"

"Fuck you, TOC, just fuck you."

Whoops, she'd been so engrossed in teasing him in an effort to keep herself from losing her mind that she'd forgotten all about his comms being open. "Sorry." She mouthed the word but didn't think he'd be able to see her in the dark despite his night vision having the dim light omitted by the penlight to give him extra help to see.

He grunted, which let her know it had been enough for him to see, and went back to concentrating on the snake. He pushed his weapon further into the hole while trying to peer over the top of the muzzle.

She was going to be forever grateful that her fingers hadn't skimmed off that snake when she'd pushed the papers in there. She shuddered in revulsion, there wouldn't have been a hope in hell she'd have been able to suppress a scream if she'd known that snake was there. The men who'd been outside would have had days to *play* with her and that just didn't bear thinking about.

"Fuck."

India didn't wait for directions or orders; she moved her happy ass out of the way as Draven jumped back. She screamed as the snake launched itself at Draven.

CHAPTER SEVEN

"Fuck." Draven jerked back, but as he was holding his M-16, the weapon came with him, bringing the snake who was using it as a launchpad closer to him. He dropped the weapon and flung out his arm to push Indy out of the way, much like his momma used to when he was in the car next to her and she had to brake hard.

The snake launched itself up the muzzle of his weapon, aiming for his face with its mouth open. "Jesus."

Indy screamed and ran, almost getting squished by the guys as they raced in with their weapons at ready position.

The snake's momentum was interrupted by him dropping the weapon, and rather than getting him right on the nose, as Indy had warned him might happen, it latched onto the ariel of the radio sticking out of the pocket of his flak jacket.

"What the hell?" Braddock made it to him first. It was a tight squeeze with all of them in this small space. "Kilkenny, why the fuck are you playing with a damn snake?"

"I'm not," he protested. "It jumped me."

"Hey, One, you better get your ass in here, because I'm not catching this snake, and I can't shoot it or I'll blow

Kilkenny's shoulder off." He smirked at Draven. "I'm guessing the big boss might lose his shit at the medical bills if I do that."

"Quit fucking around," Kristof replied. "We need to move, because TOC has movement coming in from the north and we have to move our asses, stat."

"Shit." Braddock scowled at Draven. "I hate you so much right now, dude. Because if there's one thing I hate more than spiders, it's fucking snakes." He blew out a breath and shuddered as if he was picking up his balls and stuffing them inside his big girl panties, and wrapped his fingers around the back of the snake's neck, just below his head. "Let go, asshole, and you can go back to minding your own business just as soon as we're outta here."

"We have to grab something from the hole he came out of."

"What fucking hole?" Braddock shook the snake, trying to get him to open his mouth and let go of the radio without getting bitten.

"The one behind you."

"I'm not looking now, jackass." Braddock pulled hard on the snake as its body wrapped around his arm. "Is this fucking thing poisonous?"

"Yeah."

"No," Indy called at the same time. "Your TOC said it gives a nasty bite but won't kill you."

Jeez, could she not have let me fuck with him just a little bit?

"Thank you, Ma'am," Braddock replied. "I'd hate to have to kill him if he's not going to kill me."

"I thought you hated snakes?"

"I do." Braddock finally got the snake to release its bite. "But it's not his fault you stuck your hand into his bed and fondled his ass. I'd want to bite your face off if you did that to me, too."

"First, ew." Draven pushed himself as far away from Braddock as the cave allowed. "Second, I didn't touch him with my hand, I used my weapo—"

"Then, for once, I totally understand a snake's position." Braddock moved toward the entrance to the cave. "I'll get rid of this, then we have to remove these tangos." He called over his shoulder, "You have about five minutes to get your shit together before we move."

He'd been afraid of that. "Indy, get in here and get your stuff." He shone the light into the fissure the snake had been in. If there was another one here, then Indy's daddy could just get his butt on a damn plane and get the papers himself. Because he wasn't dealing with any more freaking snakes.

"Is it there?"

"You mean you made me disturb the fucking snake's nap and you aren't even sure it's the right damn hole?" He fisted the fingers on his free hand closed.

Do not lose your shit.

Do not lose your shit today or you will strangle her.

"I'm pulling your leg." Her hands landed on his waist as she scooted past him to go get her rucksack. "It's in there."

"If it's not, I'm telling you now, I'm going to be pissed as fuck."

"What's new?" she asked. "You've spent half of your life pissed at me. If it changed today, I'd be asking what aliens abducted you and how much me and Lizz need to pay to get real you back."

If he rolled his eyes any harder, he was pretty sure he'd be seeing the inside of his brain. "I'm starting to understand the boss more and more." He cautiously pushed his hand into the fissure and breathed a sigh of relief when his fingers brushed off papers and not a snake. As much as he wanted to snatch them up and yank them out, he forced himself to keep moving slowly in case the reptile Braddock had taken

45

outside to find a new home for had a friend or mate who was pissed at his removal.

"Did you get them?"

"Yes, Indy, I have them."

"Thank you." She held out her hand as if waiting for him to pass them over.

He opened the bottom of his flak jacket and pushed the papers behind the bulletproof plate where he kept his emergency medical kit. "They are safer here." If she thought he was handing them over until they were somewhere safe, she was sadly mistaken. "If a bullet goes into your pack, they'll be destroyed."

"It's Kevlar." She dropped her hand and thankfully didn't make an issue out of him keeping the papers and followed him out of the cave.

Looks like she trusts me not to be a nosey bastard.

A quick glance around the clearing showed him the guys were ready to move. Since they'd arrived, dusk had fallen. Here under the canopy of the jungle, he knew it would soon be almost full dark. If they were lucky enough, moonlight would penetrate the treetops, so they could use their night vision rather than the lights attached to the rig on their helmets.

"Ready?" Kristof asked.

He raised one eyebrow in Indy's direction and when she nodded, he swiped at his pants with his hands, sending dust and cobwebs flying. "Yeah. We're ready to blow this awesome joint." He scanned Charlie team, looking for any indication the movement Kristof had mentioned earlier was going to be a problem, and blew out a sigh of relief when the other man shook his head. When Kristof gave the hand signal to move out, Draven positioned Indy between his front and Archer Knox, aka Charlie Three's back. In this position, she was in the center of the team, the safest position they had. Just as they had on the way in, Kristof and Braddock took point position, scrambling up the embankment first and out of the clearing in front of the cave system.

Draven silently urged Indy to follow Archer while behind him the others took swing position, carefully erasing any sign they'd been there.

Hopefully it would be enough, because those dead bodies you all left in your wake are going to be a dead—no pun intended—give-away that something happened here.

When Indy stumbled over something in the darkness, Draven immediately steadied her with his hands. "You okay?"

"Yes, thanks."

He had to have imagined the shudder which he felt rack through her, or maybe she found him so repulsive that she did it on autopilot. He wasn't sure why that pissed him off. But it did so much that he clamped down on the inside of his cheek to keep from asking her about it. The last thing he wanted her to feel about him was repulsion.

She's not a kid anymore.

She's still Lizz's best friend.

You're adults—

He lost his train of thought when this time it was his boot which got stuck in a vine and he stumbled, almost landing on top of her.

"I'm not sure why you are Tier Two and we're Tier Three." Lucian Wolf, aka Charlie Six, grabbed him by the neck of his flak jacket, almost choking him as he hauled him to his feet. "Even Kayce doesn't fall over his own damn feet when he's out with us. And he spends most of his time back at HQ, in the fucking kitchen."

"Fuck you, just fuck you." There wasn't a single snowball's chance in hell that he was admitting to Luc that he'd been watching Indy's butt rather than paying attention to where he was going.

Never gonna happen.

He wasn't entirely sure if he meant the telling Luc, or deciding Indy was now old enough that jail wasn't automatically in his future, should her daddy take offense to their dating…

Well, considering who her daddy is… jail may still be on the table.

When he stumbled again, he gave himself a mental slap upside the head. There would be time for all the fantasies in the world when he had Indy safely out of Africa and back home in the US. He ignored Luc's chuckling behind him. That asshole had a punch coming if he kept it up.

Be grateful you aren't out here with Bravo. They'd never let you get away with a couple of snickers and whispered shit throwing.

He was grateful after the teasing he'd given both Rexar and Kentucky when they'd been trying to get their heads out of their asses when it came to the women they loved. Both would have rubbed their hands together in glee and made sure Indy heard every single teasing word which came out of their mouths. Small mercies and all that jazz… he'd take it.

She's yours then?

Hah.

Nope.

He already had an inkling that he was lying to himself. He just wasn't ready to admit it to himself. He also wasn't ready to filet open his head and lay it bare on the ground for her to stomp all over it.

He was so deep in his own thoughts that he almost missed when Kristof raised his closed fist in a silent order for them all to stop. They crouched down, and Indy dropped with them without instruction, telling him she'd at least done some training with a field team, probably Ground Branch. He'd have to remember to thank the former SEALs he knew who currently worked for the three letter agencies spec ops team.

"I have movement up ahead," Kristof whispered over comms. "Possibly tangos, or the movement TOC mentioned earlier."

As one, they silently melted into the undergrowth, taking themselves off the path they'd been following. If this was someone looking for the men they'd taken out when looking for Indy, then this could be a problem, a big fuck off problem which could potentially end in yet another firefight. He didn't want that to happen. At least she was wearing the bulletproof vest…

Shit.

No, she's not.

Because with all the drama over the snake and getting the papers he'd forgotten to take it out of his ruck and put it on her.

You are a fucking idiot, Kilkenny. A two-bit dumbass who should have installed your damn brain cells.

He silently berated himself. He knew better than to forget important things like putting the bullet stopper on his principle.

Quit thinking of her like Lizz's friend, he ordered himself.

She is a principle. A VIP. One you must protect at all costs.

Hah. If anyone, even himself, thought he wouldn't fight harder and longer for Indy than he would for a VIP, then they were whacked in the head. Indy laid her hand on his arm, and he glanced down at her. She cocked her head to one side, raised an eyebrow, and mouthed, *what's happening?*

He shook his head. *I don't know.* He nodded in the direction of the path and made a walking signal with his fingers. Her eyebrows furrowed for a split second before she figured it out and nodded in reply. He grinned as she pulled her fingers across her lips as if she was zipping them shut and tossed an imaginary key over her left shoulder. He mouthed, *good girl*, and she lowered her head before turning back to watch where they had entered the trees a few seconds ago.

He turned his head to the side which didn't have his comms unit in his ear and listened, straining to hear any movement from the path. Whoever was out there was good. He couldn't pick up on any sounds. That knowledge didn't tell him anything. A local out hunting would probably know the path well enough to avoid anything which may alert their prey to their presence. Tangos who worked or patrolled in the area would be similar, in his opinion. He barely caught the sound of something scraping off a stone, probably a boot, before silence reigned once more. This was the bit which made him crazy, and he resisted the urge to fidget. He could confirm for anyone who wanted to know that hurry up and wait still officially sucked. But he didn't dare move a muscle. Hell, he was hardly breathing. The first one to make a move died. With Indy in their midst, that was not an option. Period.

CHAPTER EIGHT

How the hell was this happening? Why on earth was she stuck in a jungle, crouching under brambles and bushes to evade someone else, probably terrorists, who were in the area? Oh, yes, because her father sent her to collect freaking papers for him, that was why.

They better be really freaking important papers, dang it. Because if this is for a memo, Imma going to be so pissed and ask Mrs. Mac to put him on a vegetarian kick for his health or something.

Something was stabbing into her arm. Its thorns were more of an irritant than painful, but soon she knew she wouldn't be able to stop herself from scratching. Which would make noise, and considering every single creature which called this part of hell home had vacated their premises or at least locked the doors and were peering out to see what strangers were in the area, making noise would draw attention to where she and the others were taking cover. She would not be the person who gave away their hiding place.

Don't think about it.

Think about something else.

Drave—

Shut up. Not him. Do not think about Draven Kilkenny.

She swallowed down the noise of frustration which threatened to erupt from her mouth. Waiting was necessary, but a pain in the rear end. She could hear the murmur of voices from the other side of the bushes which concealed them but couldn't make out the language they spoke in no matter how hard she strained her ears.

When Draven nudged her in the side, she could have cheerfully murdered him. If he expected her to keep quiet, then he shouldn't be trying to make her yelp. She frowned at his finger when he made a jabbing motion past her, and it took a couple of seconds for her brain to connect the dots and figure out what he wanted. Indy nodded in response and tapped the man in front of her twice on the arm. The man turned his head toward her and frowned darkly.

Yeah, buddy. I'm not trying to give us away to whoever is out there. But the idiot behind me wants your attention.

She moved her head as much as she dared toward Draven, silently telling his teammate that this was on Draven, not her. Hopefully, he believed her, because he didn't look like anyone she'd want to piss off.

Draven and his teammate had a silent conversation with their hands, and the one whose name she didn't know nodded, then turned around, tapped the man ahead of him on the shoulder, and had a similar hand spoken conversation with him. The leader of the team was next in line, and he was clearly irritated when he turned around. But a couple of seconds later, he glanced past, and she felt Draven's nod against her shoulder. The team leader clearly gave a silent order which she didn't understand as Draven cleared his throat loudly.

She cocked her head to one side. Had all this been for

nothing, and the people who had been out there had kept on moving and were already too far ahead to hear the noise Draven had made? She'd no sooner had the thought when the bushes over her and Draven's heads parted and the muzzles of multiple weapons pointed directly at their heads. Out of the corner of her eye she saw Draven lift his open hands in a don't shoot motion, but was aware that the rest of the team with them took aim at the new arrivals.

"If you shoot me, Wolf, Nemesis is going to be pissed at the paperwork it causes him," Draven said dryly, with a hint of amusement.

She'd met Nemesis once, when he'd rescued her after the field office she'd been working in had been targeted. He certainly didn't strike her as someone who particularly enjoyed paperwork. But then who did?

The man standing over them stared for a heartbeat before he cursed softly then muttered, "What the heck are you doing here, Kilkenny?"

"My—India—" he jerked his chin toward her "—needed a ride home. We came to pick her up." Draven got to his feet. Clearly, he knew these men, and Indy took the hand Draven offered her and stood next to him.

His India?

Where the heck does he get off calling me his? He refused to have me be his anything.

Despite her silent thoughts, she focused on what was going on around her. The dynamics of these two teams was more interesting than a rerun of her favorite TV show.

"Wolf Steel, Ma'am." The new arrival's gaze darted toward her. "These men with me are my team."

As if I couldn't have figured that last bit out by myself.

She clamped down hard on the snarky thought. Just because she was irritated with Draven didn't mean she had to take it out on this man. She took his hand, giving it a swift shake before withdrawing again. "India Fox."

"For a remote part of Africa," the man on the other side of Draven muttered, "it's getting rather crowded in here." He got to his feet in an easy movement, grinned wide, then punched Wolf on the shoulder. "Good to see you, Wolf."

The team leader's eyes flashed with something which bordered on surprise before his expression blanked again. "You too, Wolfe." They smirked before moving at the same time to smack each other on the shoulders in a bro hug, all the while dishing out insults.

"I don't understand," Indy whispered to Draven. "They are both called Wolf?"

"Steel's is a nickname." Draven rummaged in his ruck. "The other is Lucian's surname," he explained. "Don't ask me how they know each other, because I don't know for sure. But they're about the same age, so probably are Green Brothers."

She turned that information over in her head and assigned the name Lucian to the man on Draven's team, carefully cataloguing that he had a thin scar which ran from the corner of his eye and disappeared under his helmet near his ear. She'd heard that term, 'Green Brothers' before, back at Langley when she was doing some field training with Ground Branch. A new member had been there and one of Ground Branch's team instructors had come through BUD/S around the same time. Both had been assigned to Green Team before getting onto an official SEAL team.

All around her, introductions were made and she tried to file away the names. She hadn't a hope of being able to match them to faces later. Unless she had time to figure out a facial or body feature to attach to each, then she was going to forget each one in about five seconds flat. Some of them gave nicknames, some call signs, and some she assumed were their real names. At least Benny and Abe sounded like real names to her. Because if they were otherwise, it was all kinds of strange.

"What are you doing here?" the leader of Draven's team, who she now knew was Hunt, asked. "Fishing?"

"Snatch and grab," Wolf replied. "If we can find him. Have you come across any warlords in your travels?"

"Depends on who you are looking for," Hunt replied. "We had a run-in a couple of hours ago. Did the usual data collection during the aftermath." He grabbed his intel packet and waved Wolf over. "See if your guy is in here."

"Thanks."

"Here, put this on." Draven nudged her arm. "It's got to be better than the one you are wearing." He handed her a bullet-proof vest similar in style to the one they all wore.

"I have plates in this one."

"Double or single?"

Did he think she was an idiot? "Of course, I have double plates in my vest." She refrained from calling him names as she would have when they were kids. "Do you think I'm stupid?"

"Hah." He snorted. "There is one thing I'd never, ever put in the same sentence as you and that's stupid." If he'd stopped there, he'd have been fine… perfectly fine. But oh no, he had to open his mouth and stuff not one but both of his boots in there. "I might be lying, but what can you do?"

She stared at him in shock for a couple of seconds, not quite believing the drivel he was saying. Did he not notice all the other men exchanging glances and stepping back? "What exactly do you mean by that?"

"I—uh—"

Stumble and stutter about it all you want.

"Well?"

"Nothing." He stepped back, or at least attempted to, but

stepped back onto Hunt's boot. Hunt helpfully pushed him back toward her, keeping him within arm's reach. "I can beat him, right?" she asked nobody in particular. "Calling me stupid is grounds for beating him without me getting in trouble, right?"

"I'd say so, Ma'am." Wolf glanced up from where he was looking at intel the team with Draven had collected. "My wife wouldn't let me get away with that one either."

"You're not helping here, Steel." Draven sounded like a little boy who had been caught with his hand in the cookie jar before dinner. She steeled herself against how freaking adorable it was. "Do you think I'm stupid, Draven?" He better think freaking carefully before answering.

"No." Draven scrubbed one hand down his face. "I didn't mean it like that. I'm sorry. My brain sometimes still forgets to engage before my mouth opens and words fall out."

She huffed. But how could she stay mad at him? He'd come halfway around the globe to rescue her just because she'd texted him.

"I'm sorry, Indy. Truly sorry."

She huffed again and figured she could come up with a way to make him regret his life choices later. If he ever bothered his backside to come to California and visit them. "Okay. You're forgiven."

"Hah, I can see why you disappeared from the wedding without saying a word to anyone," one of Wolf's men said. "Even Tex remarked on it."

Wedding? What wedding?

"It wasn't my wedding, and Kentucky and Becky had already left." He sounded defensive. "Besides, Nem and Trev knew I was leaving."

"They got one of our dudes." Wolf paused in flipping through the images on one of the wrist-held computers. "I gotta put a call into command." He turned away, then paused and glanced back at her. "Do you think you can refrain from punching him until I'm done?" He nodded to her hands.

Men, they were all the same. Thinking the woman couldn't control her temper. She figured she might as well give them something which reminded them who they were dealing with. She slowly uncurled her fingers from the fists they were in. "I can try. No promises."

Make of that what you will, Sir.

"I like her," the one who'd been just ahead of her as they'd walked whispered. "She's got spunk, and it sounds like she has big enough balls to keep Kilkenny on his toes."

"You have got to give me some names to go on." She nudged Draven with her elbow. "All this head hopping all over the place is driving me nuts." It was like watching a freaking tennis match without knowing who the players or ball guys were.

"You won't remember the names," Draven reminded her. "Every single time I've introduced you to someone, you've forgotten their names before the end of the conversation."

That's what he remembers? Seriously?

"I'm not that bad anymore. I cannot keep saying, 'hey you or him' every time I need to mention someone's name. I caught some of them when you guys were introducing yourselves." She pointed to Wolf. "That's Wolf One." Then she turned and pointed to the other one. "That's Wolf Two. That one is Hunt, which I'm assuming is a surname, and you are dumbass." She quirked up one eyebrow. "How am I doing on the name front there, hotshot?"

"You can tell her our names, man," one of Wolf's team interrupted. "Her clearance has just been verified. Hey, I'm Abe."

"Be straight up and direct with him," a man with a gnarly scar on his face which the camo paint didn't quite hide said. "We call him honest Abe."

That made sense in her head, and she nodded. "Be direct, got it."

"Yup." He pointed to his chest. "I'm Mozart. Just don't ask me to start playing music and crap, because I couldn't fit the piano in my ruck."

"Hah." From the way he mostly kept the scarred side of his face turned away from her, she was guessing he was self-conscious about it. But didn't he know a scar wasn't anything to be self-conscious about? It was a badge of honor which proved you fought the battle and came out alive.

"The one over there..." Mozart pointed a little to the right, "...that's Cookie. If we need to swim, you latch onto him, as he's our best swimmer."

"No swimming, please." She waved at Cookie. "But noted."

"And Mozart is our medic," Abe called softly over his shoulder. "You'll let him look at that cut on your neck, right?"

"Draven patched it up." Trust an operator to have spotted the bandage. "It's only a scratch. Draven would have been carrying me as if I'd broken my leg if it was worse."

"Smart man," Mozart interjected. "You should listen to him."

"Listening to him has been the bane of my existence since I was a kid," she whispered. "Please don't encourage him."

"No promises," Mozart said mildly. "We protect women, and your Draven better do the same or he'll answer to us."

Her Draven? Hah, if only they knew he'd slammed the door on that idea years ago.

"Dude is our explosives guy." Mozart pointed to another one of the men who acknowledged with a wave of one hand. "You'll recognize him by the good looks, and he'll give you the bird with only one hand." Mozart lowered his voice. "The other has some chewed up fingers from saving our asses."

"Another medal of honor." The words were out of her

mouth before she could stop them. "Like you have on your face."

"I—uh—"

"She's got you there, bro," Dude interjected. "If you deny it, I'm telling Ice and Summer."

"Asshole."

She could tell there was no heat behind the reprimand. She briefly wondered if Ice and Summer were other operators or their significant others. She kinda hoped they were these men's wives. Men like these deserved to have someone waiting at home for them.

Mozart flipped Dude off and pointed to the last man on the team. "That's Benny. If you're in a jam and need someone to pick a lock, he's your guy."

"Awesome. Hi, Benny."

He acknowledged her with a short nod and went back to scanning the area with his night vision.

"Pop quiz time," Draven quipped. "Who is—oopf." He thankfully shut up when she elbowed him hard in the belly, giving her time to put names to the faces and hopefully remember them.

Mozart... the pretty one.
Wolf... the growly one.
Abe... the honest one.
Dude... the boom-boom one.
Benny... the escape artist.
Cookie... the fishy one.

She could totally remember them. She hoped.

CHAPTER NINE

Draven folded his arm under his head, using it as a makeshift pillow. This part of the world was a pain in the ass. Everything from the spiders to the snakes to various fractions of terrorist organizations were all trying to kill you the second you crossed their paths. He wanted to keep moving, but they needed to stop. They'd been running for two days. If they didn't stop, then they would start dropping or getting dehydrated. With the LRA after them, they couldn't afford for either to happen.

He glanced down at the woman cuddled in against his side. She'd been one hell of a trooper. His memories of India had been the socialite teenager with more money than sense and a heart of gold. She still had the heart of gold, and could probably pull off socialite, but he was pretty damn sure her level of sense more than matched at least her bank balance, if not her daddy's too, maybe even both combined.

His phone vibrated against his chest, and he pulled it out to see a notification from Trev. He tensed. Shit, if something had changed with their extraction point, he'd be tempted to scream. Hell, he might even do it, just for shits and giggles.

He tapped the notification, and it opened up to a photo. He smiled for the first time in days.

Trev and Checkmate's faces filled the screen in a selfie, both of their eyes wide as if they'd seen something neither could believe. He snorted a laugh and tapped out a response.

Draven: Stop spoiling my cat.

Trev: Checkmate is now my cat. He has decided he no longer can put up with your dry kibble torture regime.

Draven: Do not steal my cat.

Trev: But is it really stealing if he moves into my place all by himself?

Draven: Put Checkmate back at my place. His litter box is there. I'm sure you don't want to have cat piss all over your fancy rugs.

Trev: [photo]

He clicked on the new photo and scowled at the phone.

Draven: I didn't need to see a photo of Check taking a dump. Pervert.

Trev: I was showing you the litterbox in my house. [photo]

Draven clicked on the photo to make it bigger and snorted a laugh. Trev had set up some kind of tent over the litterbox. He'd even made a sign, labeling it a Porta-kitty-potty.

My fucking cat is going to get notions of grandeur.

"Hmm." India stirred against him. "Everything okay?"

"Yeah, I'm just checking in on Checkmate."

She blinked up at him in confusion. "You still have Checkmate?"

"Of course, I do." Was she insane? What did she think he was going to do with the kitten they'd rescued out of the storm drain all those years ago? "What did you think I'd do with him?"

"He must be what, fifteen?"

"Seventeen." He handed her his phone. "See the photos Trev is sending? He's meant to be feeding him, but I think he's kidnapped my cat."

"I can't believe you still have him."

"I found him. He's mine."

"Possessive much?"

"When it comes to what's mine," he told her seriously, "once I find it, I keep it." He immediately regretted saying it out loud. There was one time he hadn't kept what was his once he'd found it. But to be fair, at the time she was jailbait for him. Especially as she'd only been sixteen to his twenty-one. Nope, walking away and joining the Navy had been the smart thing to do in that instance.

He rolled his head to one side when he heard footsteps approaching, his hand going where his weapon lay on the opposite side of him from India.

"It's me. We gotta go." Wolf Steel appeared out of the dark. "Cookie and Keane have spotted a convoy coming our way. I really would prefer not to have to engage with hostiles if we can help it."

"Copy that." He and India got to their feet. "Are they between us and the extraction zone?" He huffed in annoyance at Wolf's nod. "Of course, they are. Why wouldn't they be?"

"Abe thinks he knows a way around and we can avoid them."

"No point in asking me." He figured it was better to just throw it out there. "My sense of direction would get you lost in a paper bag." He gestured between himself and India. "We'll follow your lead."

"Roger that." Wolf handed them both a granola bar. "Be ready to move in five. If we keep moving at this pace, then we should make it to the city sometime before morning."

He nodded in reply. Getting out of the jungle and into a

hotel would be fucking awesome. He could smell himself, never mind everyone else, and they all reeked. "I can't wait to have a shower, any kind of shower."

"Agreed." India shoved the wrapper of her bar into her backpack. "I'd even consider sharing one with that snake who thought your face looked tasty."

"No snakes," he promised her. "If you have to share with anyone, you share with me. Period."

It didn't take long for them to get moving, Braddock and Lucian were making one last sweep of the campsite to ensure they'd left no trace of their presence behind them.

"All good," Braddock said softly as he moved past them to take up point position once again.

Thank fuck, Draven was ready to be out of this hell hole. Wolf and his team had trucks somewhere. He'd take the ride they'd offered. It sure as hell beat roughing it through the jungle where they might stumble over more people who would take exception to their being here. Not to mention the wildlife. He could do without another close encounter with a face eating reptile.

One foot in front of the other. One step at a time. They would get there. He'd get India home and leave her there. Then he could go back to his life in Montana…

Easy day, bro, easy fricking day.

* * *

WHAT THE HELL had he been thinking? Coming here and expecting an easy freaking day had been optimistic at best, but ridiculous in reality. He wiped the sweat from his brow, nudging up his helmet and tugged it back into place.

"You're telling me we have to swing across that gorge?"

Indy narrowed her eyes at him as if it was his fault. He wasn't the one leading the show. "So it seems."

"Drav, I'm telling you now, you aren't Tarzan and I'm not Jane." Indy stepped closer to the cliff's edge as if she was calculating how far they would fall if the ropes didn't hold.

He bunched his fingers into the back of her shirt. "Don't get too close," he warned. "Because if you fall—"

"But you're going to send me swinging out over there. What if I fall then?"

"I'll take you on my back."

Her snort of distain was a kick to the balls, but there was no way he was letting her know that.

"Hell no," she muttered. "If I'm worried it won't hold one of us, there is no way I'm chancing it with both of us."

"I'm gonna go over and string a rope across," Wolf interrupted their squabbling. "We can attach you to it and you can crawl across."

"That sounds like it would take longer than swinging."

"It will," Wolf replied. "But it's probably safer." The words were barely out of his mouth when a sound from the jungle behind them had them dropping into a crouch.

Draven cocked his head to one side, listening. Every sound made ice slide down his spine. It wasn't long before the sound of voices drifted toward them on the breeze. "Someone's coming," he whispered to Wolf.

"No shit." Wolf moved closer to Kristof and whispered something to him. Both men glanced from the jungle to the gorge and back again. Their hands moved as both team leaders made the decision.

Draven's stomach clenched hard once he realized the outcome of that conversation. They were going across, and they were going now. It didn't leave much time for anyone to build up their nerve. But maybe this way was better. There was nothing like having a tango on your ass or bullets flying around your ears to make a two-hundred-foot drop more appealing. "We're gonna make a run for it," he whispered in Indy's ear. "I hope you are ready to fly."

"If God wanted me to fly, He'd have given me wings." Her whole body shuddered. But she took his hand and got to her feet. "But bring it."

He was so fucking proud of her. Maybe it was only him it was obvious to, but she was more terrified of the drop than she had been when he'd peered through the cave opening and seen her with a machete to her throat.

"Go first and catch me."

"Nope, I'll follow you."

"I can't do this, unless you are there to catch me."

As they whispered furiously, most of Wolf's guys were already swinging out with the rope, landing on the opposite side, and sending it back for the next man, a large branch giving it the weight it needed to send it across the gorge.

"Yo, Kilkenny." Kristof nudged him in the back. "We gotta move, stat."

"If you aren't there to catch me, I'm not going," Indy insisted.

Damn it.

He remembered that tone of voice. It was the one she used when it would take a freaking nuke to change her mind. "I swear to God, Indy, if you aren't across straight after me and put these men in the shit, I'll…" He trailed off because he had no freaking clue what he'd do.

"I'm next, I swear."

He had no choice but to believe her as the sounds of whoever was in the jungle behind them was getting louder and louder. He grabbed the rope and moved as far back as he could before running forward. By the time he made it to the edge, he was running full speed. Hopefully it would be enough to get him to the other side, because underneath him was a whole lot of nothing.

"I got you." Hands caught him, tugging him onto the ledge and pulling the rope free from his hands. "Sending it back," Mozart said. "Your woman better find her courage, and she better find it fast."

He agreed with Mozart, but he just wasn't sure she could do it. Because the Indy he remembered was terrified of heights. "I should have sent her first," he muttered more to himself than anyone else.

"Why didn't you?" Dude didn't even look at him as he spoke. Instead, he kept his gaze on where his scope was trained on the opposite side.

"Because she refused to try if I didn't go first."

"Making sure you were safe first," Dude observed. "A woman who cares about your safety more than hers is one you should keep forever."

"She's not mine to keep. She's my baby sister's friend."

"Keep telling yourself that, bro." Dude shifted against the stock of the rifle, adjusting his view. "When I find me a woman who puts me before her, I'm telling you now, she's the one, and I'll be all in, and I don't give a fuck whose friend she is."

As he watched Kristof rigging something to keep Indy attached to the rope if her grip wasn't strong enough to hold her, Draven considered Dude's words. Maybe in another time and place, it would have been possible. But with the life he led... it wasn't fair to drag a woman into his world and expect her to deal with the jobs he did. Even if she worked for the CIA—it just wasn't right. He held his breath as across the gorge, Kristof ran next to Indy as she raced for the edge. Just as she stepped off into air, Kristof gave her a push, and she was swinging toward them.

Draven was grateful when Mozart stepped to one side and allowed him to take his place. He reached for Indy and snagged the pants leg closest to him.

"Eep."

She was obviously working hard to keep her fear under wraps. But he could tell by how pale her face went under her tan that she was terrified. "Easy, baby, I got you." He stumbled when her momentum threatened to pull him over the edge, but one of the men gripped his vest, giving him the purchase he needed to get her onto the ledge next to him.

"Fuck. Shit. Fuck."

He tugged at each finger, conscious that Kristof and two of Charlie team were still on the opposite side. "You can let go now."

"Hold on, don't let go."

Damn, her eyes were still shut. He wasn't even sure she was aware she was safely on the other side. "Hey…"

"Send the rope back, Kilkenny, fuck," Wolf ordered. "Hurry the hell up, we are down to minutes."

Being pushed by the guys combined with the fear he could see on her face clearly did something to his brain. Caused a short circuit or something, because his next move ranked right up there with pissing on an electric fence. He wrapped his arms around her and tugged her into his chest, then claimed her lips with his own, kissing her deep and slow, until he felt her hands bunch into his shirt. He sidestepped them out of the way, relying on the guys to ensure he didn't walk them right off the cliff.

For a couple of glorious seconds, she kissed him back until a soft wolf-whistle made her stiffen in his arms before she ripped her mouth away from his and pushed at his chest.

"What are you doing?" she hissed.

"Kissing you." He swiped his thumb across her lips. "Sorry, I had to get you to let go of the rope." He winced internally the second the words were out of his mouth, knowing he'd fucked up.

"Asshole." She pulled away from him. "You are still the

biggest asshole on the planet, Draven. Still. An. Asshole." She punctuated every word with a stab of her finger into his chest.

"Finish that argument later," Wolf ordered. "As soon as Charlie One has that rope cut, we're popping smoke."

Damn it. Just damn it.

"Yes, Sir." He turned away from him, fighting to get himself under control. It was meant to have been a way to distract her. Instead, he was the one all kinds of distracted. He blew a long slow breath out through his nose.

Time and a place.

She's a kid.

She's Lizz's bestie. If you fuck around, holidays at home will **not** *be fun.*

Time and a place.

But no matter how much he reminded himself of all of the above, now that he'd had a taste of India Fox... he wanted more.

Idiot. I'm an idiot.

By the time Wolf gave the order to move out, he'd mostly convinced himself that he'd only done what was necessary. But he wasn't quite sure he believed it. He also knew he wanted to kiss her again. He fell into formation and followed behind Indy as they headed toward where Wolf promised they had vehicles waiting. He was more than ready to get the hell out of Africa, and away from the temptation Indy offered. Yup. It was time to go home.

CHAPTER TEN

Her bones were going to rattle right out of her body. They couldn't have found a paved road or something. Of course not, why would that have happened? Instead, she had to deal with almost landing on Draven's lap every time they went over one of the huge ruts caused by the rains. "Sorry." She leaned to the opposite side, trying to sit in her own seat and hit the broad shoulders of Draven's teammate.

"No worries, Ma'am." Braddock smiled down at her.

"If we had seat belts, this wouldn't happen." She was being a bitch, and she knew it. These men had risked everything to rescue her. The next time the truck went up on two wheels to get over a rough patch, Draven pulled her onto his lap. "I'm fin—"

"Leave it out, Indy," he growled in her ear. "Every time you bang your head off the window, it pisses me off. Either sit here or I'm going to slit Kristof's throat, and it's not his fault the road is in shit condition."

He was right. As much as she hated to admit it, she was being stupid by insisting she was fine. She wasn't. It sucked, but there was nothing she could do but sit on his lap and let him hold her in place. She huffed in annoyance, but settled back against his chest, ignoring the equipment and gear strapped to his vest. She could deal with them digging into her back, as it meant she didn't have to feel his body heat seeping into her skin.

"Good girl."

His breath washed over the side of her neck as he whispered to her. She had no business wanting to arch her neck as if inviting him to kiss her there. No business, but she did it anyway.

Hussy!

His hands wrapped around her waist and he shifted her against him, this time her butt was pressed against something attached to the lower end of his vest.

"Can you move what's digging into me?"

He chuckled softly against her ear. "Nope, it's attached to me."

It took a couple of seconds for what he meant to sink in. "Oh." Even she could hear the mortification in her voice. Heat climbed up the back of her neck and given how she was sitting on his lap and the amused noise he made behind her head, she knew he saw her blush.

Asshole. Imma going to make you pay for being a dick.

Dick... hummm... remind him that two can play that game.

She waited for the next rough patch on the road. It would never do to be so obvious. When the truck rolled, she moved her body with it, half standing out of his lap, before slamming down as the truck righted itself again. Indy bit her lip to keep her groan from escaping. She was more than willing to torture herself if it made him growl like that. Next to them Braddock snickered. She turned her face to him, grinned, and winked.

We're all adults here. No reason to be embarrassed.

She snorted in her head.

You sure talk a good game, sister.

She shifted, wriggling on his lap. Teasing herself hadn't been the plan. She wasn't sure what she'd been expecting him to do, or how she'd thought he'd react, but holding her in place while his penis pushed against her butt hadn't been it. But the stubborn bitch inside her refused to veer from her path.

"If you keep doing that," Draven muttered, "one or both of us are gonna be very embarrassed right quick."

She glanced at him over her shoulder, her eyes innocently wide. "Are you telling me you have no staying power?"

Braddock guffawed and slammed his fist into his chest as if to stop himself from choking. "You are killing me."

"Behave, damn it."

Make me.

He didn't think he could kiss her like he had back there. Then tell her it was just to distract her and think there would be no payback, did he? It was almost as if he'd forgotten who she was. "No."

"Indy."

The warning was clear in his voice, but she chose to ignore it. A dangerous path to take—maybe—but she was already on it and peddling full steam ahead. She could barely move with how his grip was holding her in place. But she was determined to make every tiny movement she could manage count.

"You better not be jacking off in the truck," Kristof drawled from the front seat. "If you are, then Wolf will lose his shit and make you clean it."

"Oh my God." Draven's words were barely audible. "I'm going to kill you."

"Can't do that," she dragged out the last word. "Because if you do, then have fun explaining to your sister that you murdered her bestie for turning you on."

"Jesus," Lucian called from the row behind them. "Boss, tell me we can sell tickets to this show. We'd make a fucking fortune at the sexual tension pouring off those two."

"Better than a strip joint, that's for sure," Brodie agreed.

Indy refused to let their teasing get the better of her. That she could feel the tension they spoke about pouring off Draven both thrilled and unnerved her.

Maybe you are going a teeny bit too far.

But before she let common sense prevail, the truck gave one last dip and jerk and then righted again.

"Fucking finally," Kristof muttered. "A straight road."

"We'll be in a town in about twenty minutes." Braddock tilted his arm to show Kristof the map on his wrist-held device. "At least I'm assuming that's where we're heading."

"Yeah, Wolf said they have a hotel in the area which doubles as a safe house."

"Thank fuck," Draven muttered, "I need to take a leak."

Everyone snorted at his comment, including her. He could use that as an excuse all he wanted. But they all knew that was not how one relieved pressure in your dick. Not that she had one, mind you. But she'd kind of paid attention in biology class. She moved off his lap and into the center seat again. Now they were on a decent road, there was no need for her to still be on his lap.

"We are not done," Draven whispered into her ear. "I'm warning you; we are not done."

She ignored the shiver which ran through her and turned to smirk at him. "Bring it, big boy, show me what you got." She decided once they got to the hotel, she was paying for her own room and there wasn't a thing he could do about it.

* * *

IF SHE'D BEEN EXPECTING some kind of resort or a typical hotel, she'd have been disappointed. Who was she kidding? She was disappointed. When Kristof followed Wolf down a side street and in through a set of gates which had miraculously opened as they'd approached it, she scanned the courtyard as the trucks pulled to a stop. "I thought we were going to a hotel."

"This is a hotel." Draven pushed open the door and climbed out. Despite the display they'd put on in the truck, he clearly remembered the manners his momma and Mrs. Mac had drummed into them as children and he turned, blocking her exit, clearly scanning for trouble, before he turned and offered her his hand to help her out. "At least it's what counts a hotel in this place."

"I don't understand."

"You aren't meant to." Instead of forging ahead, he was almost a step behind her with one hand placed squarely on her lower back, guiding her forward.

He's comfortable here. He's been here before.

She eyed the tall man in fatigues who stood waiting for them at the doorway. At least a couple of inches over six foot, with blond hair and piercing green eyes which flicked over her before moving onto Draven.

"Who invited you to my little piece of paradise, Kilkenny?" the man asked. "Because you weren't with the guys when they went on safari."

It didn't take a genius to guess safari was a euphemism for a mission.

"We stumbled across 'em," Wolf answered before Draven could. "And decided it was better to bring them here. They'd get into shit if we left them wandering around in the jungle causing shit you don't want to deal with."

"Yeah," the man replied slowly. "It's probably better that you brought them here."

"Who's he?"

"Classified," Draven whispered back. "If he wants you to have his name, he'll give it to you."

"And here I was thinking you still had the manners your momma and Mrs. Mac gave you."

"Hah."

"This your wife, Kilkenny?" The man turned to them. "Nobody told me you got hitched."

"Hell no." As if realizing how he sounded, Draven huffed out a breath. "She's a friend. I'm giving her a ride home."

Even if what he said was mostly truth, yet another rejection from him stung more than she would like. "What he said."

"Good, then, you won't mind sharing with him." The corner of the man's mouth quirked up on one side. "Because this ain't no Hallmark movie and my momma would kick my butt into the middle of next week if I made you share a room with a stranger."

"I... um—"

"Thanks." Draven nodded to their host. "I appreciate that."

"I bet you do, you ole dawg." He turned away from them. "C'mon in the house and get out of the sun. I'll have Mucy find all y'all some grub and something cold to drink."

"Thanks, man." Draven urged her to follow him into the house, almost stepping on her heels until the door had shut behind them.

"Wolf." Their host pointed to a corridor. "You and your men can take the same rooms you had before. Take everyone but Kilkenny and his—er—friend with you. They can stay in my guest room."

"Man, I thought we were friends." Wolf smacked his hand off their host's. "And you are sending me off with the minions while Kilkenny and his woman get your fancy guest suite."

76

"When you go boobs instead of balls, you can stay in my guest suite," their host shot back. "Mucy will have refreshments ready in about half an hour. You know where you'll find them."

"Yeah, I remember," Wolf replied. "Thanks, man."

"No worries," their host replied. "Anything for a brother, and you know it."

Indy turned that little nugget of information over in her head. *Anything for a brother.* Was this man a SEAL? A former SEAL? She supposed it didn't matter who he was. She walked next to Draven as they followed him deeper into the house. If it mattered, she'd figure it out when she needed to.

"I wasn't expecting guests." Their host opened a door and stepped out of the way to let them enter the room. "I'll have Mucy come in an' dust."

"Nah." Draven waved him off. "It's perfect as it is. Seriously, we appreciate you putting us up."

"Yes, we do," she added on. "A little dust never hurt anyone."

"My social skills are a little rusty." He shrugged. "My ma would have a shit fit." He grinned again. "Thankfully, she isn't here to do it." He leaned into the room. "But at least you don't have to share a bathroom with everyone else."

"I appreciate it more than you know." Indy smiled at him. "I've been trucking through the jungle for days." She wrinkled her nose. "I can smell myself, never mind them."

"If you go now," their host nodded to a door, "the bathroom is through there. You better shower fast, or all the hot water will be gone."

She could take a hint when one was so blatantly given. As much as she wanted to know who this man was, she would take her smelly nosey self into the bathroom and wallow about it under the shower. "Thank you."

She took her rucksack from Draven and headed to the

bathroom, closing the door behind her. She dropped the bag on the floor and rested her forehead against the door. "What was I thinking? I wasn't—that's what happened. I wasn't thinking."

Murmuring of voices filtered through the closed door and she pressed her ear against it, trying to make out the words.

"If you see my brother, tell him I'm vertical…"

She didn't catch the rest of the words as it sounded like they had moved out into the hallway. She'd ask Draven about it later. But for now, the shower was calling her name loud enough that she could no longer resist. She flipped on the water, used the toilet, and stripped off the filthy clothes she'd worn for way too long. "I'll deal with you later," she told her pants as she dropped them on the tile floor and nudged them to one side to step under the water. "Mmh, he was right, this *is* paradise." Conscious that the men would probably also like a hot shower, she hurried through washing her hair and slathered on some of the conditioner she found on the shelf, then soaped up her hands with the bar of soap next to it to scrub her skin as best she could with no washcloth, the lack of one telling her it was mostly men who stayed here.

When she was done, she switched off the water and wrapped herself in one of the towels, twisting the other one into a turban to keep her hair from dripping all over the floor. After donning clean clothes from her ruck, she put the filthy clothes into the large plastic bag she kept for just this purpose and put them in the back before zipping it closed.

"Bathroom is fr—" She cut off on a yelp as her wrist was caught when she emerged from the bathroom and she was pushed against the wall.

"Did you mean it?"

Draven!

"You scared the shit out of me, asshole."

78

His breath was hot against her ear, his voice gravelly when he rasped, "Did you mean it, Indy, or was it just teasing to you?"

Yes. Yes, I meant it.

Oh, lord.

Doing this changes everything.

It's sex. It doesn't have to.

That's a steaming heap of bullshit and you know it.

She pushed back against him and spun to face him. "Did I mean to drive you crazy?"

"Yeah." He braced his hands on the wall at either side of her head, enclosing her between them. "Was it just teasing…" He paused and blew out a slow breath. "Or you telling me you want more from me?"

She opened her mouth to answer, but he stopped her with a finger to her lips.

"Before you answer that…" He captured her mouth, sipping from her lips as if they tasted of the finest cabernet. His dancing tongue and the hand massaging her scalp drew whimpers from deep inside her. She didn't know how long they kissed, but when he broke away, she sighed and tried to pull his head back down.

"Now you can answer," he whispered softly. "I wanted to taste you again before you told me no, or kneed me in the balls."

She was going to knee him in the balls if he didn't kiss her like she was his last breath again. Did she dare believe this wasn't just a one and done? But somehow, with Draven, she knew better than to expect anything more.

"I want you to tell me you want me too."

Stunned, that was the only way to describe her reaction. Her jaw dropped, and she shook her head. "You are asking me if I want you too?" Was he dense? Did he think she was like this with everyone?

"Yeah."

She wrapped one hand around the back of his neck and drew him down until his mouth hovered over hers. "Kiss me."

He kissed her again and again and again, slow, exploring, and deep, then scorching hot and wild until she couldn't tell where he began and she ended. He whispered, "Be sure, because I do not want to fuck things up between us."

Fingers trembling, she lifted the hem of her shirt, and whipped it over her head, baring her bra covered breasts to him.

"Jesus, Indy." There it was; the sexy growl he didn't even appear to know came from him. "I want to touch you. Will you let me?"

She shot him a sidelong glance, and her heart skipped a few beats. Never had anyone look at her like that, with such burning intensity that she felt it all the way down to her toes.

"May I?"

"God, yes, please." If he didn't, she was going to burst into flames any second. She swallowed hard, unable to look away as his stare held her spellbound. She nodded, her hands reaching for his shirt, tugging it out of the waistband of his pants. As he kissed her again, she was grateful that he divested himself of his flak jacket and gear while she'd been in the shower.

His hands, hot, large, and insistent, covered her breasts, squeezing and releasing, before tugging down her bra to flick over her nipple with his thumbnail.

He slanted his lips over hers and wrapped his other hand behind her back, keeping her close to him. She ran her hands up his back, using her nails, reminding him that while she may be the woman, she would not be a passive partner. She refused to have half measures from him. Especially not from him.

She pressed her lips to his throat when he released her mouth and bent his head to suckle at her nipples, sending excitement and desire surging through her.

When his thick fingers slid down, popped the button on her pants, and delved under her panties, she didn't know how her knees were holding her up. But she didn't have time to figure it out as he skimmed one finger down between her folds, ramping up the heat and desire between them.

He moved a finger, and then another. "Jesus, look how wet you are, Indy. I love how easily my fingers slide over your pussy."

She pressed her head into the wall, arching toward him with her body, and swallowed against her rioting emotions.

"When we make love," he ran his finger in a circle over her opening, "I promise, I am going to worship your pussy with my mouth until you come on my tongue."

She clutched onto his shoulders as the promise in his voice went to her head. He pressed at the bundle of nerves and sent sparks of lightning scorching her body from the top of her head to the soles of her feet. Her hips rocked against him, craving more of the pressure he gave.

"Ready, baby?" He tilted her head up and brushed a soft kiss across her mouth. When she nodded, because words were impossible right now, he pushed a finger into her, then another.

"Ahh." She arched against him, closing her eyes against the intensity on his face as he watched her.

With excruciating slowness, he withdrew his fingers and then plunged back in.

"Draven," she sighed.

He twisted his hand and pressed the heel against her clit while his fingers moved in and out of her pussy.

"Faster."

"Demanding little thing." But he did as she asked.

It wasn't enough. She clenched hard around his fingers. "Harder." A scrumptious wave of something she'd not felt before swept through her, wrapping around her. Pulling her along, urging her higher until she was almost at the point of exploding. She just needed... "More, please, Draven, more." He pinched that aching spot in the center of her folds, and she shattered, shuddering and moaning as her sex clenched around his fingers. The delicious waves of her orgasm went on and on, until she sagged against his chest and he carefully withdrew his fingers.

He pressed a kiss to her temple and fixed her bra back into place. "So damn beautiful." He caught her hands when she skimmed along the top of his pants and drew them to his mouth. He turned first one and then the other over and kissed each palm.

She knew. She just knew this was it. He was going to walk away. She clamped down on the disappointment and hurt which splashed over her like a bucket of cold water.

"I'm gonna go shower in the guys' area." Draven pulled a key out of his pocket and placed it on the small table next to them, then grabbed his ruck. "Lock the door when I leave. Don't open it for anyone but me."

He's leaving now? What a jerk.

Fabulous, he thought she was stupid as well as wanton. Leaving her now after what they'd just done was a dick move. She clenched her hands into fists. She could punch him now... right? That was allowed?

"Have another shower. We'll go grab dinner when I get back. And, Indy?"

Despite the fact that the thought of another hot, steamy shower reminded every muscle in her body they ached from running and from the orgasm which had raced through her a couple of minutes ago, she refused to cry in frustration. The jackass would probably think she was upset and there wasn't a hope in cornflakes that she was going to know let him know that. "What?" She couldn't keep her voice as even as she'd wanted to. She didn't mind if he thought she was pissed, it was much preferable than him knowing she was hurt and upset. He didn't get to give her one glimpse of what it could be like between them and then disappear to jack himself off in the shower somewhere. It would serve him right if she'd taken off and found her own way home by the time he got back.

"Be here when I get back, because I swear if you make me chase after you, I'm gonna be pissed as fuck." His growl was low. If he'd been a dog, she'd have been tempted to say it was feral. "I'll be listening to hear the lock turn."

The asshole is reading my fricking mind.

She'd never been so tempted to throw a key at someone's head before. She gritted her teeth and waited for the door to close before ramming the key into the hole. She turned the key and repeated the phrase Mrs. Mac had drummed into her. "Patience is a virtue. Patience is a freaking virtue. My ass."

"Patience and you do not mix."

"Bastard." She gave the closed door a middle finger. It wouldn't be polite to yell the words which ran through her head. If she had any hope of retaining her sanity and being able to pretend nothing had happened between them, then polite was the only thing she could be.

Ugh. Men are freaking infuriating.

CHAPTER ELEVEN

Draven listened for the sound of the lock engaging. Just because they were in a safe house didn't mean they could afford to be lax on security. He scanned the hallway both ways before pressing his palm to the bulge in his pants. Walking away from Indy had been one of the hardest things he could ever remember doing. But staying would have caused bigger problems. She was meant to be off limits. Just because he'd let her sweep in under his defenses wasn't an excuse to take advantage of her.

It's not taking advantage if...

He slammed the door shut on that thought without prejudice. What he wanted didn't matter, she was vulnerable even if she didn't believe it. He knew it. Which was why he was on this side of the door and regretting his life choices.

Argh.

He turned back toward the front entrance of the house and went looking for the guys. Spending time with them, farts, burps, and all the stink which came from running around in the jungle for days on end, would hopefully remind his dick that while this mission may be helping a friend, it was work and his brains needed to be in his head and *not* in his balls.

He paused just inside the front door and glanced around. He could almost feel the cameras he knew had to be here watching his every move. There was no way an operator with Sawyer McKinnon's experience didn't have a way to monitor every inch of his house.

Raptor. He's Raptor.

He took the corridor Sawyer had directed the teams to earlier and walked past the first three doors until he came to a fire door and pushed against it. It moved a little, then refused to open. He angled his head to peer through the small glass windows and scowled at the bicycle lock threaded through the door handles. "Fuckers." They should have known he'd be coming. He knocked heavily on the door and waited.

Dude stuck his head out of the room closest to the fire door, his hair dripping wet.

"Yo, Cooper, it's Kilkenny."

"One sec." Dude disappeared into the room and returned with a towel wrapped around his waist and unlocked the bicycle lock, then pulled the door open. "Did your lady throw you out already, man?"

"Nah, but she needs to shower and shit." That sounded reasonable. "I figured you guys might be quicker."

"Don't bet the house on that, man." Dude led him into the room. "Benny takes about six years to get clean."

"Damn." He dropped his ruck on the floor and took the glass of whiskey Dude was pouring from a bottle on the table next to the TV. "Even so, he can't be as long as a woman in the shower. I have a sister—I remember how it goes."

Dude filled a glass for himself and swapped the glass to his non-dominant hand before clinking it against Draven's.

Draven narrowed his eyes at Dude. "You don't have to

hide your hand from me. Those missing fingers tell me that you do the hard jobs. You are the one who faces down the IEDs, so we don't step on that shit."

"It's habit, at this point." Dude shrugged. "It weirds some people out."

"I'm not one of them, Cooper." He jerked his thumb over his shoulder. "Neither is a single man on Charlie team. That hand means you put yourself between danger and your team. That says a hell of a lot about you in my book."

"Noted." Just like most other men he knew in the community, Dude shrugged off the praise, if you could call it praise, drained his glass, and started pulling clean clothes out of his go bag. "Yell at Benny to hurry up," he said over his shoulder. "Let him know you're waiting, or you'll be here all week."

"Nah, I can wait, and cold water doesn't bother me." He flopped into a chair. Dude didn't need to know that a cold shower was exactly what he needed.

Dude looked at him in disbelief but dropped the towel and pulled on a pair of boxers. "Suit yourself."

* * *

By the time Draven's skin was wrinkled and he shivered under the water, he figured any arousal he'd had had retreated. He was as clean as he was going to get. He switched off the water, stepped out onto the bathmat, and grabbed his towel.

"Kilkenny, hurry your ass up." Dude opened the door and stuck his head around it. "We're gonna go and get some grub. You might want to go grab your woman."

His belly rumbled at the mention of food, reminding him that way too many hours had passed since he'd had the granola bar for breakfast. "Two minutes. I just have to pull on pants or I'll get yelled at by Raptor."

Dude winced. "Yeah, good thinking. He gets kinda pissy about manners and shit." He withdrew from the bathroom and left Draven to get dressed.

He had no idea why Raptor was so finicky about manners, because most of them had all met his brother Hawk and his men. None of those three had one single manner between them. At least in the field, the only one with manners in that triad relationship was Micah Kennedy's K9 Delta. Draven made short work of getting dressed and ran the towel over his head one last time, which was all his closely shaved head needed to be dried. He gathered the towels he'd used and folded them on the rail before bagging his filthy clothes and leaving the bathroom. "I'm just gonna go grab Indy." He followed the guys out of the room. "I'll meet you in the dining room."

"Don't be too long." Kristof's voice followed him toward the guest suite. "Our Wolf eats like a starved hound. Combine him with the other Wolf and you'll have scraps if you aren't snappy."

He was tempted to give the Charlie team leader the bird, but remembered the cameras he was sure were there and restrained himself. If he fucked up this safe house, Nemesis would fire him for sure. He paused outside their room and blew out a slow breath.

She's Lizz's best friend; keep your dick in your pants and your paws to yourself.

He knocked on the door loud enough to be heard over the shower if she was still in it and waited. Draven frowned when Indy didn't answer the door, and he knocked again. "Indy, are you ready for dinner?"

The sensation of swarms of ants crawled up his skin and around the back of his neck, warning him that something was off. He put his hand on the doorknob and twisted, but of course he'd made her lock it when he'd left so it didn't fucking open. He hammered on the door. "Indy, open the door."

"What's wrong?"

Draven almost jumped out of his skin when Raptor called from a door further along the hallway.

"I don't know, Indy won't open the door." He dropped his ruck and rifled through the pockets for his lockpick kit. "I'll pick it."

"Not if the key is in it, you won't." Raptor strode toward him. "Come with me, we can pick the French windows." He opened the door next to the guest suite. "It's faster if we go through here."

Draven didn't need telling twice. He was almost stepping on Raptor's heels by the time the man had entered the room. They crossed to the windows and Raptor placed a fob-like device against the mechanism, opening it and leading him out into a small garden.

Draven almost tripped over Raptor when he stopped dead in his tracks in front of him. "Jeez."

"Fuck," Raptor muttered softly. "Would your friend go walk about without telling anyone?"

"No. Why?" He tried to see around Raptor, but the other man's bulk and the shrubs prevented him from seeing anything.

"The door is open." Raptor pulled out his side arm. "Whatever we see in here, do not lose your shit."

Draven echoed his movements and followed him to the French windows. When they entered the room, Raptor went right and Draven to the left. It didn't take more than a glance to clear the bedroom, and two more seconds to tell them the bathroom was also empty.

Fuck. Fuck. Fuck.

She can't be gone.

He raced for the French windows, calling over his shoulder, "She must be in the garden."

"Unless she's shrunk like those kids from the movie from when we were kids, no, she's not. It only goes past the door."

Raptor was correct, a wall ended the space. "How the fuck did this happen? She was meant to be fucking safe here." He slammed Raptor against the wall. "How the fuck did this happen, Raptor? What the hell did you do?"

"I swear this isn't on me." Raptor didn't fight back against him. "We will find her and then hell will reign down. I swear it."

He had to have something to do with it. There was no other explanation. Draven slammed Raptor into the wall once more before turning away. He ran for his phone; he'd plugged it in earlier when Indy was in the shower the first time. His fingers were stubborn and fumbled as he picked it up, and he dropped the phone. "Fuuuck."

"Hunter, we got a problem…"

He gathered the pieces of his phone and put it back together as Raptor called Kristof and flipped the lock to open the door into the hallway.

"Bring everyone," Raptor ordered. "We're gonna need a plan." By the time he'd finished speaking, the sound of pounding boots could be heard from toward the other part of the house.

Wolf Steel and Kristof both tried to enter the room together, and after a slight struggle where their shoulders were trapped in the door frame, Kristof popped through the door first. He strode toward Draven and skidded to a stop in front of him.

"We'll find her." Kristof gripped him by the shoulder and held eye contact. "I swear we'll find her. If they'd wanted her dead, they'd have put a bullet in her brain in the room or slit her throat. They wouldn't have taken her with them."

DRAVEN (SPECIAL FORCES: OPERATON ALPHA)

"Jeez, bro." Wolf tossed the stress ball he held directly at Kristof, hitting him in the back of his head. "You are meant to be calming his ass down, not giving fuel to the fire which will make the top of his head explode."

"How the hell did they manage to get in here?" The two team leaders could argue and bitch all they wanted. Draven had better things to do. "This whole place is locked down." He glanced at Raptor. "At least I'm assuming this place is locked down."

"Yeah." Raptor paused at the door. "I'm gonna go check my cameras and shit. Be back." He disappeared out of the room.

"I don't know how they got in here. This place is usually like Fort Knox." Wolf pulled a sat phone out of his pocket. "But…"

"Who are you calling?" The last thing they needed was for Wolf to call Navy Command on this. Not only was Indy not supposed to be in the country, but Draven wasn't meant to be here either.

"The only person I know who has any hope of finding her before whoever has her kills her or sells her." Wolf punched in numbers and put the phone to his ear. "Yo, Tex, I need a favor."

"Tex?" Draven remembered him. "Keegan, right?" A tiny spark of hope unfurled in his gut. He was an idiot and clearly had forgotten how to use his brain cells, as the first thing he should have been doing was calling Trev back at HQ and asking him to help find her. He finished putting the battery back into his phone and pressed the button to switch it on.

Archer clicked his fingers and pointed to the phone he had to his ear to and mouthed, "Trev?"

Wolf nodded in response to Draven's question, but spoke to Tex again. "Yeah, we have a woman who was taken from the safe house within the last half an hour. We need to find her." He glanced at Draven. "He's on it. What was she wearing?"

Nothing. She was naked as a jay bird and sexy as fuck.

"She was getting in the shower when I left, so depending on how long after I left the room, she might have been naked." He went into the bathroom and picked up her ruck. "I don't see a change of clothes here, just the ones she was wearing earlier. But I have no idea what she changed into."

"Don't worry," Wolf replied. "There can't be that many blond American women in this town. Tex will find her."

CHAPTER TWELVE

"Men are jerks." Indy glared at the door again. She pulled on her pants and tucked her t-shirt into them. As much as she'd love to go barefoot, she knew better. She sat on the end of the bed and turned her boots upside down, shaking them before putting them on. It would be totally sucky to find a flesh-eating spider or something had crawled in there where she was in the shower plotting murder and revenge on Draven fricking Kilkenny.

Once she was dressed, she huffed again in annoyance at herself. "You freaking knew better than to do that with him. Childhood crushes turn into adult jerks." She grabbed a book and fanned her face with it. Even with the ceiling fan, the room was hot. Maybe opening the windows would help. She twisted the lock on the French windows, threw them open, and walked straight into the muzzle of an AK47.

"You will come with us quietly, Miss Fox."

"Shit." Where the hell was Draven when she needed him? She slowly raised her hands in the air, showing the men who surrounded her that she wasn't armed.

"For you, maybe." The man grabbed one of her arms and

shoved it into what looked like a burka, while another man kept his weapon trained on her chest. "For us, no. It is easier than expected."

Within seconds she was being hoisted over the wall and dropped on the other side with no care for her wellbeing. Her head hit the ground with a thud, and everything went black.

* * *

BY THE TIME Indy regained consciousness, she was tied to a kitchen chair in what looked like the bedroom of a house. The windows were shuttered so she couldn't tell if it was daylight or not. Her fingers tugged at the bonds which held her in place, trying to tug at the knots.

"There is no point in trying to open these knots," a voice directly behind her said. "The only thing which will open them is maybe my knife." She flinched away from the touch of steel against the back of her fingers.

"What do you want?" If she was striving for confidence, she failed, as even she could hear the wobble in her voice.

"Information."

Everyone wants information, buddy. But I'm not giving you anything.

"Tell me about the CIA man whose house you are staying in?"

"I don't know what you mean." If their host in that house had been a CIA operator, she'd eat her hat. He didn't move or talk like any CIA operator she'd ever met.

He could be ground branch.

He could be, she supposed, but she'd bet any chance she had of getting out of here that he wasn't.

"I don't know what you mean," she repeated when the man behind her chuckled in her ear. "I am on my honey-

94

moon with my husband. I've never been there before, and I don't know the people who own it."

"Don't lie to me," he snapped.

Pain radiated out from her fingers and up her arm, and tears involuntarily filled her eyes. "I swear I'm not lying. I don't know who he is." Pain exploded up her arms again, this time she recognized a crack which reminded her of Mrs. Mac's wooden spoon on the countertop when she lost her mind over a mess in the kitchen.

It's just smacks on the fingers, you can deal.

Don't cry.

Don't scream.

Don't cry.

Don't scream.

"Pay attention." The command was followed by a rap on the arm.

She caught a glimpse of the walking stick out of the corner of her eye just before the blow fell, and despite her resolve, she cried out.

"Are you Johnson's woman? What is he doing at the compound? How many men does he have?"

"No, I swear. I didn't even know his name was called Johnson." She'd bet every penny in her trust fund that their host was not called Johnson. He probably wasn't John anything.

"What is his real name?

"You will tell me everything about him.

"How many men does he have?

"What is he doing here?

"How long is he staying?"

Each question was punctuated by a rap of the walking stick. How on earth did he expect her to answer when she was choked up on snot and tears? Even if she'd wanted to, there was no way a word was going to make it past the fear strangling her voice, never mind answers. "I—I—don't know," she wailed and spluttered, her breath sawing in and out of her chest.

It sounded like the door slammed open behind her. For a split second, she thought Draven was here, but her hopes were dashed when a heavily accented voice growled.

"What is going on in here?"

She had the impression that the man behind her jumped back, but as she was relying on the movement of air, she couldn't swear to it.

"I am getting you answers."

"Did I request that you get me answers?" This man was definitely higher ranking than the first one. Authority rang in his voice, even if his tone was mild. Falsely mild, if she had to guess.

Indy took the reprieve as these two men argued softly behind her to gather up her emotions and made a valiant attempt at locking them down. Although she wasn't sure if that was the best course of action given that she'd told the first man that she was just a woman on her honeymoon.

Draven will find me. He found me in the jungle.

He had freaking coordinates for the jungle.

Shut up.

She needed to keep her wits about her. Had to maintain the cover she had already started to use. There was no way these men could know who she really was.

They know your name.

Nope. She was India Kilkenny, and she would convince them and make them believe it. They had to believe it, as if they didn't, then she'd found the proverbial creek and was fresh out of paddles. The slamming of the door behind her made her jerk against the ropes and she squeaked in pain. Not being able to see and not knowing what was coming was terrifying, but she would not let the terror win. It could not win. She just had to hold out until Draven figured out where she was.

"Now, India." The man in authority walked around her chair and placed a chair directly in front of her within kicking distance. "I apologize for my brother's actions." He smiled at her. "Sometimes, he is rash."

She noted neither of them had used names. That little nugget of information told her these weren't your run of the mill LRA soldiers, which meant they were most likely connected to ISIS or a similar well-organized outfit.

I'm so screwed.

"Tell me, India, how is your father? He will be angry that we have taken you… no?"

My father? What has my father got to do with this?

She had to think on her feet to come up with an answer fast. "He will be upset that his daughter has been kidnapped while on her honeymoon."

None of this makes sense.

Just like the CIA operatives who were my backup turning on me doesn't make sense.

The change in tempo from the abuse of her knuckles to this man talking to her like they were at a café in Paris or Rome was disconcerting, but she knew it was a ploy to unsettle her.

"Come, come. Miss Fox, we are all friends here—"

"That's Mrs. Kilkenny," she snapped. "As I told your brother, I am here on my honeymoon. My family doesn't even know where we are. I didn't know we were coming to see the gorillas until we got here."

"Whose house were you staying at?"

"It's a hotel my husband booked. I don't know who owns it."

"Are you Rourke Johnson's woman?"

She filed away the name he gave her, but she was almost

one hundred percent sure that wasn't their host's name. If it was a cover name for the CIA, it would most likely be Black, White, or Green, and not Johnson, further reenforcing he wasn't a CIA operative. The surname Johnson put their host firmly under one of the Department of Defense's black ops teams. "I don't know who Rourke Johnson is," she insisted. "My husband booked the hotel for us to rest before we traveled on to see the gorillas."

Please believe me.

She could tell by how his jaw tightened that the man questioning her didn't like this answer. "Who is Rourke Johnson? Who does he work for?"

"I don't know who Rourke Johnson is. No matter how many times you ask me, I can't tell you what you want to know." She glared at him. "Unless you want me to lie, I'm not going to lie, because my mother would turn over in her grave."

"Tell me about the work your father does for the CIA?"

"What? Are you crazy? My daddy is an investment banker." So far, it didn't seem like he knew that she too worked for the company. "He is an old man and doesn't work for the CIA. You've lost your mind if you think differently."

"You are lying."

"Sir." She could pretend politeness; she had enough practice from earlier today to be convincing, she hoped. "I have no reason to lie to you. I'm nobody, we're nobody. I work at a mall and my daddy has been in banking for as long as I can remember."

"And what does your husband do, Miss Fo—Mrs. Kilkenny?"

Is he buying it?

Does he believe me?

She didn't dare hope that was true. "He's a wrangler on a

ranch. We're just normal people on the trip of a lifetime for our honeymoon."

"I don't believe you."

"I work for my sister-in-law." She kept dropping information from the back story she'd memorized in case this situation ever happened. "Kilkenny's Lingerie store in Riverton, California, is how I met my husband. Through my boss."

He didn't need to know how true that was.

"Give me the phone number." The man leaned to one side and pulled a phone from somewhere behind him.

She was going to assume it had been in his pocket as he wasn't wearing a belt that she could see. She rattled off the number for the store. "I don't know if they are open. The time difference…" She trailed off when he held up one hand with his palm facing her and she held her breath.

You have reached Kilkenny's at Riverton Mall. We're closed right now, please leave your name and number and we'll call you back during opening hours.

Her voice filled the room from the recording at the store. The second she heard the beep, she spoke as fast as she could. "See, I told you. I work there. You didn't have to kidnap me. I am nobody. Please take me back to my husband."

"Shut up." The man glared at her as his fingers jabbed at the phone.

Thankfully it wasn't a smart phone, and hopefully the call would be logged on the store's voice mail. She silently prayed it wouldn't be too long before Lizz came in to open the store and found that message. "What did I do? I'm sorry." She cowered as low as she could in the chair as if in fear when he stood and brought his arm back and smacked her in the mouth with the back of his hand.

He paused when the sound of women's voices yelling and children crying filtered in from outside the room, turned his head toward the roof, and sighed heavily. "You better hope your husband's family has money and can pay a ransom, or things will go very bad for you."

"I just told you my husband is a wrangler. The only thing he owns is his truck, his boots, and his hat. If money is what you are after, then I'm afraid you have kidnapped the wrong woman."

He huffed in annoyance and strode out of the room, flipping off the lights as he went, plunging the room into darkness. Once she was sure she was alone, she allowed her shoulders to slump forward and her tears to fall.

How do I find myself in these messes?

I'm quitting as soon as I get home.

She refused to believe that she wasn't going home. Draven would be ripping apart the Democratic Republic of Congo looking for her. He would not leave here without her. She knew it. She believed it right down in her soul. All she had to do was stick to her story and hold on until he found her.

CHAPTER THIRTEEN

Two days. Two fucking days and they hadn't had so much as a sniff as to where India was. The security footage had shown them a group of men climbing over the wall and taking her as she'd opened the French doors. But despite all the people they'd spoken to and the money they'd offered, everyone claimed to know nothing. His phone buzzed and he glanced at the screen, then swiped it to answer the call. "Trev, did you find something?"

"I have your sister Lizz on the line." Trev ignored his question. "She insists on only talking to you."

"Tell her I'll call her when I get back."

"I can't," Trev replied. "She says she has information about Indy, and you need to hear it right now."

Excitement bubbled in his belly. This was the break they were looking for. It had to be. "Put her through."

"Hello? Dray, are you there?"

He swallowed hard enough that he knew Lizz heard him. "I'm here. Tell me everything."

"When I came in the store this morning, I had a voice message from a number I don't recognize. It's in Congo, but

Indy used all of our code words and said she'd been kidnapped."

"When was it left?" Hope flared and he tamped it down. He needed the fear to help him concentrate.

"A couple of hours ago."

If he hadn't been sitting in the back seat of a Humvee, he'd have fainted or fallen on his ass in relief. "Give me the number."

"What's happen—"

"Not now, Lizz," he snapped. "Give me the fucking number."

"I'm going to let you get away with speaking to me like that just this one time," his sister muttered. "But if you ever do it again, I'm going to pop you in the mouth and then tell Momma."

"I'm sorry." He was being a dick and he knew it. "Give me the number, please."

She rattled it off and added on, "Where is Indy? Is she okay? Is she really kidnapped?"

He pinched his fingers into his eyes. "She's missing. I'm looking for her. This helps."

"Dray…"

"Not now, I need to have our tech guys run the number and see where it gets us. I promise I'll call you back."

"You better or—"

"I know, I know, you'll call Momma."

"Now he gets it," she answered. "Maybe McDonalds does do brains after all." The phone went dead in his ear. He lowered it to hit speed dial for Trev. "It's me, Indy left a voice mail on the store's phone sometime in the last few hours."

"Hit me with the number." He started to give the number Lizz had given him, but Trev cut him off. "Give the number for your sister's store; we'll trace it from there."

"Okay, I'll shoot you over a contact card from my phone."

"Good." Trev was clearly working on the computer as the sounds of the keys on his keyboard could be heard clacking over the line. "Do it now."

"As soon as I hang up." For the second time in five minutes someone hung up on him and he didn't even care. He immediately pulled up his sister's contact number and sent it to Trev.

"What's happening?" Wolf Steel looked over his shoulder then put his eyes back on the road.

"Indy left a vm on my sister's shop phone. Trev is running a trace now." Even saying the words gave him hope. But he couldn't hope... hoping for good intel or a lucky break was asking for trouble.

"If she was talking, she's good."

"I know you mean well, Steel, but don't—just don't. 'Kay?"

"Yeah." Wolf nodded. "Just know I know how you feel. Most of us do."

Before he could answer, the phone in his hand buzzed and he swiped answer. "Go."

"Tex found something," Trev said. "Coordinates are coming on Wolf's team's wrist devices now."

"Thanks." He leaned forward. "Check your wrist for coordinates."

"Got it," Dude answered next to him. "I'm getting a hold of Tex to give us directions."

"Roger." Wolf slowed the Humvee as they approached a crossroads. "I just need to know where we're going."

DRAVEN BUNCHED his fingers into fists. He'd spent most of the last decade and a half kicking in doors and clearing houses. Everything about the lead up to tonight had been so fucking routine it should have calmed the nerves which rioted inside him. Everything except that the hostage they were searching for was Indy. His knee bouncing up and down in the back of the Humvee and his opening and closing fists were the only outward sign that he was upset. But he figured they'd all been around the block often enough that none of the guys would comment on it.

Dude pointed across him. "Tex says go straight here, then left on the next street."

"His left or mine?" Wolf asked.

"When has it ever been our left when Tex is giving directions?" Dude replied. "Just drive where he says and we don't get lost."

Wolf smacked at Dude when he tapped him on the back of the helmet. "I'm not gonna get lost."

Draven ignored the bickering going on around him. They sounded enough like his own team for him to be comfortable that they would still get them to where they had to go. The shit talk was a way to keep their emotions on lockdown.

The Humvee rolled through the streets, taking them from the suburbs out of town and down a deserted road. It wasn't long before he could tell by the feel of the vehicle going over ruts that they'd moved from a paved road to a dirt track.

"Right, then an immediate left," Dude ordered. "Then it's the gate directly in front of us."

Draven braced himself against the side of the Humvee and flipped down his night vision rig when Wolf flipped off the lights of the truck.

"Thanks, Tex," Dude said. "I'm leaving the phone open so you can hear what the hell is going on." Clearly Tex had replied with a question, as Dude responded with, "Copy that."

After making the final turn, Wolf pulled the Humvee into the side of the road, hugging the edge close enough that Draven would have to scoot across the seat and get out on the other side or risk falling down the embankment they were parked against. Every man in the vehicle checked their weapons were ready and scrambled quietly out of the vehicle.

Within seconds they were joined by Charlie team, who were given comms units so they were connected to the same tactical operations center as Wolf and his team were, and were making their way toward the compound ahead of them.

Draven held his breath while Mozart and Benny approached the big door-like wooden gates cautiously and checked to see if they were locked. His stomach fell when Mozart shook his head and moved back to the wall where the rest of them were lined up. Benny cupped his hands and Mozart placed his boot in them, taking the boost to get up on the wall.

The routine of an infiltration he'd done more times than he could count in Iraq and Afghanistan did more to snap his brain to where it should be on the mission than anything else could have. But unlike in the Middle East where most of the gates were unlocked, this time they had to wait for Mozart to let them in.

Finally, the gate opened a crack, and Draven held his breath, waiting for it to creak or an alarm to go off. But if there was an alarm, it was either a silent one, or only sounded in the house. They moved in formation across the open space between the wall and the house and stacked up on either side of the door while Dude moved into the breacher position and made short work of picking the lock.

Both teams entered and together they flowed through the house, clearing room to room. Just before the final door at the end of the hallway, Wolf held up his closed fist, and they immediately all stopped. Wolf touched one hand to his ear and cocked his head to one side, silently telling them to listen.

Draven strained his ears, listening for the familiar sound

of Indy's voice, but all he could hear was soft snoring. Ahead of him, Wolf and Mozart communicated in hand signals. Even though all of Nemesis' teams also used hand signals and sign languages, and he himself had come from teams, the ones Wolf and his guys used were slightly different, but he got the general gist of it. It looked like this part of the DRC was similar to the Middle East in having the women and children sleeping in one room. He glanced at the ceiling.

Does that mean the men are on the roof?

Fuck, I hope Indy is with the other women.

A tap on the center of his back snapped his focus back into place in time to see Wolf pull his head back out of the room and shake his head.

Damn, she's not there.

Lucian and Archer stayed at the room where the women and children were sleeping. Hopefully, they could find Indy and get her out of here before anyone was any the wiser. They continued clearing the house, making their way to a staircase which the house plans Tex had somehow produced earlier showed led to the rooftop.

Just like when they went after bomb makers, insurgents of doing different things, different bad things, they had the intel packet Tex and Trev had put together and sent them. Draven hated that tonight felt almost like a mission in any other theater of war he'd been in across the globe. Almost, but not quite, because tonight every move he made, every room they cleared, and each step he took to the roof, was tinged with fear for Indy.

They paused just below the open door to the roof as Wolf peered through the fly curtains. Waiting while the mission leader scanned the area sucked, until Wolf turned and gave him a thumbs up.

She's there? He mouthed the words, barely daring to believe it. Indy was there.

Wolf repeated the thumbs up sign and emphasized it by nodding his head twice. *She's there!*

They moved through the curtain-covered doorway carefully, ensuring the beads didn't rattle as each man stepped onto the roof. Draven's eyes darted around, searching for the person he wanted to see most of all. His gaze landed on her, hogtied on the roof between two tangos who slept on either side of her. Not an ideal position, but he knew they could make it work.

Indy.

As if she heard him saying her name in his head, her eyes opened, and she stared at him. Draven raised one finger to his lips, asking for silence. She blinked once, and he smiled at her acknowledgement. At least it better be a freaking acknowledgement, as he was already reaching for the set of zip-tie cuffs from one of the pouches on his belt.

Across the room at the tango he was standing over, Wolf opened one hand wide and dropped each finger to count them down until his fist was closed. The teams moved as one, carefully sliding the cuff over one wrist and zipping it closed while their targets slept.

It never failed to amaze him how often these tangos didn't wake as they cuffed them.

He doesn't know I'm right here. I could take his life and he'd never know about it until it was too late.

The tango snorted out a snore as Wolf gave the signal for the next step. Draven figured the man on the sleeping mat was probably dreaming that he was being flipped over in his sleep. Draven and the guys rolled the tangos over to put the zip-tie on the men's other hands. He zipped his wrist in nice and tight and glanced around to make sure all the others were ready.

On Wolf's soft command, Draven gripped the man and shook him hard. "Wake up, motherfucker."

The tango jerked awake, already struggling. With hands tied behind his back, he bucked and rolled, flopping around like a fish out of water. Draven flipped on the light on his helmet. "America's here, asshole."

"Draven," Indy whispered, her voice hoarse as if she'd been screaming or shouting a long time.

"Brat." He nudged the asshole further away from her. "Wha—"

"Look after your woman." Dude smacked him in the center of his back, making him stumble forward. "I've got the asswipe."

"Thanks." He dropped to his knees next to Indy, and used his knife to cut the rope which tied her hands to her ankles. "Are you okay?"

"Yeah, I am now." She shook her hands out and rubbed at her wrists. "Kick that one." She nodded to the man he'd captured. "He's a dick who likes to hurt people."

He stilled, fighting against the rage bubbling up inside him. "Did he hurt you, Brat?"

"Yeah, but also his kids. Assholes like him should never be allowed to have children." She allowed him to help her to her feet. "Just let me…" She stepped around him and drew back her leg. As much as Draven wanted to allow that kick to land, he wrapped his arms around her and pulled her away from her target.

"Get her out of here, Bravo," Wolf ordered. "We've got this."

"Yes, Sir." He totally agreed. Getting Indy out of here was the best option. She'd been here long enough, and maybe by the time they made it to the Humvees, he might have found those nerves of steel he usually had. Right now, he was holding his crap together by a rope which was unraveling by the second.

"Thanks, because one of these assholes is going to tell me

the combination to the safe downstairs." Wolf scowled at the captives.

He'd been expecting that; there was no way a SEAL team wasn't going to gather every bit of intel they could find. You never knew when or if there was a thread the DOD analysists could pull which would lead to more missions.

CHAPTER FOURTEEN

Something twigged on the edges of Wolf's memory, and he reached for a pocket on his vest. He was almost certain one of the men they'd captured was on the wanted list. He flipped through his intel packet, looking at the playing card size images of people on the most wanted lists. Every man on his team had a similar set of cards, except his had one card extra. The card with the code BL47 printed on top– Blacklist number forty-seven. "I'm gonna check the cards against them." He nodded to where the tangos sat against the wall.

"Sure thing," Dude replied, just as Wolf had known he would. Checking the cards was protocol for them, especially when they were hunting in this neck of the woods.

Wolf separated out the cards for known terrorists in the region and stepped up next to the first man. He flipped through them, glancing from the guy's face to the cards and back again. "Nope, it's not him." He showed the card to Abe.

"Agree, it's not him." Let them think this was an organized hit and not a rescue mission for Indy. "What about him?" He pointed to the next man in line.

"Yeah, I don't know, man." Wolf studied the card, and then the man. "Whatcha think?"

"Nope, you need your eyes tested, Boss. That doesn't even look remotely like him." Abe plucked the card out of his hand and held it up next to his face. "See? No resemblance whatsoever."

Wolf snatched the card back and shoved it under the deck and moved to the next guy. "You're right."

They did this song and dance often enough that he knew Abe was expecting the words he'd say next. "I'm getting closer, I feel it."

Abe sighed heavily as if he were dealing with an idiot. "No. No, you're not getting close. I'm telling you to have the missus organize you an eye test the second we get home."

Wolf showed him the picture. "It is him... right?"

"No, put that card down and move on."

"It could be him."

"Boss." Abe moved onto the next guy. "Check this one, because that one ain't on the list."

"I'm in charge here," Wolf reminded him. He glanced from the card to the tango. "Oh yeah, you're right, that could be him." He knew full well that this guy wasn't BL47.

"You sure?" Abe asked.

"No, he's similar, but not quite a match. Show me the next one," Wolf ordered.

"You got it." Abe stopped in front of the last man on the row, the one Indy had tried to kick on the roof. "Lift up your head." The tango ignored him, and Abe pushed the muzzle of his weapon under his chin. Clearly the threat of a bullet through the windpipe was enough, and the man lifted his head.

"Get him on his feet." Wolf waited for Abe to do as he asked and leaned forward to study the man's face.

That's him. Holy shit. That's him. Blacklist number forty-seven.

The tango leaned back on his heels and slammed himself forward in an attempt to headbutt Wolf. Even with his hands tied behind his back, he was still trying to jump on him. Wolf leaned his head back and to the side really fast, then kicked out at him, sending him flying across the room. "That's BL 54, which means his almost double is his brother, aka this one." He flipped through the cards until he found the one he wanted. "Bag both of them, we'll bring them with us." Command would lose their shit when they saw the gift he was bringing home with him. Maybe it would be enough to earn his guys some down time.

Now that he knew for sure who he was dealing with, they needed to take every scrap of intel out of this place. Having this terrorist and his brother in their grasp was too good an opportunity to pass up. He gestured to the safe on the far side of the room. "Who knows the combo to this safe?" Wolf growled. The men they had captured just stared at him.

Seriously? This is what they were going to go with? Selective mutism. Assholes.

"Who knows the combo to the safe?" he demanded again, even though he knew what the outcome would be. Just as he suspected, nobody said anything. If they wouldn't answer him, then it was time to bring out the big guns: the man who valued honesty over almost everything else. He glanced at Abe and nodded.

Abe gave him a silent chin lift and cleared his throat. "Okay. The next person who doesn't know the combo to the safe is getting shot in the kneecaps."

Wolf started counting in his head as the captives glanced from one to the other as if trying to decide if Abe's threat was serious or not.

One.

Two.

Three.

Abe clipped his M-16 to its sling and allowed the muzzle to drop before fishing out his Glock.

Four.

Five.

Wolf tensed as Abe cleared the rack and pointed the muzzle at the man sitting closest to him. The tango didn't need to know he hadn't tabbed off the safety. He wrinkled his nose against the stench when one of the captives pissed themselves, and tapped Abe on the back of the shoulder, gesturing toward the one he was going to take a wild ass guess was the weak link.

Abe strode toward the captive sitting second to last on the row and crouched in front of him. He pressed the muzzle of his weapon against the man's kneecap and tilted his head to one side.

The captive swallowed hard and spilled the beans, giving them the combination to the safe.

"That better be right," Abe warned. "If it's not..." He trailed off and shrugged, letting the captive fill in the blanks for himself.

Wolf went back to the safe and punched in the numbers he'd memorized. Thankfully, the lock clicked and the safe opened. "No more fun today," he called to Abe. "That combo works." It pissed him off that threatening people worked better than just asking a question. But he wasn't here to make besties. He and his team had a job to do. They would do it. Period.

He opened up the safe and his eyes widened when he saw it was stuffed to the brink. "Shit, Benny?"

"Yeah, Boss?"

"Toss me a garbage bag. All this shit ain't gonna fit in our rucks." It was way above his pay grade for him to decide what he brought with them and what was left behind. Everything in the safe was classed as intel.

"Here." Benny handed him a folded black plastic sack. "It's the only one I have."

Wolf eyed the body bag Benny had provided and decided it was kind of fitting to use it to carry the Congolese Francs, passports, and everything else which classed as intel. The loss of the contents of this safe would hopefully put a minor dent in the acts of terror the LRA carried out on a daily basis.

"That's one hell of a big year score for us," Benny whispered. "Command will have a field day with that lot."

"Yeah." Wolf stuffed everything into the body bag, zipped it shut, and put it on his shoulder. "Wrap them up." He nodded to the captives. "We're going to exfil, stat."

"Yes, Sir."

We saved the girl and won the day.

As they prepped for exfil out of the property, a whoosh followed by a boom snapped their attention to the outside. Wolf peered out the window just in time to see the explosion.

"Shit, RPG." He flattened himself against the side of the wall. "Move your asses, we got shit coming in." Fuck, he hoped Kilkenny and his woman were well out of the way. Already he could hear Kristof shouting orders from deeper into the house.

"Is that for us, or did the asshole piss off someone above his pay grade?" Cookie hauled BL47 to his feet while Abe grabbed the man next to him.

"Fuck knows," Wolf muttered. "Let's blow this joint before we have to find out."

"Yes, Sir."

"Copy that."

"Hooyah."

CHAPTER FIFTEEN

"I can walk." Indy wriggled against him. "Put me down."

"Not a chance in hell." He'd just found her, and she expected him to be okay with not having her in his arms for the next dozen lifetimes. She was crazy? Well, maybe he was the one who'd lost his mind as he had no business insisting on holding her, he admitted silently to himself. "I'm not putting you down until we know how badly you are hurt."

"The only thing hurt is my knuckles and my pride," she muttered. "They walloped me on the hands good, like an old-fashioned school mistress."

With Braddock and Lucian on his six, he made his way out the open gate and toward the Humvees. "Bastards."

"Yeah." She sighed heavily, but stopped struggling, which made it easier to move her. "I'm not hurt, I swear," she whispered softly. "I'm just mad at myself that I got caught off guard twice in one week. That has to be a record, even for me."

He stood to one side as Braddock opened the rear door of the first Humvee, then leaned in to place her on the seat. "Stop that. It's not your fault."

They all ducked when a sound which haunted the dreams of every soldier who'd ever deployed knew, better than the sound of his momma's voice swept over them.

"RPG," Braddock called.

"No shit." They stared in horror as the flying bomb raced toward the house they'd just been in. "Wolf, you got incoming," he called over comms, giving the guys in the house as much warning as he could. He could hear both Braddock and Lucian doing the same for Charlie team. Before he'd finished speaking, the RPG struck a building on the back wall of the compound. "Fuck. TOC, Bravo Three. TARFU. I need eyes, stat."

"Bravo Three, TOC, what's happening?" a voice he didn't recognize asked. He knew from having worked in this area while he was military that this was possibly someone in the Navy based out of Naples, most likely U.S. Naval Forces Africa (NAVAF), the forward-deployed naval component of U.S. Africa Command who had led on the mission Wolf and his team were on. Or if it was totally a wholly spec ops mission, then possibly command had their own tactical operations center (TOC) in place, with a liaison from the other alphabet agencies.

"RPG just struck the compound."

"I got a target," Braddock said from where he had taken between the Humvees.

"You are engaging?" TOC asked. "You aren't supposed to be engaging right now."

What the fuck did he want them to do? Wave hello at the tangos and ask them if they wanted freaking tea? "No, sir." Draven scanned into the dark with his lasers. "Wolf, his team, and some of my guys are still in that building. I need to know how many tangos we have incoming. But I'm picking up a bunch and they just sent an RPG toward our guys."

"Drone footage shows approx fifteen tangos maybe one

hundred meters out." Clearly TOC had got their act together and were pulling up drone footage.

Fif—fucking-teen. Jeez.

"Hey, you see this guy?" Lucian called.

"Yeah, got him," Braddock called back as he too hit a target with his laser. "Have you got this one?"

"Yup, got him."

"Bravo Three, TOC, confirm you are just lasing targets?" TOC demanded.

"Confirmed, TOC, we're lasing and watching them move up," Draven confirmed they were identifying targets by shining their lasers on the people approaching from the open field across from them. Lasing ensured everyone got visibility. Thankfully the bad guys wouldn't realize they were being lased, because one needed night vision to see the laser.

TOC was either reading his mind or a script as he asked, "Those tangos don't have night vision?"

"Confirmed, no night vision, TOC."

"Roger," the voice replied. "Our guys are headed to exfil with their packages. The women and children have been escorted out the back of the property," he said. "Cover the guys."

"On it." Draven kept his scope moving. With his night vision, he could make out a group of people coming through the front gate. By how they were moving, he recognized their guys; they were pushing two captives ahead of them. Rapid gunfire made them all duck and one of the captives bolted for the jungle as fast as his legs could take him.

"I've got a captive squirting off target without a weapon," Draven called. "He's running right toward us."

"Got my weapon on him," Braddock confirmed. "He's coming right for us."

Draven knew without being asked that Wolf would be pissed to lose one of his captives. But they didn't have time to lose their shit about it right now. He tracked the tango as he took off to the left. Clearly, he didn't even know the rest of them were there. But as he didn't have a weapon, Draven wouldn't shoot him. The tango dived into the jungle and kept moving toward them until he was scrambling through the bushes behind the Humvees.

"I'm going to creep up on him," Lucian whispered.

"Copy." They had to deal with the cat, aka the tango, so they could get on with their exfil and try not to draw the attention of the people who still beelined for the compound.

Braddock and Lucian turned to go creeping up on the tango. Through night vision, Draven saw when he spotted them as he turned and took off running toward the teams. He kept on tracking him with the scope.

"Arrrgh, I can't shoot him as he's not armed."

He got on comms and advised, "There's a squirter coming onto the target. There's a squirter coming onto the target."

"What?"

But clearly TOC didn't need an answer to that question and must have passed on the intel, because the next thing Draven knew was he could see lasers from the teams coming toward them.

The tango stopped, backtracked, and moved off to the right before crouching down and flipping up what looked like a blanket. At this point he had what resembled a flower petal of lasers. It didn't take a genius to figure out what would happen as soon as he stood with a weapon in his hands.

"Strap yourself in, we're gonna be peeling out of here like our asses are on fire," Draven ordered Indy. He leaned into the first Humvee and switched on the engine as Braddock and Lucian did the same with the other two. Within minutes the guys arrived, and they piled into the Humvees. The tangos who'd been targeting the compound came racing toward them, attracted by the gunfire.

Draven dived into the back seat next to Indy and slammed the door behind them. "Go. Go."

"I knew we should have parked Fallujah style," Wolf growled as he slammed the gear into reverse and followed the other vehicle down the track. "Driving out of here would be a hell of a lot easier than fucking reversing."

Draven agreed, but taking the time to maneuver the vehicles before they'd gone in would have given the people in the house more time to know they were coming. They hadn't wanted to risk that happening, and had agreed the risk of parking facing the property was an acceptable risk.

As Wolf reversed out onto the main track, switched gears, and hit the gas, making them all lurch forward at the change of direction, Draven was regretting that decision now. He glanced out the rear window. "They're running after us."

"Won't be long before someone finds the vehicles in the compound and uses them." Abe checked his weapons and ducked his head to look out the side mirrors. "If my head is in your way, Wolf, just shout, 'kay?"

"Yeah, you're good," Wolf replied. "I'll worry about what's in front of us, you watch our six."

"All is see on our six right now is the nose of Charlie Team's wheels."

"Bravo Three, Charlie Four," Braddock called over comms. "I've got a white pick-up on my ass." As he finished speaking the rat-tat-tat of machine gun fire filled the night. "Tell Wolf to floor it, our asses are taking lead."

"Hit the gas, Wolf. Charlie Three is getting their asses whooped."

"This thing doesn't have any more power to give." The engine growled in response when Wolf dropped a gear and hit the gas. "Raptor skimped on all the bells and whistles on this shit."

"I heard that, Wolf man," a voice crackled over the radio on the front dash. "Keep going straight on the four cross-roads and you'll see me coming in on your three o'clock."

"All Stations, TOC, your ride out is on its way," TOC advised over comms. His advisory competed with the voice on the radio for air space.

"That's me," the voice on the radio confirmed. "I'm your expediated exfil. Move your asses, because chatter says there is a mob on the way and they're pissy as fuck over someone taking their paydirt captive."

"Paydirt captive, my butt." Indy's nose winkled up, just like it had when something had pissed her off when they were kids.

"Is that our ride?" Abe pointed to the right. "That's a damn helo. Does command have—"

"I told you, I'm your ride out," the voice on the radio cut him off. "Watch for the tracks to turn in," he ordered. "If you miss it, you're gonna get stuck in the dyke and then you're hotfooting it across the grass, because I can't come any closer with the electrical wires."

"Roger that." Clearly Wolf was taking him at his word. He dropped gears again and whipped the Humvee into a narrow opening with a post on either side of it, making a beeline for the helo which hovered on the far side of the clearing.

Draven glanced over his shoulder to make sure the other Humvees made the turn. Because he wasn't paying attention when Wolf slammed on the brakes, he went flying forward. Only Indy's arm shooting out to press against his chest prevented him from breaking his nose on the seat in front of him. "Shit."

"Move, move!" Wolf yelled. "Bail out, now."

They scrambled out of the Humvees, hauling their captive

with them. By the time they were all on the helo and rose into the air, the Humvees were surrounded by the tangos. Once Draven was sure they were high enough not to be hit by any stray bullets, he tugged Indy close to him and buried his nose into her hair.

She's okay. She's safe.
She's okay. She's safe.
She's okay. She's safe.
She's okay. She's safe.

He chanted it in his head like a mantra, over and over. Maybe if he said it enough he might actually believe it.

CHAPTER SIXTEEN

"Who saved us?" The fear she'd been suppressing for way too long tasted sour in the back of her throat. She peered around Draven, trying to get a look at the helicopter pilot.

"Raptor."

"From the house? Why would he come save us?"

"Because me house is fucking burning!" the pilot whose seat they were pressed up against yelled over his shoulder. "We're gonna be flying over it in about thirty seconds. Bastards sent three fucking RPGs about half an hour ago."

Shit. Is that because of me?

"It's not your fault," Draven whispered in her ear. "So, stop thinking that right now."

He was reading her mind because she hadn't said it out loud. As least she didn't think she had. She chanced a look up at his face.

"It's written all over your face," Draven told her. "I know you well enough to recognize guilt when I see it."

"I'm gonna drop you at your original exfil point." Indy heard Raptor tell Wolf when the team leader stepped over them and sat into the copilot seat. "From there, you have a bird to Djibouti."

"Thanks, man. We appreciate the ride." Wolf grabbed a set of headphones and put them on. "What can I do?"

"Sit your ass still, this old girl doesn't like movement too much," Raptor replied.

The prisoner clearly heard it, as he almost immediately started flailing around, and the helicopter shuddered as if it was going to fall apart.

"Jesus, someone sit on that fucker!" Raptor yelled. "If he makes us crash, Imma gonna be a hell of a lot more pissed than I already am."

Benny and Abe managed to corral the prisoner, flatten him on the floor of the helo where the seats should have been, and keep him in place.

By the time they were landing at what looked like a disused airstrip, Indy was so relieved to be on the ground she considered kissing it like the pope would.

Don't you dare. You've had quite enough germs over the last few days.

I was thinking about it, not actually going to kiss the ground. Jeez Louise.

Grumbling in her head, she waited for Wolf's guys to pull the prisoner off the helicopter and half carry him into the belly of the plane which waited for them on what remained of the tarmac. There had been a couple of times over the last few days when she'd been concerned she wouldn't get out of this country alive. Then Draven and the guys arrived, and her odds had grown big time. But still, Indy decided there was nothing quite like seeing a US military plane filled with soldiers waiting to bring them home. She scrambled to her feet with Draven and paused to thank the pilot. "Thank you." The last thing she felt like doing was smiling, but she forced her lips to curve upward and prayed it didn't look too much like a grimace.

"You might want this, Miss. Fox." He reached down to one side and pulled her ruck sack out of somewhere she couldn't see. "I had it in my safe and grabbed it along with everything else when the first RPG hit my house."

She winced in apology. "I'm sorry—"

"Don't worry about it." He flipped some switches over his head. "We'll go back to square one and start all over again. No biggie."

While she appreciated the reassurance, she knew he was lying. An undercover role like he'd clearly been playing wasn't easy to set up. Sometimes it took years, and this situation had screwed that up. "They were asking me about you." She remembered the interrogation, if you could call it that. "They wanted to know who you were and what I was to you."

"Whatcha tell 'em?"

"That I was a tourist on my honeymoon." She could feel the heat building under her cheeks. "I told them Draven knew you and we were just on our honeymoon."

"Good thinking." Raptor reached for his pocket and pulled out a small card. "When you get a chance, send me an email with all you can remember, because we don't have time to go over it now." He nodded toward where Wolf, Mozart, and Charlie team waited next to the door of the plane with some of the soldiers. "I don't think they are gonna wait for you to give me all the nitty-gritty."

She glanced at the blank card and turned it over to find just one line written on it, an email address. "Thank you. If you ever—"

"While I do like to gather favors," he cut her off with a slash of his hand, "I don't need any from the CIA."

"Wow—"

"Dude," Draven growled in warning. "I'm grateful for the save and all, but rein it in before I have to punch you."

"Hah, you and what army?" Raptor snorted. "Get the hell off my bird and get your asses back where they belong." He looked and pointed to the plane. "On that fucking plane before it leaves without you."

"Thank you." She laid a hand on his shoulder. "I mean it."

"I know you do, and you're welcome." He nodded to her, then glanced at Draven. "Remember what I asked you to do?"

"Yeah."

"Don't worry about it," Raptor said. "My location is changing and there isn't a damn thing Hawk can do about it. Just tell him to let my momma know I'm still standing up straight and that I'm not losing weight and all that shit."

"You got it," Draven replied. "Do I tell him…"

"Nothing other than that," Raptor said. "Now git, because they're waiting on you."

"C'mon, Indy, let's go." Draven nodded to Raptor once more before he was tugging her to the door and leaving the helicopter. They strode side by side to the plane and up the ramp. Once they'd cleared the entrance, the ramp rose behind them, closing them into the belly of the cargo plane.

"Where are we going?"

"Don't care." Draven guided her to one of the red mesh seats which lined either side of the plane. She noted he put them on the end of the opposite row to the prisoner, ensuring there were plenty of men between her and the captive. "I only care that it's out of here and I'm bringing you home."

Crap, she didn't know if home was where she needed to go. That depended on her handlers when she got in touch with them. But she figured that being on her way out of Africa with the papers she'd been tasked with retrieving was enough for now. As the plane took off, she settled into her seat and leaned her head on Draven's shoulder. Exhaustion and achiness from running, being captive, and being rescued twice, finally hit hard. With the murmur of voices from men she trusted around her, she drifted off to sleep, secure in the knowledge that they could and would handle any trouble which managed to find them at twenty thousand feet.

CHAPTER SEVENTEEN

Draven's eyes opened, instantly awake as the change in altitude and the sound of the wheels descending brought him out of his sleep. He glanced at his watch. It had been almost seven hours since they'd boarded the C-130 for their escape out of Africa. With the flight time, he could guess where they would land. He turned to Kristof. "Napoli?"

"Yeah." Kristof nodded. "We'll head back to Istanbul from there, unless you need a backup to get home?"

"No, we'll be good from here." He stroked one hand over Indy's head and tugged lightly on one ear, hoping to wake her slowly. She swatted at him, but her eyes remained closed. "At least we should be, but we can call Nemesis and see what he thinks."

"Good thinking." Kristof nodded to where his fingers tugged at Indy's ear again. "If you keep doing that, she's gonna stab you in the balls."

"She wouldn't do—" He froze when he felt something poking at his balls and glanced down. "Shit... Indy, what the fuck?"

"Stop pulling my ears, dumbass, you know I hate that."

Kristof held out his hand and made a gimme signal with his fingers. "You stole my knife right off my belt."

"If you didn't want it stolen," she pulled the knife away and handed it to Kristof, "then you should have kept a better grip on it, shouldn't you?"

"You know, Indy, I like you." Kristof replaced his blade on his belt. "And it rocks that you keep him on his toes. Kilkenny deserves every bit of shit you put him through." The plane touched down with barely any bumps and he tightened his hold on Indy as the brakes engaged and the plane slowed to a stop.

"Thanks, I think." Indy shrugged out of his hold. "What happens now?"

"We wait for them to get off with their prisoner, and then we go from there." Kristof jerked his chin toward Wolf and his team. "Someone will tell us where they want us."

Relief soaked into him. Finally, he could breathe. He had Indy back, and despite all the obstacles, she was safely back on a US Navy base. It hadn't been pretty, but it was better than the alternative... he'd take it.

Wolf came back up the ramp. "There are a couple of liaisons waiting on you guys," he said.

"Thank you, Wolf. Thank you for helping get me out of there."

"You're welcome, Indy." He took her hand and gave it a solid shake. "Try and stay outta trouble from here on out."

Draven snorted. "That's a tall order, because Indy and trouble are besties." He stood from the seat and shook Wolf's hand. "Tell your guys I said thank you, too."

"Will do." Wolf nodded. "We'll be wheels up again in less than twelve hours, but if you need something before then, ask command to call me." He smiled and turned away as Charlie team and Draven gathered their gear.

"Leave your weapons with me," Kristof ordered. "The

Navy frowns on unauthorized weapons on base. Nemesis will take care of getting them back to us."

"Yeah." Draven stripped off all the weapons, dropping them into the go bag Kristof had at his feet. "Indy, your weapons."

"I—uh—um—" He knew what she was going to say before she continued. "I don't have any."

"Excuse me?" She better not be telling him that she was running around one of the most dangerous places on the planet with no weapons. He swallowed down the urge to reprimand her.

"I had a knife, but the assholes took it when they captured me."

"A knife?" He picked up her ruck. "You don't have a gun? Or a—anything?" He already knew the answer, and it pissed him off so much it hurt not to yell at her for being an idiot.

"Unless a set of brass knuckles count, no." She snatched the bag from him. "I don't." She clutched the ruck against her chest as if he was going to snatch it from her.

Don't yell at her.

He opened his mouth and snapped it shut again. Now was not the time nor the place. But they would be having a conversation about this just as soon as they were somewhere they couldn't be overheard.

Not now.

Say it later.

He scowled at her and turned back to Kristof. "That's it."

"Okay." Kristof zipped the go bag shut and shouldered it. He glanced at the guys as if counting them in his head. "I don't know how long it's been since you came through here last, but be prepared to be searched," he warned as they strode to the door of the plane. "It ain't fun, but Nem says we gotta behave and comply."

* * *

A COUPLE of hours later and Draven was grateful for the warning Kristof had given. Being searched and the questions and answer session from the brass hadn't been fun. Thankfully, there had been one person who knew Dalton Knight, and despite reprimanding him for sending a team through the base without prior arrangement, had let them go after speaking to his boss.

He glanced at Indy in the passenger seat of the rental car Dalton had provided for them along with directions to a safe house in northern Italy. "How you doing?" he asked softly.

"There are very few things I prefer the way the CIA does them." She clasped her fingers around one knee. "How we go through Navy bases in Italy is one of them."

"I'm sorry…"

"It's not your fault." She reached for the paper mug in the holder and took a sip. "It just sucked is all. After the last few days, I don't want anyone touching me, never mind being strip-searched to make sure I'm not wearing a suicide vest."

"I hear that." He resented the fact they'd even checked behind his balls. "While it's awesome that they make security a high priority, I couldn't hide enough C-4 behind my balls to cause damage to anything but my freaking balls."

She spluttered into her mug and smirked at him. "Are you saying you've got small balls?" She quirked an eyebrow up at him. "Because if you are…"

"Shut it, brat."

Just like that, all was right between them again. But he was going to shatter the uneasy truce they seemed to have called at the first opportunity. He should do it now, but he didn't want to. He needed a minute to just be.

"I gotta pee."

He glanced at the sign on the side of the highway.

"There's an auto-grill about ten miles up. Can you wait until then, or do I gotta find a ditch?"

"I can wait." She shifted on the seat. "Is there a reason we aren't on a plane back to the US right now?"

He'd been waiting for it to come up. "My boss, Dalton, remember him?"

"Yeah."

"He has some of the guys digging as to why your dad sent you over here and why everything about the job seemed … off? Is off the word I'm looking for?"

"Yeah, off about fits it."

He changed lanes, getting ready to take the exit for the auto-grill, and in the rearview mirror spotted the black SUV behind them doing the same. "He wanted to look into it some more. While I was waiting for them to finish up with clearing you through the base, I spoke to him and he said he'd sent a couple of the guys down to California to talk to your dad in person. We both felt it was best to wait until we have their input before we put you back in the path of the alphabets." He switched lanes again, this time squeezing in between two slower cars on the right-hand lane, all the while keeping an eye on the rearview.

"Are we being followed?"

He glanced from the mirror to her face and back again in time to see the SUV behind them do the same. "Maybe." He lifted one shoulder. "But I could be paranoid."

"I don't need to pee that badly." She placed her feet back on the floor of the car and slipped them into her boots. "Keep going and see if they follow."

"I'm probably imagining it—"

"How long have you been an operator?" She glanced up from tying her boots.

"Long enough."

"Exactly, long enough to trust your instincts." She jerked

her thumb over her shoulder. "If it's nothing, then we've booted it down the road for a couple of miles and maybe earned a ticket or two for Nemesis's bank account. No biggie."

"And if it is them, then we let them know we see them."

"Nah." She grinned at him. "We are gonna have a mock argument the second you miss the turnoff and they're gonna think I'm mad that you didn't stop."

"Genius. I fucking love it." What was more normal than a couple arguing over when to make a pee stop on a road trip? He resisted the urge to give the SUV behind them the middle finger and just before the exit for the auto-grill switched lanes again to the middle one, and almost jumped straight out of his skin when Indy yelled in his ear.

"What the hell? I wanted to stop there." She went full on for the Italian experience with her hands flying as she spoke.

Behind them, multiple horns blew as if someone else cut the lanes too short. But he didn't have time to look as he was too busy trying not to go under the wheels of the eighteen-wheeler. "Jeez, don't do that." He got way too close of a look at the underside of the truck before he got the car back under control and firmly between the white lines. "You scared about fifteen years off my life."

"Just giving them a good show." She swatted at his head. "Did they follow us?"

He ducked his head out of the way to avoid her hand and peered into the wing mirror. There it was, the front nose of a black SUV. "Yeah."

"Damn, they are following us."

He didn't want it to be the case, but he wouldn't lie to her either. "Looks like it." He chewed on the corner of his lip. "Grab my cell out of my pocket, will ya?"

"Should I make it look like I'm still wailing on you?"

He eased them into the fast lane and hit the gas. "Go for it, just don't make me crash or I'm gonna be pissed."

"Damn, and I thought you'd crash and I could take off running for the hills." She swatted at him again, her hands flailing. This time they were completely out of sync with the words coming out of her mouth.

"Grab my phone," he reminded her. "We need to talk to Nemesis, or at least Trev."

She nodded and dug into his pocket for his phone. "Code?"

"Four, seven, one, nine, two." Out of the corner of his eye he saw her frown as she recognized the last five digits of her phone number. "Speed dial one," he hurried to add on before she could question him on it.

"Okay." She hit the button and held the phone down on her lap where it wouldn't be visible if the men in the vehicle tailing them managed to develop super vision and were able to make out the shape of the phone in her hand.

"TOC," Trev answered. "Is everything okay, Bravo Three?"

"Hey, Trev, I've got Indy with me—"

"I should hope so," Trev snorted. "She's why you took off from Kentucky's wedding Hallmark style after all. If you didn't have her with you, I'd be sending you back to either Napoli or the Congo depending on where you parted ways."

"Shut it." He scowled at the phone, his expression darkening when Indy snorted with laughter and waved her hands around again, clearly still in the couple fighting zone. "Indy is my friend."

"And here I thought she was your sister's friend," Trev teased him. "My bad."

Indy cut off the bickering by clapping her hands together. "All right, all right. We got a problem, TOC, because we've

BELLA STONE & ANNABELLA STONE

picked up a tail," she said. "Me and Draven think it's probably the CIA."

There was a pause and Draven knew Trev was scanning through the mission notes, looking for something which may have alerted the CIA to her presence in Italy. "Do you still have your phone with you?"

"Crap." Indy leaned between the seats to grab her ruck. "I do." She rummaged through the pack and came up with her phone. "It's dead, though."

"Is that one that you can replace the battery on?" Trev asked.

"No, an iPhone."

Trev's sigh was audible. "Then they are probably tracking it. Toss it," he ordered. "I don't have the patience to talk you through checking it tonight, and Tex is busy so I can't call him to do it."

Indy pressed the button to lower the window. "You want me to toss it right now, even though they can see it?"

"Yup," Trev replied. "GPS on the rental shows you're on the A1 and headed toward Florence. Toss the phone, lose the tail. I'll give you a new target location shortly."

He knew from past experience that Trev was about to hang up, so Draven hurried to ask, "Just to be clear, I'm to lose them at all costs including any traffic tickets which might come because of it?"

"Yeah," Trev muttered. "I'll clear it with Nem."

"Thanks." That was all he needed to know. "Toss the phone, babe, then let's raise a little Cain on this here motorway."

"Oh, damn, you've gone country. We're screwed." She dropped the phone out the window and saw it disappear under the wheels of a truck in the lane beside them.

"Hah, you called her babe," Trev crowed. "I fucking knew it. Hallmark for the win."

If Draven hadn't needed both hands on the wheel as they picked up speed, he'd have scrubbed one of them down his face in annoyance. He'd assumed Trev had hung up, just like he did every other time the conversation was done. Trust that the one time he didn't double-check that Trev would hear him slip and call her babe. The teasing in his future was going to suck.

"What does your TOC keep talking about Hallmark movies for?"

"Inside joke."

"Nope." She popped the end of the word and Draven just knew she wasn't going to let it go. "You don't get away with it that easy. Spill."

Thankfully this time they weren't squeezed between two eighteen wheelers and he could scrub one hand down his face. "I'll pay you in coffee…"

"Buddy, with those jackasses behind us, I'm not likely to get a pee stop, never mind a coffee stop in the next hundred miles or so," Indy shot back. "Spill. Now."

He could probably refuse to answer, and she might let it go. But, and it was a big but, he liked the easy vibe they had going on. He didn't want to lose it. "When I asked Trev to help me figure out where I was going to find you, he figured out that you are Lizz's friend," he said. "Trev being Trev added two and two together, and instead of four, he got about seven, I think." He took a non-descript exit at the last minute, shooting across in front of a truck, nearly killing them in the process.

Indy yelped and braced her hand on the dash, pressing herself back into the seat. "Jesus. Give me a little warning before you do that."

"Sorry, I'm just trying to lose our tag-a-long friends."

"You still could have warned me."

He could have warned himself, for a second there he

139

thought he'd misjudged the space and it was pure damn luck that he wasn't stinking up the car and in need of a new pair of shorts. "I'll warn you the next time," he promised.

"I think you're just trying to get out of telling me about the Hallmark thing."

He wasn't, but he also wasn't going to look a gift horse in the mouth either. "Is it working?"

"Not a chance. Tell me the rest."

How did he know that would be her answer? "So anyway, Trev was doped up on happily ever after shit because of the wedding or something and came up with seven and not four," he explained.

"You know this doesn't make a single bit of sense, right?"

"It will, I promise." He wove them through a small town and came to a stop at the traffic lights before moving forward again as it turned to green. "I think the wedding shook something loose in Trev's brain or something, because he decided that me coming to save you is like one of those Christmas movies on the... you know?"

"Hallmark channel?"

"Yeah, the Hallmark channel." He nodded. "Remind me to tease the shit out of him for knowing about Hallmark movies, will ya?"

"You knew about them, too."

"That's completely irrelevant." He slipped them down a side street with no idea of where they were going, but he supposed there were worse places to get lost than in the Italian countryside. "You and me, we aren't anything like the movies."

"If you say so." She glanced over her shoulder, checking each vehicle which came up behind them. "But they sound like the movies Lizz likes to watch, and one of those plots is rescuing your sister's best friend and falling in love with her while you did it."

CHAPTER EIGHTEEN

Indy slapped her hand over her mouth to hold back the laughter as Draven choked. She was totally teasing him, but she couldn't resist it. He was freaking adorable when he got all flustered. She ignored the twinge of disappointment that he rejected the idea of them so thoroughly. But what could she do? She was a grown ass woman who, despite what they'd shared in the DRC, could take no for an answer. "Remember to breathe, Draven."

He thumped his closed fist in the center of his chest a couple of times. "You're mean."

She shook her head at him. "No, I'm not. I'm just filling in for Lizz and reminding her brother that he isn't Captain America or GI Joe," she teased, hoping to lighten the mood.

"Hell no, baby, I'm better than either of those two smucks," he growled just as she'd hoped he would. "I was a SEAL."

"Go Navy."

"Damn straight." He snorted and overtook a tractor. "Navy rules, and Army drools!"

Now that he wasn't driving like a bunch of NASCAR

drivers who'd heard there was an invasion happening south of the Mason–Dixon line, she relaxed into the seat. "What about the Marines?"

"No fucking clue, they're too busy eating crayons and getting lost."

"I thought getting lost was your specialty." She poked the bear just a little bit more. "Are you telling me you identify as a Marine?"

"Wash your mouth out, baby, before I do it for you."

There he went, calling her baby again. She refused to consider it meant anything more than a habit. Maybe it was something he'd picked up over the years and she'd not noticed.

I haven't spent enough time with him to notice.

She shook it off. Nope, he'd made it clear that he wanted to be her friend, and nothing more. As much as that hurt, she'd respect it. She forced joviality into her tone. "Maybe we should stop at a store and see if they have any crayons and test that theory out." She cocked her head to one side. Winding him up should not be so much fun, but it was. At the mention of stopping, her bladder reminded her it had needs too. Ones which were becoming more urgent by the second. "Or maybe an auto-grill for a pee stop, they might have crayons."

"Crap, I forgot you need to pee." He nodded to the phone. "Find us a gas station." But before she could, the phone rang. "Sorry." He hit answer. "Go."

"Bravo Three, TOC. Get your butts to La Spezia." Trev didn't bother with pleasantries. "The Four X's have a plane coming this way tomorrow, and a safe house for you for tonight."

"Thanks, man."

"Do I need to send you a route?" Trev asked. "Or can you find La Spezia without getting lost?"

"Fuck you, Trev, just fuck you." Draven smacked at the phone.

She knew he'd meant to end the call, but he ended up knocking the phone off its holder and it dropped into the footwell near her feet. "So are you getting your Marine on and stopping for crayons to draw the route on the map so we don't get lost on our way to La Spezia?" She reached for the phone as muffled laughter filtered through the speaker.

Shit, it's still on.

Her fingers fumbled over the screen as she tried to hold back her own laughter. She hadn't meant for Trev to hear her teasing him. Finally, she managed to end the call as Draven whipped the car into a shopping mall parking lot. Her shoulders shook with the laughter she refused to allow out of her mouth.

"Sometimes I wonder why I even like you." He unclipped his belt and pushed open the door before glancing at her over his shoulder. "Stay right there, I'll come around and get the door."

He didn't give her time to reply but got out of the car. She could tell by the way he was standing that he was scanning the area. It was a stark reminder that there had been people chasing them only a short while ago. She unclipped her belt and took his hand when her door opened. "Why thank you, kind sir."

"I'm not sure if you're being sarcastic or not." He guided her out of the way while he locked and alarmed the car.

"I'm not." Her breath caught in her throat as she smiled up at him. "I swear I'm not. It was kind of you to open the car door."

"Baby, if a man doesn't open the car door for you, drop kick his ass to the curb. You deserve better."

"Um." She made a noncommittal sound as she wasn't

quite sure how to answer that. "Didn't you teach me to kick them in the balls if they don't show respect?"

"Yeah, but let's not get you arrested this week, please. We've had enough drama for a couple of months." He scanned the signs overhead and pointed to the right. "Ladies room is that way."

"Thanks. I'll be back." She hurried off in the direction of the restrooms. She didn't care how strong a bladder someone had, there was nothing like a car journey to make it forget how to work. Stretching her legs was also welcome. "Why do men never seem to have this freaking problem?" She wrinkled her nose against the smell of bleach. At least it was clean, because at the last stop, she'd taken one look in the door and changed her mind, deciding she hadn't needed to go that badly. After locking the stall behind her, she did what she needed to do and pressed the flush before going to wash her hands. When she opened the door, Draven straightened off the wall he was leaning against. "You didn't have to stand right there waiting."

"I wanted to be sure you were good."

She could hear a weird undertone in his voice. Was there something he wasn't telling her? "What happened?"

His jaw tightened, but he kept walking until he stopped at the coffee counter. "I'll tell you in the car."

Oh, that's not good.

She nodded and turned around, putting her back to his so she could keep an eye out while he ordered them more coffee and some pastries.

Someone should have told me that Draven Kilkenny speaking Italian would sound so freaking sexy.

Two men caught her attention as they wandered around the chips stand and paused to look at a massive lollipop which was probably filled with a bunch of smaller ones. With

144

their suits and briefcases, they shouldn't have looked out of place. But they did.

Who brings their briefcase into a mall just to wander around looking at chips and lollipops?

"Black suits near the big pink lollipop." She took the take-away mug from Draven's fingers, placed it on the high table, and doctored it with sugar and a couple of single milks. "Are they watching us?"

"Nah." He took a sip of his coffee, winced, and reached for the brown sugar packets. "It's bitter." He ripped open the sugar, dumped it into his mug, and stirred it with one of the plastic spoons from the holder on the table. "What makes you think they are following us?"

"The briefcases." She loved that while he thought she was mistaken that he was taking the time to investigate. "Look around you, do you see anyone else in here with briefcases?"

"People gotta work."

"And I'd normally agree with you," she said, then added on, "if it was a weekday. But it's Sunday... right?"

"Yeah." His eyes closed briefly as if he was cursing in his head. "Damn. If it is them, how did they find us?"

"I don't know." There were a million ways. "But if I come around there and snuggle in next to you and we take a selfie which just happens to get them in the background, do you think Trev can find out who they are?"

"Yeah." Draven opened his arm and smiled at her. "Get over here. Trev sent me a selfie with Checkmate, so now it's time to send him one with you."

"You and that cat."

"Hey, Checkmate is awesome." He wrapped his arm around her from behind, tugged her into his chest, and angled his phone in front of them. "He'll be happy to see you." He took the photo. "I mean, if you ever come to

Montana, he'll be happy to see you. If Trev ever gives him back to me."

"First, there isn't a hope in heck this valley girl will ever survive in Montana, even if it is to visit Checkmate," she quipped. "And second, Trev better not try to keep your cat or he'll find out that some of us have calls and we aren't called Checkmate."

"Come on, trouble, let's get going before they figure out that we're onto them."

There was a weird tone in his voice, and she didn't think it was because he was concerned about the two men in suits. Even if they were from the CIA and wanted to talk to her, she'd done nothing wrong. Besides, if they were going to do something to threaten her, Draven could take both of them, probably without even breaking a sweat. She slid her hand into his and walked with him to the parking lot. She turned the conversation over in her head, trying to figure out if it was something she'd said which made him look like he was eating a bunch of lemons.

Was it the comment about me not surviving in Montana?

She didn't have time to figure it out as he was already unlocking the car and holding the door open for her. He leaned in and buckled her seat belt. "When we're on the road, send the photo to Trev." His smile was tight. "It's the top chat on the list."

"Okay." At times like this she wished she was double jointed so she could kick her own butt. Gone was the open fun-loving boy she remembered from childhood, and he'd taken the man who was making her girly bits remember they existed and had wants and desires with him. In his place was a closed off warrior who was all business. Her heart ached at the difference between the two faces of the man.

I'm such an idiot. It had to have been the comment about Montana.

But he has no reason to take exception to that. It's not as if we are a thing.

He doesn't want us to be a thing.

Damn it.

She fiddled with the phone as he got the car going and drove out of the parking lot. "What do you want me to tell Trev?"

"Just what you told me in there." His words were clipped. "He'll figure it out from there."

"Okaaaay." She tapped out the message, attached the photo, and sent it to the chat. Immediately the phone buzzed in her hand. "He sent a thumbs up."

"That means he'll take care of it." He slid the car into traffic. "Pull up directions to La Spezia, please. I'm ready to be somewhere safe for a bit."

"Me too." She did as he asked and placed the phone in the holder on the dash, then sat back to sip her coffee. Maybe the drive to La Spezia would give her time to figure out how to fix the mess she'd made of things.

CHAPTER NINETEEN

He was sulking, he knew it. Her words had stung. They shouldn't have, but they did. He just wasn't entirely sure why.

"At the roundabout, take the first exit."

"Yes, Ma'am."

"Did you just answer GPS lady?"

He paused at the roundabout for traffic to make a space for him and glanced at her as she stretched and yawned, waking up from her snooze. "I sure did. She managed to get me to La Spezia and didn't ask me to make a freaking U-turn once."

"Shh, don't say that too loud or you'll jinx us."

"Ha." He braked hard to avoid the driver who had no clue that the flicker lever was for more than decoration under the steering wheel. "I have a fair idea of where I'm going now. I did some training missions with the Comsubin Incursori near here a few years back."

"Yeah, I heard they have a base near here."

"Out by the reserve." Small talk, he could do. Hell, he was a level expert at small freaking talk. But he wanted more between them than small talk. "Do you know any of the McKinley brothers?"

"I've run across them a time or two."

Up ahead he spotted the signpost for the garage he remembered being at the exit to The Four X's group villa and hit end route on the GPS before it could tell him to take the turn. He glanced in his rearview mirror as he flipped on his indicator and frowned when the vehicle behind them did the same. "Shit."

If that car behind him was the CIA, then they too probably knew exactly where he was going. He punched speed dial one with his finger.

"Go."

"Trev, tell The Four X's that we're coming in hot, and I think I've got spooks on my tail."

"On it."

She glanced over her shoulder at the sedan he was watching follow him up the side street. "You think it's them?"

"I don't want to take a chance that it is. If I say nothing and bring spooks in his house, Gunnar will shoot me."

"You're bringing me."

"You don't count."

"Why?"

As he approached the massive electric gates at the end of the street, he eased his foot off the gas, allowing the car to coast up to the gate. "Because you're mine, that's why." There was just about enough room for their car to squeeze through when he hit the gas again and drove down an elaborate driveway and around the big circular hedge with the other car right behind them. "Get inside now. Go."

Thankfully she didn't question him but unclipped her belt and bolted for the double doors of the villa the second he'd slowed the car enough for her to safely jump out. He yanked up the handbrake and bailed out just as Gunnar McKinley let Indy into his home.

"Stop. Stop right now." One man jumped out of the other car and ran after Indy. He made it to the steps just as she disappeared inside.

"Who the fuck are you?" Gunnar growled. He closed the door behind him and glared at the potential spook.

Draven side stepped around the spook who spluttered, but thankfully stopped short of trying to push Gunnar out of the way. Draven put his back to the house. He trusted the people who were in there and stood side by side with Gunnar on the top step.

"This is an outrage," the man said.

Out of the corner of his eye, Draven saw Gunnar's eyebrows fly almost into his hair line.

"What's so outrageous about it?" Gunnar asked mildly.

"We are guests here." The man gestured to his friend who came to stand with him. "And our sister has been kidnapped by this man."

"That's what you're going with, huh?" Gunnar reached behind his back and pulled a weapon from under his shirt. He handed it to Draven. "It's loaded. If they try to come in my house while I'm inside asking your woman if these two are related to her, kick them off my marble steps before you shoot them. Marble is a bitch to clean blood off of, it smears everywhere."

He was going to kiss him. No bro hugs for Gunnar McKinley today, he was going to kiss him right on the damn mouth. "You got it, bud."

"You can't stop us…"

"Wanna bet?" Draven grinned at the asshole. "You really want to piss off The Four X's?" He lifted one shoulder. "I suppose you could, but good luck the next time an alphabet agency wants someone to…"

"She's never seen you before in her life." Gunnar came back out of the house. "I suggest you remove yourselves from my property before I call the police. They don't take kindly to people trying to break into a resident's home here."

"This is a hotel…"

"This is not a hotel." Gunnar flung his arms wide. "*This* is my house, and you don't have an invite. Get out. Now."

Draven could see the indecision on the men's faces, and clearly Gunnar could too as he stuck his fingers into his mouth and gave a short sharp whistle. Immediately the door opened, and Draven moved out of the way to allow the three men to stand next to Gunnar.

"We," Gunnar pointed to each man, and then himself, "are the McKinley brothers. Either get the fuck off my property or tell the CIA to lose my fucking phone number, because we no longer will be taking their calls."

Draven opened his mouth to tell Gunnar not to go too far— the CIA was a huge contract to lose—but he snapped it shut again when Gunnar's brother Remi made a signal with his hand.

The two agents on the steps glanced at each other and for a second Draven thought it was going to come down to war to get them to leave, but they exchanged glances and turned away. "This isn't over," the one getting into the driver's seat called. "Tell India we will be waiting."

"You touch her, you die." Draven wasn't letting Gunnar take the lead on that decision. Indy was his to protect.

"By the way," Remi interjected, "you ought to know, Nemesis is calling in that favor you two jackasses owe him."

"Nemesis?"

"Yeah." Remi smirked and pointed at Draven. "He's Nemesis's man, and that woman in our house is his woman." His smirk grew to a full-on grin. "Do you understand what that makes her?"

152

"Shit…"

"Nope, quite the opposite," Remi replied. "It means she's off limits. The way I see it is the CIA has two companies they call to get people like you out of shit. Us and Nemesis. If you touch her or come after her, you piss off a lot of people. Who's gonna save your asses then?"

"Get off my property," Gunnar repeated the order. "And don't come back. This house, my house, is fucking Switzerland as far as the CIA is concerned. Period."

They watched the men leave without talking. When the car reached the gates, Gunnar pulled a remote from his pocket and opened the gate before closing it behind them again. "What the hell, Kilkenny? You've brought shit to my front door. I fucking hate when something stinks in my house."

"I'm sorry, Gunnar. I wasn't expecting that to happen."

"You know the second we go out that gate tomorrow to take you to the airport that they're gonna be waiting to follow behind. Right?"

"Yeah." Fuck, he was going to have to call Nemesis himself and figure out a way to evade them. This shit couldn't fall on the McKinleys.

"Good thing," Gunnar clapped him on the shoulder, "we have an alternate way out that nobody knows about."

"I swear to god you guys are like rats on a ship. You always have an escape route." And he was so freaking grateful, it wasn't funny.

"Your girl pissed off a lot of people." Talon, the quietest of the brothers, led the way into the house. "They have advisories out to every agency that she's to be brought in by any means necessary."

"Fuck."

"Yup."

Indy jumped up from a seat partially hidden behind a plant in the massive entranceway. "What happened?"

"They left, but they will be waiting." Draven caught her hand and tugged her closer to him, grateful that she followed his lead without protesting. "What's going on, Indy? Because the CIA doesn't blackball people for nothing, especially not the deputy director's daughter."

"Shit," Gunnar muttered softly. "Come with me."

Draven and Indy glanced at each other, then followed Gunnar through arched double glass doors into what turned out to be an office. The sound of a child crying somewhere in the house had the other three brothers disappearing, closing the doors behind them, leaving just Draven, Indy, and Gunnar in the room.

Gunnar crossed the room and plucked a decanter off a shelf along with some glasses. He lined up the glasses on his desk and poured a couple of measures into each one. "Brandy. We're gonna need it."

For a brief second he considered how much he could reveal. But this wasn't an official mission. No orders had come down that he was aware of, so he figured an open conversation was in order. "How bad is it?" Draven took the glass Gunnar nudged toward him, handed it to Indy, and took another for himself.

"There's talk of stolen documents…"

"I don't have any documents," Indy interrupted.

"Said like a true spook." Gunnar studied her. "It doesn't matter if it's documents or not, but you have something they want." He rolled the glass in his hand, warming the brandy. "And the agency is almost willing to piss us off to get it." He sipped from the glass, peering at them over the rim. "Almost willing." He repeated himself.

Draven worked to keep his face neutral, because the up and close encounter with the snake in Congo told him she

154

did have documents. "Is there any indication what these documents contain?"

"Nope." Gunnar tapped a keyboard and typed with one finger before turning the laptop toward them. "This is the BOLO."

"Crap."

Draven stared at the photo of Indy on the top left of the notification issued by the CIA. "Who else got that?"

"Hell, man, it's on Interpol's most wanted list." Gunnar flipped screens. "I'm surprised you guys got through Napoli without triggering a lockdown on base."

"You have a child in the house. It's dangerous for me to be here." Indy drained her glass as if the booze would give her some extra strength. "I'll leav—"

"You won't." Gunnar glared at her. "The kid is leaving tomorrow. I have enough men to take on the agency if needed. It will take them a while to find where they stored their balls before they come back here."

"Hell no." Draven spun her toward him. "If you leave, you are vulnerable. We'll figure out a way to fix this…"

Indy reached for one of the green leather armchairs in front of Gunnar's desk and sat in it. "I don't understand what's going on," she said softly. "I just did the job I was ordered to do." She looked up at him. "I'm not sure what's going on or why. But I think it's time to call Dad."

"He's compromised somehow," Draven reminded her. "I think we should call Nemesis and see what the guys found out."

"I agree." Gunnar picked up the phone, flipped through a rolodex, and punched in numbers. "We should call someone, but I'm not sure Nem is the one we need. We need someone with way more clearance than Dalton Knight."

"Who—" She stopped talking when Gunnar's brows narrowed and sighed. "Fine…"

Draven hoped Gunnar knew he was on dangerous ground when she said 'fine' in that tone. But he wasn't about to warn him of it either. Despite the fact they did need Gunnar's help, seeing him get all flustered while Indy lost her shit might be epic.

CHAPTER TWENTY

She had no idea who Gunnar was talking about. There weren't many people who had more clearance than Dalton Knight. At least, she didn't think there was.

There is one person who has more clearance than everyone.

Don't be ridiculous, he'd never call...

"Good afternoon, Mr. President." Gunnar leaned back in his chair and placed one foot on his opposite knee. "I have a situation, and I'd like your input, preferably before I piss off a lot of people."

"Is that really...?" she whispered to Draven.

"Yeah, they are old buddies." He kept his eyes on Gunnar. "Their fathers served together, way back in the day."

"I—no wonder he didn't care about tossing the CIA agents out on their ears."

"Even if he didn't know him, Gunnar wouldn't give a shit either way. He has his lines in the sand. Coming to his house without an invite is one."

"We had one... an invite... right?"

"Yeah. Nemesis and Gunnar are tight."

Their whispered conversation clearly annoyed Gunnar as

he tapped his knuckles on the desk, then slashed his hand across his neck in a silent but clear 'shut up' order. "The president wants to know if you picked up the information packet your father sent you for."

She blinked at him. "I don't—"

"Cut the crap, Miss Fox," Gunnar growled. "The president is who gave the order for those papers to collected."

Indecision gnawed at her insides. She'd never, ever compromised any job she'd worked. Ever. Even when her father had asked her for something, when he wasn't on the need-to-know list, she'd refused to tell him anything. "How do I know you are even talking to the president?"

"Because I'm not a liar." Gunnar stared at her for a heartbeat, then pressed a button on the phone and dropped the handle into the cradle. "Mr. President, you are on speaker, Sir."

"Thank you, son."

Her mouth dropped open as she recognized the voice from the TV, but she wasn't quite ready to trust it.

Crap.

"How do I know that's not recorded or a trick of some kind?" She shook off the hand Draven placed on her arm and glared at Gunnar. "Prove that is the president and give me a reason why I should trust you."

"You trust him." Gunnar jerked his chin in Draven's direction. "That—"

She snorted, interrupting him. "You aren't him."

Chuckling filtering over the phone stopped their argument. "I'll call you on video in about ten minutes, just as soon as I have a secure channel set up."

"Yes, Sir. I'll be waiting on your call." He glared at her across the table. "That was rude."

"Maybe it was," she acknowledged. "But I'm also not going to break promises I made on your say so." She could feel Draven's gaze as he studied her like a bug under a microscope, but refused to be distracted and held eye contact with Gunnar. "I'm sorry if that annoys you, but tough luck, because my word means something to me."

Gunnar leaned back in his chair and blew out an audible breath as if he was striving for patience. He turned to Draven. "You picked well. Look after her."

"I intend to."

"Smart." Gunnar steepled his fingertips together. "What's the plan, Kilkenny?"

Draven snorted and leaned forward to grab his glass from the desk. "Keep Indy safe, and burn the world to the ground if that's what it takes to do it."

Gunnar shook his head. "You're gonna lose your clearance and burn your career to the ground."

She hated that Gunnar was probably correct. By calling Draven to rescue her in Congo, she'd set wheels on a bus which couldn't be stopped in motion. She turned to him. "Walk away now. Mayb—"

Draven glared at her, drained his brandy, and placed the glass back on the desk with a thud. "Not a chance in hell."

Her hands balled into fists. "But—"

He plucked her glass out of her hands. "If one sip of brandy makes you think I'm leaving you to deal with this alone, you've had more than enough of it." He tossed her drink back too and placed her glass next to his. "Fill those up again, Gunnar, because I have a feeling I'm going to need the fortification for what's coming."

He's an idiot.

He should walk away from me right now.

She opened her mouth, but couldn't find the words she needed and snapped it shut again. With Draven, it was sometimes better to say nothing until you had your ducks in a row. Her ducks weren't in a row. They weren't in the same room, and at this point she was pretty sure one of them was a pigeon or a chicken.

The chicken is you. You should just tell them thank you for the help and leave.

"I think your lady is trying to protect you," Gunnar said mildly as he refilled the glasses. "If you want to keep working for Nemesis, maybe you should listen to her."

"Don't—" Draven was cut off by chiming from the computer and a simultaneous knock on the door.

Talon stuck his head in the room and pointed at Gunnar's computer. "Remi says that's the POTUS for you. Answer it."

"Thanks." Gunnar tapped the space bar on his computer and moved it until the screen was where they all could see it and tapped answer. The screen flipped a couple of times before it finally steadied.

"Sandra, this thing isn't working," the voice from before grumbled. "I can't see anything."

"Dan, we do this every single time," a woman chided softly. "With the amount of calls our grandkids make, you would think you'd have the hang of it by now. Move the phone back and prop it on the stand and don't touch anything."

"I'm doing it," Dan grumbled. "You'd think these things would be easier to manage."

"You're just spoiled with all the aides and secretaries running after you to fix everything for you," Sandra replied. "What are you going to do when we are done here? You have got to learn how to use the technology the kids have."

"Maybe the aliens will have invaded by then, and I won't have to worry about it."

The screen finally came into focus and the President of the United States filled it.

Oh, no. I screwed up.

That classifies as a crapola for sure.

Aliens are real?

"Hello, Miss Fox," the president said. "Do you recognize me now?"

"Yes—um—yes, Sir." She was so freaking proud that her nervousness didn't bleed through in her tone. Mortification marched up her spine and she knew she was blushing, as the heat in her cheeks begged for her to press her palms against them. She resisted the urge—barely. "I apologize for my rudeness earlier."

He snorted. "India, if I had a problem with everyone verifying who I am, I'd never get anything signed, never mind done." He leaned forward, almost blocking their view, then sat back down.

Is he buttering toast?

Shit, we interrupted his breakfast.

"Now, India." The president placed the butter knife across his plate. "I understand you are the person who picked up a package in the Democratic Republic of Congo. Is that correct?"

"Yes, Sir, Mr. President."

"Good, good." The corners of the president's mouth curved upward in a smile which didn't quite reach his eyes. "You are to give that package to Gunnar McKinley. He will make sure it gets to where it's meant to be going."

"My orders were to bring it to my father."

"That won't be possible," the president said, his tone matter of fact. "Your father is not currently available to the CIA."

What is he talking about?

"I'm afraid I don't understand, Sir?"

"Your father is currently under investigation and will not be returning to the office for the foreseeable future."

Oh, god, do they think I'm involved?

Guilt slammed into her. Her first thought should have

been for her father and not for herself. Guilt was swiftly followed by confusion.

"What is he supposed to have done?"

"I'm afraid I can't tell you that," the president said. "We have managed to keep it out of the press, and I would like to keep it that way until the investigations are complete."

"Of course, Sir."

Oh, Daddy, what did you do?

But she knew she wasn't going to get any answers. If it was anyone else telling her to hand over the papers, she'd have told them to shove it. But that wasn't exactly something one could tell the president. She reached for her rucksack and pulled it up onto her lap. "I have them here." She glanced at Draven. "You will sign as witness that I am handing them to him?" She nodded toward Gunnar.

"Of course."

"Smart." The president nodded his approval. "Sign and stamp a receipt, Gunnar."

Gunnar grabbed a sheet of paper from the printer. "Yes, Sir."

Indy reached across the table. "Nope, not a handwritten receipt," she said. "Type it up on the computer, and I want it emailed to my account, and to…" she glanced at Draven with an eyebrow raised in silent query and gave him a small smile in thanks when he nodded, "to Draven."

Draven cleared his throat. "Send a copy of it to the main TOC email at Nemesis, too." He reached for his phone. "I'll let Trev know to expect it."

"Anyone would think you guys don't trust me," Gunnar grumbled, but he minimized the screen after the president waved at him to do as she asked.

"I'm not feeling very trusting right now," Indy said. "If my father is in trouble, I'm no good to him behind bars, am I?"

"Agreed." Gunnar typed with his index fingers, scanned

the screen, then jabbed his finger on a button and the printer behind him fired into life. He leaned back and grabbed the page, read it, then handed it to her. "Does this work?"

She read it and handed it to Draven. "What do you think.?"

He too read the page and nodded. "Sounds good to me, too." He handed the page to Gunnar. "Send the email to Trev, and once he has it then you can sign this one and we hand over the papers."

I freaking love you!

He was backing her all the way. She had been almost sure he would, but seeing it play out was such a relief. "What he said."

She and Draven exchanged glances when Gunnar scrawled a signature on the end of the page and turned away to place it on the scanner.

She leaned in and whispered in his ear, "I'm doing the right thing—right?"

He nodded silently.

Thank God!

She'd figured she was, but having Draven confirm it was a relief. She'd heard so many stories about agents being burned by the CIA. If they survived, their lives were never the same again. Maybe it was time to go home and run the store with Lizz as she'd been promising her for years. "How do we clear my name?" She wasn't sure who she was asking the question to, but with the president on video call, she wasn't going to pass up the opportunity to ask it. If anyone could override the CIA, it had to be POTUS... right?

"I'm sending through a notification that you were acting on my behalf," the president said. "As soon as that works its way through the channels, you will be free and clear."

"The second that happens..." She knew what needed to happen. She wasn't entirely thrilled about it, but she knew it was the right decision. "...My resignation will be on the relevant desks the following morning."

"Whoa." Draven breathed. "Are you sure?"

"I'm sure." She knew this was the only way she'd ever be free. "My father is compromised, and there's a whole host of agents who think I am in on it. Or who at the very least are following orders which say I am." She stared at Draven, willing him to understand. "I won't live my life looking over my shoulder waiting for someone to decide if I'm guilty of something else."

And I won't compromise your security clearance.

He squeezed her knee lightly and nodded. Thankfully, he didn't try to change her mind. She might have been out of the country when whatever it was her father did happened. At least she thought she might have been. But she was done. Over it. Finished. If the president was clearing her name and letting her walk away without involving her, then her father could think she was letting him down or betraying him all he wanted. She never had, and would not, break the vows she'd made to her country. Walking away was the only way to ensure she didn't have to choose between her father and her country. She figured they all knew it. The men were just too polite to say it outright.

Draven's phone pinged, and she watched him open it and check the message. "Trev got the email, and it checks out."

"Okay." The contents of her stomach rose into the back of her throat, and she swallowed hard against the bile, but she did as she'd promised and handed over the package of papers she'd collected in Africa. "Here you go."

"Thanks."

She opened her mouth to protest when Gunnar immediately stood after taking them and left the room. It took everything she had to keep her mouth shut.

"He'll be back." Draven must be reading her mind. "He's probably going to put them in a safe."

"Okay." She inhaled deeply through her nose and breathed out slowly through her mouth. Maybe if she did it often enough, she wouldn't panic or freak out.

"India?"

"Yes, Sir, Mr. President?"

"I've just sent the notification to Langley that you were following my orders on a matter of national security and that you are to be removed from the most wanted lists, effective immediately."

"I—ah—thank you, Mr. President."

"You are welcome," he replied. "Thank you, India, for your service to your country."

"It was my honor." What else was she supposed to say? Railing and crying about her service ending would make her look like an idiot. But damn it, it hurt. She'd given the CIA everything since she turned eighteen, and this was how they repaid her. "Will you grab me some paper, please?" she asked Draven. "I'll write up my resignation letter right now."

"Are you sure? You have a couple of hours."

She shook her head. "No, I gave my word, and it's better to just get it over with."

He got to his feet and got some paper from the printer. "Ripping off the Band-Aid, huh?" He plucked a pen from the holder on Gunnar's desk and handed both to her.

"Something like that." Her pen hovered over the page and her mind went blank. "I don't know what to write."

"India." The president called her attention back to the screen. "If I may offer a suggestion?"

"Of course." She could hardly tell him 'absolutely not,' now could she?

"State your name, date of birth, agent number, and then 'I hear by state that I have tendered my resignation to the President of the United States,' on today's date. Then something like the president has accepted or similar. Make it flowery, if you wish," he said. "Have Gunnar and your man Draven witness it."

"Thank you." She placed the papers on the desk and carefully wrote out what he had suggested, filling in her date of birth and agent number before dropping a line and carefully writing out, "I, India Fox, have tendered my resignation to the President of the United States, which he has graciously accepted on today's date. Does that work?"

"Yes, Ma'am, that's perfect."

She read over it twice, checking for any stray commas or misspellings, then scribbled her signature underneath it. Indy handed the page to Draven, who in turn scanned it and scribbled his signature under hers and dated it just as Gunnar returned to the room.

"What's going on?"

"Sign and date Indy's resignation, will you, please?" Draven tapped his finger on the blank space under his signature.

"Sure." Gunnar did as he was asked, then rounded his desk and picked up a stamp. He inked it and placed it just next to his signature.

From where she sat, she could make out the barbed wire encircling four X's with an eagle over the letters. The Four X's seal was almost as solid as one from POTUS. It would have to do.

"I'll scan this and send it to you, Mr. President. I'll also send it to Trev." He glanced at her. "Do you have an email you want me to send it to for your records?"

"No, not right now that you can have.." She nodded to the paper in his hand. "I'll take a hard copy and Draven will make sure I get an electronic copy."

"Okay." Gunnar sat back at his desk. "I'm emailing those

now."

"I'll confirm with Trev." Draven tapped a message into his phone and almost immediately got a response back.

Draven: There's an email coming for India from Gunnar McKinley. Can you forward it to her?

Trev: Got it. Same email as before?

"Same email as before?" Draven showed her the phone. She nodded. "Yes."

Draven: Yes, same as before. Copy me in too, please.

Trev: Done.

Draven scrolled through his screens, bringing up his inbox and opening the message from Trev. He scrolled down before showing it to her. "Got it."

"Thank you." She really hoped he didn't think she was being short with him. It was hard enough to keep herself together while this meeting, if you could call it a meeting, went on.

"You're welcome."

Are we done?

They better be done, she needed to find a corner and sulk for about ten years, then she might be okay. Her whole career path had changed in an instant. Somehow, she made it through the small talk. Mostly by making noncommittal noises, but she did it. By the time the president had ended the call, she folded her fingers together, mostly to stop them from shaking. Indy squeezed her eyes shut, blinking back tears of frustration because she knew Draven and Gunnar would assume she was upset.

Breathe through it like a boss.
You still have a business to go back to.
And you aren't running from the CIA.
Bright sides and silver linings.
Bright sides.
Silver. Linings.

CHAPTER TWENTY-ONE

Draven nodded when Gunnar held up the brandy decanter. "Sure." He answered the other man's unspoken question and nudged his glass closer to him. "Indy—" He stopped in his tracks and narrowed his eyes when he caught sight of her closed eyes, and lowered his voice to a whisper. "Are you sleeping?"

"She zoned out before we ended the call with POTUS." Gunnar filled his glass again. "Just curled her feet under her and settled in."

"Your chairs are comfier than if we were at a debriefing."

"Damn straight, I sometimes sit in those." Gunnar settled into his own chair. "I wanted comfortable chairs, damn it, so I bought them."

"I hear that." Should he ask Gunnar's opinion on how things would play out? Draven trusted his judgement and figured it couldn't hurt. "Do you think she'll be in danger?"

"I don't think so. But I'd maybe give it a day or two before you leave here. Give the paperwork time to process."

"You mean we stay here a week then. Because we both

know, paperwork works at the speed of treacle coming out of a jar."

"It does," Gunnar agreed. "But there are worse places to be stuck than in a fancy ass villa in Italy."

They grinned at each other.

"It sure beats a hooch in the Hindu Kush, doesn't it?" Draven eyed Gunnar. "I just never figured you for a bells and whistles kinda guy."

"Right? I'm a work for a living kinda dude." Gunnar scratched at his beard in a habit Draven remembered meant he was wandering into uncomfortable territory. "My folks funded us to get off the ground. But we needed a place in Europe, and this place came up for less than it cost to build a barn at home. My mom talked us into it, then redecorated and all that shit." He looked rueful. "Before I knew what was happening, we each had an apartment, and the ground floor for family stuff." He lifted one shoulder. "But it works."

"Yeah, I'll bet it does." Draven drained his glass again, but shook his head when Gunnar tilted the bottle toward him. "I'll take her to bed if you have one for us."

"Just one, or do you need two?"

It was official, he was an asshole, and he didn't even care because he didn't want Indy in a separate room to him. "One."

He only mentioned beds, not rooms. He could have a room with two beds.

Shut up, brain.

He schooled his face into what he hoped passed as impassive, but given the way Gunnar smirked, he was guessing that wasn't successful.

Gunnar thankfully didn't call him on it. "If she asks me for another bed, I'll provide one."

"Noted." He stood, turned to Indy, and carefully scooped her into his arms. "Shh, it's just me."

"I got your stuff." Gunnar grabbed Indy's ruck and held it up. "Just this one?"

"My go bag is in the rental."

Gunnar opened the double doors and stood back to let him through. "Ah. No worries. I'll have one of the boys grab it for you." He led them to a sweeping marble staircase. "Sorry, no lifts here."

"I remember how to climb stairs," he replied. "And she weighs less than those rucks we had for cardiac hill."

"Yeah, I'm pretty sure the chief was stuffing mine with rocks or something." Gunnar opened a doorway at the top of the stairs which led into a corridor. "Guest suites are through here."

"Thanks." Draven turned sideways to ensure he didn't bump Indy's head or feet on the door as he went through it.

"We have three suites here on this wing," Gunnar told him. "One is occupied, so I'm gonna put you two down at the end. They don't have kitchens, but they do have coffee machines and a mini fridge."

"You lied earlier," Draven whispered. "This is a freaking hotel."

"Nah." Gunnar snorted. "We like to keep an eye on the people we have here. Making them come to the kitchen or having us bring them up food means we get to do that." He pushed open the door at the end of the hallway, and once again held it open for Draven to enter with Indy. "Besides, most of the people who stay here are as good as family, and we want them to come to the kitchen to eat with us."

He kinda thought Gunnar had contradicted himself there, but he wasn't going to call him on it, even if he was curious as to why. "Can you grab the covers for me, please?"

"Sure."

He waited with Indy in his arms, her breathing soft feathery wisps of air on his neck while Gunnar did as he asked. Draven placed Indy gently on the bed and patted her much like his momma did with her grandkids when they slept restlessly, when she shifted and murmured in her sleep. "Shh, you're safe."

"Drave."

"Yeah, baby, Drave." He stroked one hand down her hair and she settled, snuggling into a pillow as he drew the covers over her. "Go back to sleep." He straightened and gestured to the door before leaving the room with Gunnar on his heels. "I don't want to leave her…"

"Stay. I have shit loads of work calling my name in the office." Gunnar leaned into the room with one hand. "Here's two keys for the door. One for you and one for your woman. If it shuts, you'll be locked out. I have master keys downstairs, so come find me if you need to."

"Thanks. I'll be sure to tell Indy." It should be all kinds of weird to hear someone calling Indy his woman. Should be, but it wasn't.

"I'll leave you to it." Gunnar turned away. "If you want to join us for dinner, it's at eight. Kitchen is two doors down from my office."

"Thank you." At this point, he was repeating some version of thanks or thank you every couple of minutes. He'd owe so many people a heck of a lot of favors after this. But as he went back into the room, closed the door, and stood at the end of the bed, watching Indy sleep, he knew it didn't matter. He'd owe the pope favors if he had to. When it came to people he cared about, he found she was top of a very short list.

I can't wait to take off my fucking boots.

Shit. Indy's boots.

What a dumb fuck, I put her in bed with her fucking boots on.

He glanced from the woman sleeping in the bed to the

chair and back again. If he woke her, he'd be annoyed with himself. But if he let her sleep in her boots, she'd be mad with him. He decided it was no contest, and carefully moved the blankets from the end of the bed until her feet were exposed. He unlaced her boots and carefully pulled off the first one before doing the same to the second. That she didn't stir concerned him.

Is she sleeping, or is she sick?

She'd seemed fine when they were in Gunnar's office. Ridiculous or not, he needed to check. More to reassure himself than anything. He knelt next to the bed and placed one finger under her nose, being careful not to touch her. In her sleep she swatted at him, as if, even as she slept, she was aware of his presence.

Thank fuck.

He scooted back and got to his feet. Now that he was sure she was breathing, he could look after himself. His ass was just about to hit the chair when a soft knock at the door stopped him. He hurried across the room to open the door in case the noise woke Indy.

"I've got your gear." The McKinley brother at the door handed him his go-bag and a holster.

Talon's voice was low as if he'd been warned Indy was asleep, and Draven made a mental note to thank Gunnar for doing so later. "Thanks, man."

Talon nodded and turned away. It was then Draven saw the dog lying at door leading into the main part of the house. The dog got to its feet and waited for Talon to reach him with its tongue lolling out one side of its mouth. Talon's fingers rubbed one of the dog's ears. Draven couldn't hear the words spoken, but the tone was affectionate. When the dog kept staring at him instead of following Talon through the door, Talon glanced over his shoulder and gave him a sharp salute in acknowledgement. Draven waved, stepped back into the room, and softly closed the door behind him.

Boots off first. Then figure out the rest.

He didn't remember the last time he'd slept properly, and as he unlaced his boots, he decided a nap was definitely in order. He toed off the boots and moved them to the other side of the room near the windows. Because eww, nobody needed to get a whiff of how badly they stank after him wearing them for days on end.

After a quick stop at the bathroom to do what needed doing, he pulled out his phone and sent a text.

Draven: I'm crashing for a couple of hours. C.D.T. if needed.

Trev: Copy.

He figured it was better to follow protocol and tell Trev now that he'd be asleep, as if he missed a text, shit would fly. By sending him a C.D.T.—call don't text—the notification would also be sent to Nemesis. He fiddled with the settings on his phone to set it to 'do not disturb' and found the charger. He turned to the bed and paused to watch Indy sleeping. Maybe he should have asked for a suite with two beds, or even a suite each for them. But right this second, he couldn't bring himself to regret his choices. He went to the side of the bed near the door and plugged in his phone, placing it on the side table next to the bed.

Pants on or off?

Decisions, decisions.

When he wasn't on missions, he typically didn't wear boxers. But thankfully, today he was still wearing the pair he'd put on at Raptor's house in Congo.

Pants off. It's comfier.

He stripped off his pants, folded them, and placed them on the floor next to his side of the bed. Then carefully

174

climbed in next to Indy, who like a five-pound cat, had sprawled herself across the bed. With his butt hanging over the edge of the bed, he gathered her into his arms and scooted them across the bed.

"Huh—wha—" She stirred and blinked sleepily up at him.

His heart did a weird flip-flop thing which impacted him right down to his toes.

That's a cramp, not my heart coming online.

This isn't going to be a Hallmark movie, dammit.

"It's just me, baby." He liked denial. Hell, correction, he fucking loved denial. He planned on embracing it like it was going out of style. Denial was a state of mind. If he didn't admit to it, it wasn't happening. "Go back to sleep. We're safe here."

She turned over and half-asleep, snuggled into his chest. "You sure?"

"Promise." He kissed the top of her head and settled in around her, trying not to rouse her any more than he already had.

She leaned back to look at his face, then cupped his cheek with one hand, her thumb stroking over his stubble. "I believe you." She pressed a soft kiss to his lips before resting her face against his heart. "Night."

Hell, as he readjusted his stiffening dick, he had to admit that not only was she damn cute, he was more attracted to her than he should be. It just blew his mind that since she'd been taken from Raptor's house, *she* seemed to be completely oblivious to him. "Night, baby." That single soft kiss landed on his heart with the impact of a cruise missile… kaboom… right then and there, he knew denial wasn't going to cut it. He was screwed. Because this woman, this one right here in his arms, was one he shouldn't touch again. But he craved her. Needed her. Wanted her. And there would never be anyone else who would be able to fill the void which remained when they went back to their lives, her in California and him in Montana.

Shit.

I'm so fucked.

CHAPTER TWENTY-TWO

Sneaking out of this bed is like trying to get past Mrs. Mac when I was sneaking back into the house at sixteen.

Indy carefully moved Draven's hand for the second time, and immediately it went straight back to her boob. A spark ignited where his skin touched hers and she peered up into his face.

Is he awake?

If he's awake, I'm going to knee him in the balls.

Her knee was in prime position to do it, given how he was wrapped around her. But untangling their legs would take a hot minute. She tried to ignore what his hand was doing, and there was no way in this lifetime that she was ever going to admit that while his fingers were stroking where they had no business stroking, she wanted more.

You are a glutton for punishment.

He'll just walk away again.

Start what he doesn't finish.

Get out of bed and go freaking pee.

She bit back a moan when his hand cupped her breast and squeezed lightly. She caught his hand and wrapped her fingers into his, backward thinking that would stop him. Instead, he just used her hand to plump at her flesh, his throaty growl sending a shiver right down to her pussy.

Oh, god.

That should not feel so good. But it did. She opened her mouth to speak, but no sound came out. She swallowed and tried again. "Drave?"

"Mmh?"

She wanted to kiss him. To have him enfold her in his arms and not let her leave. But she really did need to go to the bathroom. "I need to pee."

"Huh?"

His eyes blinked open, and for a brief moment they just stared at each other before it was too much and she lowered her lids to hide from his gaze. "I need to pee."

What did you say that for?

Are you crazy?

You are in bed with Draven. He's not wearing pants and you are talking about peeing?

"Um—okay."

"I—ah—" She could hear the confusion in his voice and glanced at his face. "I'm kind trapped here."

His eyes followed her gaze to where their hands were intertwined over her breast, and if it hadn't been so mortifying... no, not mortifying... exhilarating, exciting, thrilling, all those words fit better, she'd have laughed outright at the stunned look on his face.

"Shit. Sorry." He tugged on her hand, obviously trying to untangle himself, but inadvertently pulled her with him until she was sprawled across his chest.

Graceful and her had never, ever belonged in the same sentence, but who the frick-frack knew that applied to when she was lying down, too? But there slap her butt and call her a biscuit because she wasn't going to let him see it. And seriously, if there was a woman on the planet who objected to laying on Draven Kilkenny's chest as he woke up, then her girlie parts needed looking at. "Um—hi."

"I was asleep." He was freaking adorable when he got all flustered. One hand moved the fingers on the other, as if the hand clasped in hers was reluctant to let her go. "I swear I didn't know what I was doing."

Mortification receded, and she couldn't resist teasing him just a little. "Call all the newspapers. I have a front-page story for them." Now free of his hand, she sat up. "Draven Kilkenny doesn't know what to do when a woman is sprawled on his chest in bed." She giggled for all of two seconds when his mouth opened and closed twice as if in disbelief. That giggle turned to a groan when he planted both of his hands on her waist and lifted his hips, pressing against her with his morning wood.

"Doesn't know what to do?" His growl should be illegal. "Are you sure about that?"

"I—"

"Go pee, baby." He shifted his hips and helped her to stand. "Before I show you exactly what I can do."

"Promises. Promises."

What are you? Five?

Before she could get herself into more trouble, she turned and fled toward what she hoped was the bathroom, and if her hips had a little bit of extra sway in them then she wasn't mad about it.

"Other door," Draven called just as her hand touched the door handle. "If you pee in the closet, Gunnar isn't going to be pleased."

Jerk.

"Thank you," she replied sweetly over her shoulder, then entered the bathroom and closed the door softly behind her. There was something infuriating about a man who could make her feel like she was sixteen and turn her on at the same time. "Get a grip, sister. Remind him you aren't that kid anymore."

"Did you say something?"

She paused mid pee and narrowed her eyes at the door. "Are you listening to me use the toilet? Pervert."

"Come out here and I'll show you how much of a pervert I can be."

"Whatever side of the bed he'd woke up on must be the infuriating 'keep me off balance' one. I'll show him off-freaking balance," she promised herself almost silently as she washed her hands. Was it healthy to be all kinds of petty? Probably not. But did she care? With that man in a bed and no pants on... that would be a big fat no. She unbuttoned the pants she'd just closed, pushed them down her legs, and stepped out of them. "I need shorts to sleep in, and they are in my ruck." She gave herself a little pep talk in the mirror. "That's my story, and I'm sticking to it." She couldn't stay in the bathroom all day, so she found her metaphorical big girl panties, pulled them firmly into place, and left the room. "Crap."

Draven caught her wrist and tugged her to one side with her back against the wall. "Did I scare you?"

"Seriously?" There was no way she was telling him that she could feel her heart hammering like she'd had multiple rounds of awesome sex or hiked up to an altitude where lack of oxygen was a serious concern.

"What?"

"Against the wall outside the bathroom door again." Not that she was objecting, mind you. He didn't need that tidbit of information though. "Classy, Draven. Really classy."

"Do you object?"

He pressed against her, hot, sexy, and a whole host of feelings which Indy knew she would struggle to describe. If he would just move his hands from the wall and onto her body, then maybe they could see where this went. If he backed off again, she wasn't going to be responsible for her actions. Maybe if she explained to a jury the reasons why, if enough women were in on it, she could avoid jail time. "Only to the fact that you have me pinned to the wall with your penis when there is a perfectly comfortable bed about five steps away."

His eyes widened slightly, and his nose flared. "Then let's take this to bed." He scooped her up and turned on his heel.

Yes. Finally.

Doing a whoop or a fist pump would be crass, right? She decided it would be, so she settled for wrapping her legs around his waist and hooking one foot over the other to keep them there.

He lowered her onto the bed, followed her down, and paused, hovering over her. "I'm not sure what we're doing here," he whispered softly. "What if this changes things between us?"

She'd wanted him off balance... she had that now, for sure. But she also wanted him to be him. She didn't understand why he couldn't be both. "I'm kinda hoping it will."

"But—"

She lifted one finger and placed it against his lips, silently asking for him to let her continue. When he nodded, relief soaked into her. "I don't see us as an either-or thing," she said slowly. If he got up now and walked away, she'd never forgive herself. But more than wanting sex to happen between them, she only wanted it if it was leading somewhere. "I don't just want to be your friend." She waved a hand between them. "I also don't want this to be just sex or scratching an itch. If we do this, I want—need it to be more." She could tell by the way he was watching her that he was thinking. She'd bared her soul, and now it was time for him to decide what she meant to him. His smile was slow, lazy, and all male when it came, and so totally, in her opinion, worth waiting for.

"I want that, too."

Sweet baby Jesus, grab your bicycle because I have a basket full of thank yous to send you.

CHAPTER TWENTY-THREE

He hadn't felt like he was a teenager since… he had been a teenager. Or if he had, it wasn't in this manner. With Indy under him, watching him as he processed her words, he stumbled. If this screwed everything up…

It won't.

It might.

She's no longer sixteen and you are both adults who respect each other enough to be able to open your mouths and do the talking thing.

It was worth the risk. She was worth the risk. Plus, she had another thing in her favor. Because if it came down to it, and for some reason this didn't work between them, his sister would neuter him with that baseball bat she kept behind the seat of her VW Beetle. He ruthlessly pushed thoughts of his sister aside; she had no place here. "I want that, too," he repeated.

He'd been ready for awkward. Ready for something. What he hadn't been ready for was a smile which warmed him from the inside out, or a split second to bask in it before Indy reached up and claimed his lips.

She kissed him, wet, deep, and hot, tugging at his t-shirt. He helped her take it off, only releasing her lips long enough to whip it over his head and discard it. The need swirled between them as they tasted, tempted, and kissed just as his whole soul craved.

Their hands stripped off each other's clothes until both were down to their underwear. "Matching undies." He dipped one finger under the side of her blue lacy panties. "I didn't know the CIA issued matching lingerie sets."

"They don't." She leaned her head to one side, giving him more access to her neck, and he obliged her by nipping up to the sensitive spot just below her ear. "Just because I was in the field is no reason not to wear decent underwear. Lizz would shoot me if I wore granny panties and didn't test how well our stock holds up."

He snorted. "It sounds like a solid plan when you have stock to—um—test." He lowered the cups of her bra and her breasts spilled free from them. "Far be it from me to prevent you from testing how they hold up…"

She rolled her eyes at his teasing, and he found he loved it. He sat back onto his heels, moving her legs apart so he had room for what he wanted to do. He ran his index finger up her side and across her chest, skimming lightly over first one nipple and then the other. "I'm going to lick and suck these beauties in a minute," he promised her. "But first, let's get you comfortable." He loved that she shivered when he told her what he was going to do to her and made a mental note to do that again—often.

He drew his finger down the center of her breasts, continuing in a straight line until he skimmed over her belly button and across her stomach just above her panties. "I don't know that they'll stand up to abuse."

"Are you going to abuse my panties, Drave?"

Fuck me, that husky voice is sexy as hell.

"Damn straight, baby, damn straight I am." Careful not to hurt her, because that would totally suck right now, he ripped the sides of her panties and dangled them between two fingers, as her eyes widened.

"You... you…" she stuttered and glared at him. "That's a three-hundred-dollar pair of underwear."

He dropped them onto her belly and leaned over her to whisper against her lips. "Don't care what they cost, baby, I promise I'll buy you more."

"You better."

"I promise." He kissed her once more on the lips until her lips were wet from their kisses, and her eyes darkened with desire. He pressed a trail of kisses down her body, licking, nipping, sucking, searching for spots which made her shiver or dragged that little whimpering noise from the back of her throat. Those spots he took the time to lavish attention on until he reached where he wanted to be. He lifted one knee and placed it on his shoulder, admiring her little pussy. "Beautiful, baby. Fucking beautiful."

"Mmh."

With two fingers, he spread her folds before licking her from bottom to top, making sure to circle her clit with the tip of his tongue. She arched almost off the bed as he captured the sensitive spot and nibbled on it.

"Oh my God."

Her taste made his already erect cock jerk in his boxers. One taste. One. And he knew if he didn't make this epic for her, he'd regret it forever. He used his tongue and added his fingers to the mix, stroking and petting her before sinking one into her opening up to the first knuckle, loving that she immediately clenched around him. "Tell me what you need."

"Umm…"

"Tell me." He peered up her body and could confirm when Indy blushed, it started at her pussy and marched up her body to her cheeks. "When it's good for you, it's mind-blowing for me."

"Suck me, please."

He pressed a kiss to her thigh, then did as she asked and captured her clit with his lips, sucking on it over and over until her juices were smeared on her thighs and his beard, and her head thrashed from side to side in pleasure. When he felt her thigh tremble against his cheek, he released her with a pop and kissed his way up her body to let her taste herself on his lips.

"No more playing," he whispered in her ear. "I need you too much."

She nodded.

"Are you sure?" He needed her to be sure. "Are you sure, Indy?"

As if she realized he needed to hear the word, she smiled up at him, one palm cupping his cheek. "Yes. I'm sure. Please, Draven, make love to me."

"Yeah, baby." He scooted off the bed and went looking for a condom before coming back to her. He shoved his boxers down over his hips, all the while watching her face. Her mouth formed a small "O" as his cock bobbed heavily once freed from its material prison. He swallowed hard and his heart thundered in his chest as he rolled the latex down over himself. His cock vibrated in his grip as his blood rushed south, driven by need and desire.

"Come here." She reached for him, and he was powerless to resist. He knelt on the bed with his knees between her thighs, watching her watch him as he grabbed his cock and placed it against her opening. She shifted her hips, making room for him. "Please, Draven, please…"

He cut off her plea with a slow, deep, sexy kiss and thrust forward, taking her in one go. Indy arched, moaning into his mouth.

She's so small. I could hurt her.

So sweet, so wet...

Draven closed his eyes for a moment to savor the pleasure of feeling his cock inside her, skin to skin.

She belongs to me.

Mine!

With his eyes closed, he let the sensations wash over him and lowered his forehead to hers, enjoying the moment.

"Please." She ran her fingernails up his side. "Please do something."

He rocked hips back and forth, thrusting in a deep move into her wet pussy, making them both moan.

He buried his face in the side of her neck, and she tilted her head, giving him access to kiss at the spot where her collarbone met her shoulder. He increased his speed, and she moaned even louder.

"That's it, baby," he whispered between kisses. "You belong to me, I belong to you. Can you feel it?"

"Yeess." She wrapped her legs around his waist, holding him close to her, and met him stroke for stroke. "More, Drave, please more."

He growled deep in his chest and shifted until he was kneeling with his hands gripping her hips as he sank into her and retreated, giving her what she asked for as she begged for more.

"I need…"

"You need?" He paused with the head of his cock spreading her opening. "Tell me what you need, and I'll give it to you."

She covered her face with her elbow. "More." The word squeaked out. "Deeper."

He smiled wider. "Behind?"

"Yeah."

Her hiccupping over what she desired was sexy as fuck

and she didn't even know it. He withdrew from her warm, wet pussy, helped her roll over, and pulled her up ass up until she was sprawled in front of him. "So beautiful, baby," he praised and pressed a kiss to the small of her back just above her butt before stroking with one hand up and down her back.

She shifted her hips back, rubbing against his dick. "Please."

"I fucking love how needy you are." He grabbed both her hands and moved them over her head, pushing on her shoulders until she was pressed against him, ass up, head down. He stroked his cock over her opening, gathering more of her juices, and pushed into her from behind in one stroke. Rough, hard, and deep, just like she'd asked him for.

"Oh, god, yes," Indy moaned. "Please, more." Her pussy clenched around his cock, making him crazy as he held her in place until she got used to his size in this position. He was big, she was small, and hurting her was not on the agenda.

"Are you sure you are ready for this, baby?"

"Yes, damn you." She glared at him over her shoulder. "You won't hurt me and I nee—" Her demand was cut off when he pulled almost all the way out and slammed home again in a thrust which pushed her forward.

He craved giving her what she wanted more than anything. Draven repeated the move, but this time when he bottomed out, he ground against her pussy, his ball sack hitting her clit. He kept his movements slow, but made each one deep, hard, and raw.

Who knew Indy had an off switch for that good girl vibe she'd had going on their whole lives? He hadn't, but he reveled in the fact she flipped it off for him. Her moans and cries urged him on.

"I won't break, damn it, give me all of you."

He took her at her word and released her hands. He

wrapped her hair in one fist, tugged her head up a little, and gripped her hip with the other before driving deep into her, and she clenched around him as he withdrew.

He groaned and released her hip to push one hand under her chest to pinch one nipple. His fingers teased, plucking, pulling, and rolling her sensitive flesh between his fingers.

"Yess," she cried. "I—"

"So wet and beautiful for me." She clenched around him in a death grip and he could sense she was close. He forced himself to do the hardest thing he'd ever done in his life and he pulled out of her.

"Asshole." She punched the bed with one closed fist. "Fuck, why?"

He wasn't quite sure how to explain it other than, "I need you more needy. I don't want this to be over yet."

"You want me to beg?"

"Yes, and more." He pressed himself against her back and kissed her neck before whispering in her ear, "I want you to need my cock, crave it. Crave me. Not be able to think of anyone or anything but me."

"If you think I can actually think right now, you've lost your mind."

He ran his hand up and down his shaft and brought it back to her pussy to run it from her opening to her clit. "It will be time to come when you need my cock more than you need to take your next breath."

"Bossy."

She was only figuring that out now? He gathered some of her juices with his fingertip and couldn't resist running it around her asshole. She stiffened for a split second before pushing back against him. He didn't bother to suppress his moan. His fingers rubbed more of her juices around her opening, and his fingertip pressed against it, teasing her.

"P—please, I need…"

"No, baby, that's for another time. Right now is for us to learn what turns us on. What makes us need each other until neither of us knows where one starts and the other ends." He pushed the head of his cock against her opening. "If you want me, take it," he told her. "Take my cock in your pussy, and make yourself come. I want to see you come on me."

Draven squeezed his eyes shut for a brief moment as she did as he asked. His cock spread her pussy lips as she worked herself back on to him. "Fucking beautiful. Do you know how beautiful you are to me, baby?"

"Mmmh."

He hoped she knew she was beautiful. If she didn't, then he'd make sure to remind her of it often. His cock pulsed inside her with each thrust, and once she had backed onto him fully, he wrapped his arms around her chest, easily lifting her until her back rested against his chest. He shifted back onto his haunches, taking her with him until she was sitting impaled on his cock with her knees on either side of his as he rested against the headboard. "You control how deep." He pressed a wet kiss to her cheek. "How hard. It's how you need it."

"Drave." Her voice was shaky as she leaned her head back, placing it on his shoulder as his hands roamed freely to play with her nipples and clit.

"Yes, baby."

She didn't answer but rolled her hips, keeping him deep inside her when she lifted almost fully off him and dropped down again.

"Fuck."

She smiled and clenched around him, then whimpered when he flicked her clit in retaliation.

He captured her lips in a sideways, messy kiss, his hands gripping her hips and holding her in place each time she dropped on his cock. He loved that she rotated her hips when he did that, as it ground him deep inside her.

"Please, I need more," she moaned. "I can't—"

"Take it, baby." He rolled both her nipples. "Show me how beautiful you are when you come."

"But—"

"Yes, you are beautiful, and this time you will come," he promised. "I already know the mewling noises you make will have my balls drawing up. This isn't me giving or you taking, it's you showing me what you need. Tell me what you need, baby."

"You behind me until I can't breathe."

"Your wish is my command." He adjusted them on the bed and ran his cock across her opening once again with one hand on her hip, tight enough to leave a bruise. "Ready?" he whispered in her ear.

"Yes, please. Now, Draven, make me feel you until at least next month."

So damn perfect for me.

Breathing harshly, he slammed into her and set a punishing pace until they both struggled to breathe. He wasn't gentle, and her cries told him she loved it as much as he did.

"I feel it.

"Need you,

"Please…"

He gave her what she begged him for, everything.

She glanced over her shoulder. "Please…."

"Your clit, baby. Touch, play, do what you need, because I'm so close I'm going to explode."

Fuck, that's it!

She did as he asked, and he felt her knuckles brush against his cock as she rubbed her fingers over her clit. He panted with the need to cum, and by sheer force of will managed to hold off until she exploded, arching and crying under him as her orgasm washed over her.

"Beautiful. Just beautiful." He sped up the pace and closed his eyelids as stars exploded inside him and jets of semen exploded into the condom, and they collapsed in a tangle of arms and legs on the covers.

Draven lay there with Indy in his arms, soaking in her scent, her skin, and how her fingers brushed lightly against his body. These were memories he never wanted to forget. Ones he could pull up during the darkest of nights and be transported in his mind right back to this very moment in time. "I—L—" he snapped his mouth shut in time to stop himself from saying something stupid, the pause filled in by the ringing of his phone.

"What?"

"Nothing, baby. Nothing at all." He reached for the phone. It was time for them to come down from their blissed-out cloud of afterglow and get back to the real world. His real world better include her in it, he decided as he answered the phone. "Kilkenny."

CHAPTER TWENTY-FOUR

She knew by how he answered the phone that he wasn't sure who was on the other side of the call. It better not be a private call, as she didn't think her legs were up to working just yet. She wasn't even sure they would be up to walking by tomorrow either.

I just had sex with Draven.

Holy cow.

Oh my word.

It didn't quite seem real, yet the delicious ache from what they'd just done told her it was so very real. How many times had she fantasied of this moment? The phone call aside, it was nothing like she'd imagined. It was better... so much better. She ran her hand down his hand and her heart leaped when he smiled at her over his shoulder.

He doesn't hate me.

He hasn't changed his mind.

"Yeah, I'll tell her." Draven winked at her. "We are just getting out of bed, so we need showers and shit." He glanced at his watch. "Do we have an hour? Perfect, see you then." He tossed the phone back on the bedside table.

She squeaked when he caught her and rolled her under him. Her lips parted when he kissed her. In contrast to the ones earlier, this one was soft, sweet, and soul achingly beautiful. When he finally pulled back and moved to one side, keeping her in his embrace, she sighed happily.

"Remi McKinley called to tell you that the closet is filled with civilian clothes of every size possible." His hand ran up and down her arm. "We are to pick what we want and wear it to dinner on the terrace in an hour."

"Do you feel like we're being summoned to dinner with my father?"

"Yeah." Draven kissed her again then sat up. "If they start asking me what my intentions are, I'm going to punch them in the mouth."

It really should be illegal for a man to look that freaking beautiful.

She scanned his body and paused where his dick stood still at half-mast with the condom barely hanging on the tip. Her eyes shot back to his and she could feel laughter bubble up inside her.

"What?"

"You have the condom hanging off..." She covered her mouth with one hand and gestured toward his nether regions with the other.

"Off what?"

He was an asshole, but she was laughing too much to be mad about it. "Your little friend."

His expression changed from one of mirth to indignation. "There is nothing little about—er—my friend."

Truth. I still feel you.

She cocked one eyebrow up at him and somehow managed to say absolutely nothing. At first, she thought he was all kinds of pissed when he stalked away from her. But when he crouched at his go-bag and grabbed something, she leaned to one side to get a better look. He turned around, ripping open another foil packet with his teeth.

"Before we go to dinner, let me prove to you that my friend ain't small."

Her eyes widened as he pounced. "Ooh."

"Plan on saying more of that, baby, because now I have a mission."

* * *

ALMOST AN HOUR later she stared at herself in the mirror. Hopefully her hair wasn't too much of a mess, because after Draven had proven to her that his friend wasn't small... twice... she didn't have time to wash it, so a braid would have to do. She smoothed the straps on the blue maxi dress and checked her bra straps weren't showing.

"Swish, swhooo."

She spun around and smiled at him. "You look rather dashing yourself."

"That dress was made for you." He stepped up behind her and wrapped her into his arms. "Are you sure you didn't have it stashed in your ruck?"

"If it had been, it would be covered in mud like everything else." She prayed it wouldn't be see through when they went out into the daylight, because the only cleanish pair of panties she'd had left, Draven had destroyed earlier.

"You make that dress look beautiful, Indy."

She stuck her hands into the pockets and showed them off. "Thanks, it has pockets."

"I hear those are important." He pressed a kiss to her left temple. "Come on, we better move or we'll be late for dinner."

Her belly growled in response. She was used to going for a long period of time with food being scarce, but this was a stretch, even for her. She took his hand. "I could eat a full-grown cow." She paused as he scanned the room before pulling the door shut behind them. "I wouldn't even need salt."

"I hear that." He placed his hand on her lower back and walked with her down the hall. "There's only so long an MRE can hold us over."

Slightly unsure of how their dynamic might have changed, she clamped down on the inside of her cheek, then promptly changed her mind. He knew who she was. He could deal. "You mean we worked up an appetite and now need to refuel for more?"

Please say yes.

If you say no, I'm pushing you down these fancy ass stairs.

He sucked in a breath, snorted, and lowered his head to whisper in her ear, "I don't know if I'm capable of more tonight, baby. Because you wore me out."

"There you are," Gunnar called from the bottom of the stairs. "I was just gonna come hammer on your door."

"Shit like that can get you shot," Draven said mildly. "I get kinda jumpy in a strange place."

She wasn't imagining his hand on her back tensing, right? She didn't think so, and leaned slightly into him, offering silent support for whatever had ticked him off.

"I don't like people who shoot me." Gunnar led them through the kitchen and out into an enclosed courtyard. "Don't shoot me and we're good." He led them to a corner where a long table had been set up for dinner.

"Don't stomp where you don't belong," Draven pulled out a chair for her, "and we're good."

I'm so confused right now.

She glanced from one to the other, trying to figure out what kind of macho stuff was flying over her head, but decided to try and defuse the situation. "Thank you so much for letting us stay." She smiled at Gunnar. "You have a beautiful home."

"Thanks, we like it too." He uncorked a bottle of wine and poured some into the glass at her elbow. "This is wine from Piemonte. It had almost died out, but a couple of growers brought it back. It costs a fortune to buy it outside of Italy." He filled the rest of the glasses, pausing to move out of the way for his brothers to place platters of crostini, cheeses, and cold cuts. "I hope you're hungry, because we may have made a lot of food."

She smiled at the other McKinleys, and nudged Draven with her toe when his face darkened. "You, Gunnar McKinley, provide better service than most five-star hotels."

"Nah, it's just a family style dinner in Italy." Gunnar sipped from his glass. "I don't believe you know all my brothers." He pointed to the one sitting across from him. "This is Colt. He's a pain in my ass, we keep telling him he's adopted as he's the only one with green eyes, but he won't listen…" Gunnar paused, "or leave."

"It's my mission in life to stay where I can make you batshit on a daily basis." Colt grabbed the platter of crostini and offered it to her. "Ignore him," he advised. "He's just cranky because Mom spent an hour chewing his head off for being a dumbass."

"Mothers will do that." Draven picked from the platter and passed it on to Gunnar. "Sometimes not having brothers is awesome, so I can see why you'd want to ship a couple off somewhere."

"Hah." Colt snorted and kept passing platters until her plate was loaded with food. "Don't eat too much," he advised her. "This is Italy, we have about ten more courses to go before we're done."

"Ten?" She was hungry, but not a bottomless pit. "I'm never going to be able to eat that much." How the frick-frack were Italians not as big as house? If this was a typical dinner, she'd have to move up a couple of dress sizes for sure.

"That one hogging all the jam…"

"It's not jam," his brother interrupted. "It just looks and tastes like it." He grinned across the table at her. "It's awesome with the cream cheese. I'll let you taste it for a price."

The crostini Draven had in his hand snapped in two and he dropped both pieces onto his plate. He drank deeply from his wine glass as if he was searching for something, probably patience at the bottom of the glass. Once he came up for air, he scowled across the table. "Remi."

"At your service." Remi McKinley offered a sweeping bow, but because he was seated at the table, only the brother next to him having quick reflexes kept a glass from flying. "Oops. Thanks, Tal."

"Stop being an idiot before Kilkenny kicks your ass," the brother she knew was Talon replied. "Rein it in, bro."

Understanding dawned. She was the idiot. She hadn't picked up on the fact they were flirting with her. Her insides warmed as she figured out what was happening. Draven was jealous.

That can't be possible.

She'd never in her life seen him get jealous of anything. Granted it had been a lot of years since she'd seen him date anyone… but even then, jealousy had never been a trait he'd shown. At least not around her.

"That's our Talon," Colt told her. "He's the peacemaker."

"We met before." She nodded to the former Delta Force operator with whom she'd worked with on a couple of intel gathering roles. "Why is he the peacemaker?" She shifted in her chair until her bare shoulders brushed off Draven's arm.

Draven's grip on the glass stem relaxed. "Because he

defuses crap before it escalates. The other two are jackasses, but good at what they do, so we tolerate them."

"What about him?" She cocked her head toward Gunnar. He didn't strike her as a jackass, although she had no doubt he could be, so she assumed Draven was talking about Colt and Remi.

"He's... um..." Draven frowned as if he was trying to figure out how to respond without insulting their host. "He's Gunnar."

"Nice save." Talon stuffed a crostini loaded with ham, olives, and truffle paste.

"Just making sure we don't get kicked out."

"Gunnar." She sipped her wine. "Gunnar?"

"Pretty much."

She considered how none of them seemed to want to describe the oldest McKinley but decided it didn't really matter. The men made short work of clearing the platters. Colt and Remi disappeared with them and returned with more plates which they placed in front of them.

"There's grilled meats next," Gunnar said. "So don't fill up on too much pasta."

"You're only saying that because you want her to prefer your pork chops over my lasagna." Remi pushed at Gunnar, almost sending him flying off the table. "That's cheating."

Confusion turned to understanding; they must have placed bets on which food she'd eat most of or something. She glanced at the huge plate of Carbonara. "So far, the crostini was awesome." She figured those had been made by Talon, given how he gave her a discreet thumbs up where the others couldn't see. "I'm sure the pasta will be fabulous too." She waited for everyone to sit back down before tasting it. "It's good. Isn't it, Draven?" Indy asked sweetly.

"I think Kilkenny has lost his ability to speak." Talon

smirked across the table. "Did you swallow your tongue, dude?"

"Fuck off."

"Draven," Indy chastised gently, then swirled more pasta around her fork. "We are guests in their home. Be nice."

"Yeah, dude, be nice."

Back and forth the boys bickered, laughed, teased, and generally drove each other crazy. Indy loved every second of it. When operators knew her to be CIA, they rarely included her in much. She'd forgotten how much fun dinner with a crowd could be. Even if Draven was grumpy and possessive, dang it was good for a girl's ego to have the man she was in love with get all kinds of territorial.

By the time they made it to dessert she was convinced she wouldn't be able to eat another bite… until she saw the gelato and changed her mind. Maybe her big toe had some room for that, because her belly was currently stuffed.

"Cheesecake?" Draven peered at the bowl. "You made cheesecake gelato?"

"Yeah, I've owed it to you since Kabul." Gunnar lifted one shoulder. "I always pay my debts."

She was sure there was a story there about that. Although from what she was seeing tonight, it was probably a bet that Draven won. She spooned a mouthful of the gelato into her mouth and flavor exploded over her tongue. "Oh, wow. That's yummy." She definitely had room for this. Zero questions asked. "I am going to need your recipe."

"Sorry, no can do. It's classified."

"Give her the recipe, Gunnar."

"Hell no." Gunnar gave Draven a shit eating grin. "I have neither the time nor the inclination to submit the paperwork to declassify it."

"I'll help you with the dishes." She'd have offered anyway,

but figured it didn't hurt to see if that held any sway over his decision.

"No, Ma'am." He shook his head and spoke around a mouth full of dessert. "In case you didn't figure it out, loser does the dishes."

"No wonder you pulled out the big guns and provided cheesecake gelato." Draven started to point his spoon at Gunnar, then swiftly changed his mind when a drip of gelato landed on the tablecloth. "You don't want to do dishes."

"Dishes are why I have younger brothers." Gunnar smirked at said brothers' protests. "The dishwashers in this house are called Colt, Remi, and Talon."

"Only if she says your dishes were best," Remi reminded him.

"They are gonna bicker for a bit," Draven whispered in her ear. "Or someone is going to flick gelato at someone."

She eyed Remi as he positioned his spoon. "If he does, then he loses by default," she said loud enough for him to hear. "Because it would be a damn shame to waste such yummy goodness by flicking it at his brother."

"Damn. You're mean," Remi grumbled and went back to his gelato.

Draven scraped his bowl clean and pushed it away from him, patting his belly. "So, which dish was your favorite?" He draped his arm over her shoulders. "If you put them out of their misery, we should have time to take a walk before we go back to bed."

She shivered at the promise in his voice. Going back to bed sounded awesome. Walking, not so much. But she knew sleeping before at least attempting to walk off such an awesome meal was asking for trouble. "Do you even have to ask?" She realized how it sounded and winced. "Sorry, boys, but... cheesecake gelato for the win."

Gunnar whooped in triumph, and even though his ego

didn't need any more stroking, she grinned when he threw his arms straight up. "Yes."

Remi narrowed his eyes at her. "Damn it. And you leave tomorrow, so we can't even have a rematch."

"Boh," Colt growled, clearly a habit he'd picked up from living in Italy.

Talon pouted dramatically, making her laugh. "I thought you liked me." He got to his feet and started gathering plates. "I'll grab coffee."

"None for me or I'll never sleep."

"Do you want tea instead?"

She shook her head. "No, but thank you. I'll stick with water for now." This evening was just what she'd needed. There was nothing quite like relaxing with friends to wash the horrors of war off your skin. Now that they'd finished eating, she tucked one foot under her and settled into her chair. "It's so beautiful here."

"Yeah," Draven agreed. "And best of all, there are no freaking mosquitoes."

She'd noticed that too. Usually eating on the terrace in Italy resulted in being covered in mosquito bites. Tonight, she didn't have one, and she hadn't had to slap them away from her either. "Why is that?"

"We screened in the porch." Gunnar pointed behind her. "But painted them black so they don't stand out so much."

Now that he pointed them out, she could see them. "It worked, you can barely see them."

"It also helps that they're alarmed," Draven chimed in. "Even two extra seconds of warning is enough when it comes down to it."

"Damn straight."

She noticed Gunnar didn't deny it. But she wouldn't expect anything less than alarms in an operator's home. Although if she lived here, she'd trip them at least a couple of times a day. As she listened to Draven and Gunnar catching up, she finally could relax. With Draven here, she'd didn't have to worry. He would make sure she was protected if need be. She refused to think of all the time in the future she now had to relax. That was a tomorrow problem. For right now, she was going to sip her water and enjoy watching the sunset over La Spezia.

CHAPTER TWENTY-FIVE

"I can't believe they lost my bag again." Draven took the papers from the man behind the help desk and turned away. "Nem will lose his shit when I send them the paperwork to submit the claim."

"Commercial airlines suck."

"You," he grabbed her bag and wrapped his arm around her shoulder, tugging her close, "have gotten spoiled swanning around on private jets with the alphabets." His brain worked furiously as he tried to figure out what they were going to say to Lizz. His sister was probably illegally parked in the drop-off lane waiting on them.

Her shoulders slumped slightly. "I don't swan anywhere with anyone. At least not anymore."

Crap. I didn't mean to say it like that.

Kicking your own backside should have been considered when humans were evolving, and whoever forgot to add that to the to-do list should have their pay docked. "I'm sorry."

She shrugged. "It is what it is."

But he knew it wasn't. When he'd transitioned out of the Navy, it had screwed with his brain for months until Dalton

Knight had called him and offered him a job. "You left to protect your father…"

"I left to save my own ass."

Ah, fuck, now he understood. He scanned the area, spotted a quiet corner, and changed direction to lead her there. As much as he hated to have his back exposed, he crowded her against the wall and peered down into her eyes. "You feel guilty for leaving the farm. For not following your father's orders, right?"

She broke eye contact. "Kinda. I don't know how to explain it."

"You feel it here." He touched her chest. "And here." Then he tapped the side of her temple. "Everything in you screams you should have followed orders to the letter."

"Yes."

"I hate to break it to you, baby." He gathered her into his arms and hugged her, resting his chin on top of her head. "You're normal. Living the life you have and having it all ripped away…" He heard her inhale and knew she was going to brush him off but he kept talking. It was important she understood this was normal. "Even if you were the one who made the call, it's still a shock to the system. Give it time to grieve and find a new normal."

"I know." She huffed, but he knew it was a deflection. She surprised him by adding on, "Logically, I know it. But like you said, it's still going to take time to get used to it."

"At least you have the store to run with Lizz," he reminded her.

"Yeah, I'm luckier than most." She finally softened against his chest. But it only lasted a couple of minutes before she stiffened in his arms again. "Speaking of your sister, what are we going to tell her?"

"That you quit. Why would you tell her any different?"

"No, I don't mean about work." She poked him in the

stomach. "I mean about us. She's my best friend. I don't want to keep this—us, from her."

Shit, he hadn't thought that far ahead. Even so, he was confused at her question. He tipped her chin up. "Do you think I want to keep what is happening between us a secret?" Maybe the airport wasn't the best place to have this conversation, but the conversation mattered. Her answer mattered more than he wanted to admit.

"No." She sighed slowly. "I just don't know how to tell her."

"Straight out like you always do, baby." He refused to believe his sister would be mad about them. "She loves you as a sister. Having us—" yup, this really wasn't the place for this conversation, but he forged ahead anyway, "—building toward a future together will—"

"Have her planning our wedding before we finish talking."

Her flippant comment made his heart ache, and he battled back the disappointment that she still hadn't figured out where he wanted this to go between them. "Is that such a bad thing?"

Maybe if you'd used words to go along with the actions, she might know.

Oh, shut up, listen to her. Brood later.

"It's too soon... we only just..."

"If you say we just fucked," he interrupted, "I swear I'm going to march through those arrival doors and tell Lizz to start wedding planning yesterday."

Her eyes widened. "Stop putting words in my mouth. I wasn't going to say that." She held up her hand and glared at him when he opened his mouth. "I was going to say I want to keep us to ourselves for a little bit. Not because I don't want Lizz to know, but because I want it to be just us before your hurricane of a sister takes off like a sprinter trying to break a world record."

"Okay, but if she guesses, I'm not denying it." She needed to understand that was a line in his personal sand box, and he would not cross it.

"If she guesses, then she guesses," Indy replied. "I won't lie to her, either. I'm not saying that." Her frustration was more than obvious in her voice. "I want us to be just ours for a little bit. I can't explain it. I just do."

He wasn't entirely happy about it, but he could give it to her if it was what she wanted or needed. "Okay. But know it's going to be hard not to let it show. We just spent days getting used to touching and sleeping next to each other... I don't want to change that."

"I know."

Now that he knew kissing her whenever he wanted was going to be off the table until she was ready to spill the beans, he was so tempted to put his aversion to public displays of affection to one side and scandalize everyone here, but he made do with pressing a soft kiss to her temple instead. "We should go. Lizz will either have a ticket or be driving around in circles, fuming at the traffic."

"Yeah."

He turned her toward the doors which led to the arrival's hall, holding her hand until the last second. He had no doubt his sister would guess there was something going on between them. The only questions were which of them she hit up for answers first and how long it took for her to do it.

He was already scanning the area for Lizz's car. The second they stepped through the doors, a long toot from a horn drew his attention and he spotted his sister's hot pink car. "There she is."

The door of the car was pushed open as they approached. "Get in, fast!" Lizz yelled. "The parking jerk is coming back, and he'll ticket me for sure if I'm not gone by the time he makes it to me."

He shook his head at his sister's orders. "Some things never change."

"Thank God." Indy pulled up the front seat. "You sit in the front, your legs are longer than mine."

He winced as she climbed into the back seat. He had no doubt Lizz would pick up on the lack of squabbling between them for who would sit in the back seat.

"Hurry up," Lizz hissed. "He's at the car behind me."

Draven ripped his gaze away from Indy's luscious behind and made eye contact with the ticket dude. He tipped his fingers to his forehead and jumped into the car.

Lizz whipped out of her illegal parking spot almost before he was fully in the seat, and he had to react quickly to get the door shut before he either fell out or it hit the rear fender of the cop car in front of them. "Jesus, Lizz, what the heck?"

"You took so long to come out that he told me I'd have a ticket if I was still there by the time he made it back from his rounds."

His head hit the top of the car when they went over a speedbump a lot faster than they should have. "Fuck." He rubbed the top of his head. "We are moving, and you aren't going to get a parking ticket," he grumbled. "A speeding one, on the other hand… that is gonna happen if you don't slow the fuck down."

"I'm telling Momma that you keep swearing at me." She zipped them in between two busses and into the fast lane. "She'll be mad."

"Hah, Mom will be so happy that I'm back in California that she won't care."

"You are going to go see her, right?" Lizz asked. "Because

I'm not covering for you again. The last time, she refused to bring me soup when I was sick."

He could tell by the way she was both babbling and avoiding talking to Indy that his sister had been totally freaked out by what happened in Africa. "She's fine, I promise." He glanced over his shoulder. "Aren't you, Indy?"

"I promise I'm okay." Indy laid a hand on Lizz's shoulder. "I'm sorry I scared you."

"You can't do things like that anymore." Lizz dashed a tear away from her face. "I get that you have a job to do, but I can't lose you." She changed lanes. "Either of you."

"It won't happen again," Indy promised.

"You can't promise tha—"

"I quit," Indy cut her off. "I don't work for them anymore. Ask Drave, he'll tell you it's true."

He heard Lizz's inhale, but he wasn't sure if Indy had. But he knew she got how stunning this turn of events would be for his sister. "It's true."

"Why didn't you tell me?" Lizz took the exit to bring them back to Riverton. "How could you decide this without talking to me?"

"It was spur of the moment. I swear, once we're home and I have the biggest glass of wine we can find in my hand, I'll tell you all about it."

"You better."

"I swear it," Indy promised and changed the subject. "Tell me what's happening at the store."

Just like that, Indy's promise fixed everything between both women who meant so much to him. He leaned his head against the window of the car and listened to Lizz as she updated Indy on the store. Gossip at neighbors, friends, and other stuff which had happened before Indy had left. Hearing them like this soothed the disquiet in his soul. He'd needed this, needed for what was building between Indy and him to not change their relationship more than he knew.

Everything will be fine. It will work out as it should.

He freaking hoped it did, because he didn't want these women at odds because of him. He loved them both, so they would have to figure out a way forward. They could do that... right?

* * *

Dinner in Italy has been amazing, and the McKinley brothers had done their best to make Indy and him feel welcome. But to Draven, there was nothing quite like having dinner with the people he considered his own family. Catching up with Lizz and talking to his mom on the phone had been the icing on the cake. He finished sorting the cutlery freshly washed out of the dishwasher and laid them all on the countertop. "What kind of heathen puts the teaspoons at the back of the drawer? My freaking sister, that's who."

He pulled the drawer out as far as possible and removed the cutlery tray, put everything in its place, and returned it to the drawer, this time with the teaspoons on the outside where under-caffeinated people didn't stab themselves with a fork every morning. When he stepped away from the counter, he had to pull up the waistband of his sweats again. His sister might think it was hilarious to have bought him three XL pants. But he didn't. It was freaking annoying, but better than having to wear her robe while his clothes finished washing. He checked his watch and did mental math to calculate the time. "They should be done by now." He opened the laundry room door and scowled at the machine which was still doing its thing. "Slow coach."

"You know the washer isn't equipped with the ability to talk, right?"

"Shit." He whirled around, hitting his shoulder off the door as he did so. "You scared about ten years off my life."

"Sorry."

Given the way she was smirking at him, he knew Indy wasn't sorry. She probably got a kick out of seeing him almost have a heart attack. "No, you're not." He stalked down the hallway toward her. "You did that on purpose."

"Indy, stop winding up hero-pants," Lizz called from her bedroom. "I'm just jumping in the shower. Do not make me come out there because he's dangling you over the balcony."

Hah, there it was, that blush he fucking loved.

"I'm not teasing him. I swear."

"Liar." He came to a stop directly in front of her and cocked his head to one side, listening for movement from Lizz's bathroom, but all he could hear was the shower running. He stepped closer to Indy, and she retreated, matching him step for step until they were in her bedroom. He closed the door behind him.

"What are you doing?"

"I've come to give you a goodnight kiss." He winced because he'd said that louder than he'd meant to. Indy, as expected, elbowed him hard in the belly. "Oomph."

"Indy?" Lizz called through the shared wall of the bathroom. "Are you okay?"

Jeez, does she have ninja hearing?

"Yes." Indy answered Lizz and thankfully didn't protest when he tugged her into his arms. "I just stubbed my toe."

"Ouch, want me to grab some ice?"

"No!" Indy yelled. "No, thank you, but I swear it's okay." She glared at him and whispered, "She'll hear us; the walls are paper thin."

"She won't," he whispered back. "If we're quiet, she won't hear us over the shower."

"You are a bad influence." She wrapped her hand around the back of his neck and tugged his head down to hers. "A very bad influence."

"And you love it."

"I do."

Damn, did she know how hot those small teasing kisses she was pressing against the side of his mouth were? "We'll have to be very quiet." He kissed her lips and her mouth opened under his. "Can you be quiet? If you can't, tell me now and I'll leave." She didn't answer him immediately. Instead, she kissed him until he didn't remember they were supposed to be quiet and he groaned softly.

"Shh." She shushed him and tugged him toward the bed. "Just sleeping, okay? I…"

He put a finger to her lips and smiled softly. "Just sleeping, I promise."

She pulled back the covers and climbed into bed, giving him an awesome view of her ass as she crawled across the bed. "Thank God, because I don't want you to leave."

He was too much of a gentleman to remind her that it had been her decision to keep their relationship quiet for now and not his. He laid down next to her, and she scooted into his arms, turning over so he could wrap around her. "Night, baby."

"Why do you call me baby? Is that something you call—"

He stiffened against her and swallowed hard, barely remembering to whisper and not speak loudly. "Don't you dare finish that sentence. I've never called anyone that but you."

"Oh." She pushed her hand under where it rested against her belly and intertwined his fingers with hers. "I'm sorry. I'm still figuring out how this works."

He sighed; she was right. This was new for both of them. "Me too, baby." He refused to stop calling her that name. He liked how it sounded when he said it to her. The warm fuzzy feeling it gave him was pretty damn awesome too. "I'll leave in a bit, okay?"

"Mmh."

He wasn't sure she heard him, but he figured it would do. He had to be back on the couch before Lizz got up in the morning.

Sneaking around like a damn teenager is not my jam.

But for her I'll do it.

• *For now.*

CHAPTER TWENTY-SIX

"Want to tell me what's going on between you and Draven?"

Indy eyed Lizz as her friend handed over money to the Starbucks cashier and waited for the change. She'd thought they'd been discreet. Obviously, they hadn't been discreet enough. Either that or Lizz had totally upped her observation game in the weeks she'd been gone for work.

Nope.

No.

I really don't.

She knew none of those would work with Lizz. "Nothing is going on between me and Draven." Crap, did she know he'd slept in her room last night?

"Hah, liar." Lizz put the car in gear and stopped at the next window. "You forget that I know you both." She reached for the coffee mugs. "Thank you." She handed Indy the to-go mugs and drove forward. "I know you both better than you know yourselves. So don't treat me like an idiot." She whipped her car into a parking spot and glared at her. "So spill."

"There is nothing to spill." She popped the lid off her to-go cup and added some sugar before shutting it again. There was little chance of Lizz dropping it. "When there is, I promise you will be the first to know."

"Hah, you said when, not if." Lizz thumped her hand off the steering wheel. "I knew it."

This was the problem of having your best friend be someone who'd known you most of your life. They knew all your tells, and Indy was sure she had some. "That didn't mean anything," she argued.

"Lie to yourself, sister, but not to me." Lizz sipped her coffee, then got them back on the road. "Don't think I'm going to forget about this one," she muttered. "We have to open the store as I have some customers coming in who want to do so before the mall gets busy."

Grateful for the change of subject, she latched onto it. It also sounded like a weird thing for Lizz to do. They rarely opened for individual clients. "Do we have some celebrity customers that I don't know about?"

"No." The corners of Lizz's lips curved into a smile, telling Indy that she liked whoever this person was. "Remember me telling you about the customer who had a flashback a while ago?"

Indy nodded. "Yes." She'd felt terrible for the woman involved and her friends. Flashbacks were horrid at the best of times, but having one in public left you with a whole host of secondary feelings, and embarrassment was usually at the top of that list.

"She and her friends have been in a couple of times to try and help Fiona get more comfortable around people." She hit the flicker at the entrance to the mall. "We both know how devastating flashbacks are, so I offered to open early so they can shop without others around rather than spend most of the time in the store watching to see if something will trigger her."

"That's really kind of you."

"I like these ladies. They are good people." Lizz parked and switched off the engine. "I'm guessing you will, too."

"Awesome." Lizz didn't typically like most people; that she did these women was high praise indeed. Indy gathered her purse and coffee and followed Lizz to the store. While Lizz turned off the alarms and set up the cash register, Indy grabbed a duster and got to work on the shelves. "What time will they be here?"

"In about five minutes."

"Okay."

"Soooo…." Lizz called from the office. "What's happening with you and Draven?"

Indy opened her mouth to deny it and snapped it shut again when a knock sounded at the door. "They're here," she called. Never mind saved by the bell, she'd been saved by the knock and decided these women could be gremlins but she'd like them anyway. "I'll get the door!" she yelled to Lizz and went to let their guests in. "Good morning. Come on in, ladies. I'm India, nice to meet you."

"Fee…"

Indy tensed at the sound of a man calling a woman's name, but when the women turned toward the voice with smiles on their faces, she relaxed again.

Do I know that voice?

The thought barely had time to form in her head before a man she recognized appeared and stopped in front of one of the women. He gathered her into his arms and kissed her soundly on the lips.

"You forgot to kiss me goodbye."

"We don't say goodbye, Hunter, we say see you later," the woman, Fee, scolded him, but stayed in the circle of his arms.

Indy's eyes widened when the man raised his head to scan the room. He scanned past her, then stilled and turned toward her again, locking eyes with her. Indy dipped her chin; she wasn't sure what protocol was in this instance. She'd follow his cues if he gave her any.

"Hunter?" The woman Fee called his attention back to her, as the other women turned toward her and narrowed their eyes in her direction.

Shit.

"She's Draven Kilkenny's woman," Hunter, or Cookie as Indy knew him said, loud enough that Lizz gasped from where she stood a few steps away.

"I knew it," Lizz crowed. "I freaking knew it." She scowled at Indy. "You and me sister are going to talk about hiding important details from your bestie. Like you are said, bestie's brother's woman."

Cookie gave her an apologetic look. "Nice to see you again, Indy." He spoke softly to Fee again for a second before giving them all a wave and leaving the store.

For once in her life, she was totally lost for words. So much for keeping things to themselves for a while. Draven was going to laugh his butt off at her. She squeezed her eyes shut briefly. If California could just give her a whopping sinkhole under her feet right about now, she'd be grateful. Lizz was speaking to her customers, and as much as Indy wanted to run out the door and hide, she went back to cleaning, because her friend would be looking for answers in about five minutes flat.

"I knew it."

She whirled around toward Lizz's voice. "Don't do that. Don't sneak up on me." She was being defensive and she knew it.

"Don't tease the crap out of you for dating my brother?" Lizz didn't bat an eyelid at her tone.

"Hah, I don't know that it can be called dating when you haven't been on any dates."

"You haven…" Lizz trailed off and tapped her index finger off her chin.

Lord, please save me from whatever is going to come out of her mouth.

"You haven't been on a date, but Fiona's husband called you Draven's woman?" Lizz screeched.

Indy glanced over her shoulder to where the women were gathered around a display stand. But instead of looking at the lingerie, they were watching her and Lizz. She didn't blame them for their curiosity. She'd have been all over it like a scabby rash if she was in their shoes. There was something about watching other people's drama play out which was too fascinating to resist.

Lizz went to the counter and grabbed her phone. "Not been on a date. Who the heck does he think he is? I'll fix that right now."

"What are you doing?"

"Indy, I'm not gonna lie. I love my brother, I really do. But sometimes I want to get in the car and run him over. Then reverse a couple of times, ya know, just to be sure he's gotten the point." Lizz typed furiously on her phone. "You are going on a date."

"Maybe I don't want to go on a date." Oh, she wanted to go on a date. But she didn't want that date to be because Lizz told her brother that a date was required. "Do not send that text, Lizz."

"Too late, sister." Lizz waved the phone under her nose. "It's already sent."

I'm gonna need that sink hole now, please. I don't know who's up there, but there has to be someone pulling levers who can open one up… pretty please.

"You know, sometimes I wonder why we are still friends."

"Because you love me, and I love you, and being a pain in each other's butts is a state of mind." Lizz dropped her phone back over the counter and left her standing there to go talk to the ladies.

"Argh." She was so temped to go in the office and move stuff around. Put the pen holders on the other side of the desk. Little things which would drive Lizz insane for days trying to figure out what was out of place.

"Excuse me?"

Indy slapped a smile on her face and turned around to smile at the woman, Cookie's woman. "Yes?"

"I—uh—I'm Fiona. You know my husband, Hunter." She chewed on the corner of her lip. "I just wanted to say hi."

"Hi, Fiona. I'm Indy, it's nice to meet you." She wasn't lying, it was nice to meet the woman behind the warrior. "Thank you for all you do to support your man's service. He gets to do what he does because he knows you are here waiting for him when he comes home." No matter how many times men like theirs went to war, there was a support system behind them keeping the lights on and the coffee warm until they came home. Wives, families, and friends rarely got the acknowledgement they deserved.

"It's weird hearing someone thank me," Fiona admitted. "But I do appreciate it."

"You're welcome." Indy smiled at her. "Is there something you need help with?" she asked.

Fiona shook her head. "No, I just came over here because we've gotten to know Lizz a little over the last few weeks, and she's kinda a hurricane when she wants something to go her way."

"Right?"

"Yeah. Anyway, I just wanted to make sure that you know you don't have to do anything you don't want to… even go on a date with her brother."

"Have you met him? Draven?"

Fiona nodded. "At Caroline's house before Christmas."

Oh, boy, she hadn't known he'd been in California last Christmas. She wondered if Lizz knew. "I could hug you right now." She backtracked when Fiona's eyes widened. "I won't, but I could," she corrected. "You may have just given me a way to divert Lizz's attention from the me and Draven thing."

"I did?"

"Oh, yeah." She winked at Fiona. "Draven didn't tell her he was here for Christmas. The second she starts going on about the dating thing, I'm going to drop that little nugget of info."

"Won't that drop your man in it?"

"It will," she admitted. "But he's a big boy, he can handle a little bus dropping on his head."

"That's kinda mean… but a good diversion tactic."

"Yeah. I'll think about using it or not." She probably wouldn't, but she was tempted—so freaking tempted. "Did you find something you like?" A change of subject was needed before she drove herself insane trying to wrap her head around what to do.

"Not yet."

"Then let's find you something you love, and which tempts your husband to refuse to follow orders the next time Command tells him he needs to go out." She linked arms with Fiona and led her back in between the aisles of clothing. "What's your favorite color?"

CHAPTER TWENTY-SEVEN

Draven walked out the door of the gas station just down from Lizz's house and sipped on his coffee. Maybe stopping for coffee and donuts after running wasn't the most healthy of options, but he wasn't going to worry about it. This morning, he needed the sugar fix. He spotted a man dressed in jeans and a t-shirt filling gas into a large pick-up and smiled. "Yo, Dude, that you?"

The man at the pumps turned around and waved. "Hey, what the hell are you doing here?" Dude smirked. "And didn't we just have that conversation but in a different corner of the world?" He hooked the gas pump back into the machine. "Are you following me, Kilkenny?"

"Nah, bro, my sister lives a couple of blocks from here. Me and Indy got back last night. The girls went to work, so I came out for breakfast." He held up the sack of donuts. "It's gas station coffee, but I was hungry after my run."

"Same." Dude eyed the bag of donuts. "You driving?"

"Nah, I don't have a car, and Lizz took hers with her. I walked."

"If you hang on a sec, I'll drop you off on my way to

Wolf's," Dude offered. "I just gotta run in and pay. Car's open."

"Thanks. I'll take you up on that." He balanced the take-away cup and the donuts in one hand and opened the car door. His butt has barely hit the seat with his phone buzzed in his pocket. He was tempted to leave it and to pretend he hadn't heard it. It vibrated again, multiple times.

What if it's Indy?

He pulled the phone out and placed it on the dash, wincing when he saw the notifications lighting up the screen.

Lizz: I didn't know our momma raised an idiot.

Lizz: WHY HAVEN'T U TAKEN HER ON A DATE?

Lizz: You are an idiot.

Lizz: TAKE HER ON A DATE, DUMMY!!!!!

Lizz: Don't make me beat you because you're being an idiot.

Lizz: I'm booking you two dinner!!!

The driver's door opened and Dude got into the car. "Are you gonna answer that?"

"I'm still deciding on that."

Dude placed a bag of donuts onto the seat behind him. "Why are you still deciding? Is it work? Because Nemesis doesn't strike me as the type of man who likes to take no for an answer." Dude grinned at him. "Kinda like Command. They don't want you to ask how high when they say jump, they just want you to jump."

"Truth." He handed the phone to Dude and munched on a donut. "Sorry, I should have asked if it was okay to eat in here."

"You're fine." Dude took the phone.

"Read the screen, but don't open a message or she'll see I've read them."

"Hah." Dude took the lid off his coffee and sipped. "You haven't taken your woman on a date? Are you crazy?"

"We got back last night," Draven replied. "There hasn't been time for dates."

"Better hurry up." Dude nodded at the phone. "It sounds like a hurricane is gonna take over and you'll be shit outta of luck to make that first date special." He sipped his coffee. "Assuming you want it to be special, that is."

"Of course, I do."

"Better get to planning, man." Dude smirked at him. "Unless you are planning on bringing her to Aces."

"No." Draven glared at the phone. "I like Aces, but it's not first date stuff. At least not what I'm going for."

"Agreed." Dude handed him back his phone, then drove forward and out of the parking lot. "Where's your sister's place?"

"Oak Tree Apartments on Copper and Fifth."

"I know where it is." Dude turned right out of the gas station. "Sooo, first date planning, huh?"

"Yeah." Draven handed Dude a donut from his stash. "Indy insisted she didn't want Lizz to know about us yet…"

"Why?"

"Beats me."

His phone pinged again, and he scowled at it when he caught a glimpse of the sender's name. "That's Lizz again. Jeez." He was ignoring her for now. "We're in building two. That okay?"

"Sure." Dude turned into the apartment complex. "Tell your sister to back off, man. What you and Indy have reminds me kinda of the guys and their women. It may happen fast, but once it does, it's a done deal."

"Yeah. I thought that, too," he told Dude. "Until Indy said to keep schtum."

"Make the first date epic." Dude pulled to a stop in front of the apartment block. "We'll be at Aces Bar and Grill tomorrow evening though, if you want to stop in and introduce her to everyone. If she lives here, it might be helpful to have some women friends who knows what it's like to be the one waiting at home."

"I appreciate that." He hadn't considered that fact for Indy. She was used to being the one in the field with the CIA. Being the one at home when he went out with Nemesis was going to be a change for her. A big change. "Thanks for the ride, man. I appreciate it."

"No worries."

He got out of the car and closed the door behind him. "If the guys and their women don't object, and Indy agrees, we'll meet you at Aces tomorrow."

"Awesome, text me and lemme know."

"I will." He stepped onto the grass and waved at Dude before turning back to the apartment building. He'd had a brainwave for what he could do for their date... Now he just needed to put his plan into place. He let himself in and dropped the donuts and coffee on the counter before opening his phone.

Draven: Don't you dare plan our first date. I already have it planned. Send Indy home at lunch time.

Lizz: I'm mad with you.

Draven: Mad enough to send Indy home at lunch time?

He opened the freezer and grabbed a package of chicken, then put it on the counter to defrost, and went back to the freezer to search for the lemonade mix Lizz usually had on hand.

Lizz: Fine.

Hah, his sister was cranky with him, but thankfully didn't appear to be annoyed that her brother was taking her best friend on a date. He'd take it.

Lizz: If you hurt her, I'll neuter you without a second thought. I don't need nieces and nephews unless they are Indy's kids.

He winced and cupped his balls. There was nothing like the threat of neutering for a man to go looking for a safe place to hunker down. But Lizz had lost her mind if she thought he was going to hurt Indy.

Draven: If I hurt her, I'll lay still for you to do it. I'll even buy you a plate to serve my balls up to her on.

Lizz: Good, then we understand each other.

"She's a piece of work, but Momma would be pissed if I make her disappear." Grumbling to himself, he went about making the marinade he needed for the chicken. He placed the chicken in a Ziploc baggie and put it in the fridge. He'd cook it later, but for now he needed to do some research. "Perfect first date, coming right up."

CHAPTER TWENTY-EIGHT

Indy slammed the apartment door behind her and yelled, "You summoned me?"

"What?"

She scowled at Draven when he stuck his head around the kitchen door. He could act confused all he wanted. "Lizz drove me home, as she said you ordered her to."

"My sister is a busy body." He stepped out of the kitchen and took her purse from her, dropped it on the side table, and crowded her up against the wall. "I know better than to summon you without at least coffee, a pentagram, and about five different types of chocolate."

"Hah. Very funny."

He brushed his nose against hers in the sweetest of Eskimo kisses. "That has been known to happen every now and again." He ran his hand down her arm and interlinked his fingers with hers. "Will you come on a date with me?"

"She is a pain in the ass."

"If you think I needed prompting from Lizz, then you are mistaken." He stepped back and tugged her gently behind him, leading her into the kitchen. "I've made a picnic and have something I think you'll enjoy planned."

Her eyes widened when he opened the cover of the basket. "You made all this?"

"Yeah. Lemonade chicken sandwiches, chocolate covered strawberries, and I even made some of the peach tea you used to like."

She couldn't stay miffed with him when he'd gone through all this effort. When Lizz had insisted she had to go home to get ready for a date with Draven, she'd assumed he'd felt pressured into it. But this... this changed everything. "You are pulling out all the stops, huh?"

The doorbell rang, and he gave her a beautiful smile before turning away. "That will be the truck I had HQ send from the hire fleet we have access to."

She leaned out of the kitchen to see him signing a clipboard and taking keys from the man standing there. She waited for the door to close before asking, "Where are we going?"

"It's a surprise." He glanced at his watch. "Change into comfy people clothes and wear shoes you don't mind getting dirty."

"Huh?"

"Chop, chop. Time's a wasting." He clapped his hands together and shooed her toward the bedroom. "I'll gather everything, just bring you and we're ready to roll."

Excitement bubbled in her belly. A picnic? She didn't remember the last time she'd had a picnic. MREs in the jungle didn't count. Those were survival. A picnic was indulgence, in her book. She stripped off her slacks and blouse and stepped into a pair of jeans, then grabbed a tank and her favorite Vans. She considered changing them out for a different pair of shoes, but decided she could clean them later if needed. "Comfy clothes also means comfy shoes. Right?"

"Yeah."

She felt the corners of her eyes crinkle as she hopped around on one foot to face him while putting on her second shoe. "Please tell me where we are going."

"Nope. You'll see in a little bit. I promise."

"Can I have a hint?"

"You'll love it."

She followed him back to the kitchen. "That's it? That's all you are giving me?"

"Yup." He grabbed the picnic basket and the keys. "Will you come on an adventure with me, baby?"

God, she loved when he growled that word... 'baby.' "Yes, yes, I will."

"Your chariot awaits you downstairs." He offered her his elbow and together they left the apartment, making sure the door was shut behind them.

* * *

It was ridiculous to be this excited about a picnic. A signpost caught her attention as they took an exit. "Are we going to the Cuyamaca Rancho State Park?"

"Nope." He reached for her hand again and held it on his thigh as they drove toward Alpine.

She briefly thought about teasing him, stroking his leg or something else, but decided she didn't need to. Being here in this moment in time was perfect just as it was. "I'm ridiculously excited," she admitted.

"Me too." He glanced at her briefly, smiled, then put his eyes back on the road. "Almost there."

She craned her neck trying to see where the 'there' was. A small green and white sign was the only indication they were heading to a destination. He turned off the road onto a narrower one. Shortly after, he turned again, this time pausing for an electric gate to open.

"We're here."

"A petting zoo?"

Mind blown. He remembered.

She adored animals but had never been allowed to own one as a kid. Now as an adult, she lived in an apartment, and because her job had taken her away so much, she'd decided it wasn't fair to own one. As a kid, her favorite days out had been when Mrs. Mac and Draven's momma had taken them to a traveling petting zoo. "You remembered."

"It's not dumb, is it?"

He sounded so uncertain. How could he not know how awesome this was? "No." She didn't wait for him to open the door for her and jumped out of the rental. He could bitch about that later. Right now, she had better things to do. As he rounded the hood of the truck, she launched herself at him and hugged him tight before planting a kiss on his lips. "If there weren't those kids over there by that car, I'd kiss you until you forget how to walk."

He stumbled and almost dropped her as he put her back on her feet. "I almost dropped you anyway."

Indy did a happy bounce, and she didn't even care if it made her look like the toddler at the other car. "What animals do they have?"

"I don't know for sure, but from what I can find online, they have everything from peacocks to buffalo and everything in between." He laughed at her antics as she almost dragged him to the entrance. "Not a dumb idea. Phew."

"I told you it wasn't." As he paid for their tickets, she peered through the gate and caught sight of a small white animal. Squinting to get a better look, her heart jumped when she finally figured out what it was. "It's a coo, Drave, they have a mini highland coo."

"That's our Galloways, Miss," the man behind the counter said. "We have two of them, Poncho and Star." He beckoned her closer. "If you scratch under their chin, they will follow you around looking for more." He reached for a package from a shelf under the till. "They also love these pellets."

"We'll take four of them." Draven reached for his wallet.

"No, no," the young man replied. "It's not often someone knows a mini coo when they see one. It's on me."

"Thank you." Indy caught Draven's hand and dragged him through the door behind her. "Best date ever."

"We haven't even started yet. So, you…"

"Shh," she scolded over her shoulder. "I've got you. We have a picnic, and you found a mini coo who looks just like Moooobella."

"Moooobella is why I chose this place." He wrapped an arm around her shoulders and walked with her toward the enclosure. "When I saw those beauties on the website, I hoped you'd get a kick out of it."

"It's perfect." She couldn't believe he remembered Moooobella, who'd lived on her bed until she got lost when she and Lizz had moved from their rental house into the apartment they'd bought together. She reached her hand through the gate and clucked softly with her tongue. One of the two Scottish Galloway mini coos came trotting over to investigate. "Oh, aren't you pretty? Hi, little one," she crooned to the beastie as the coo allowed her to scratch under its chin. "You're so beautiful." The second coo came to investigate, nudging the first to one side to get its fair share of scratches. "Can we move in and stay forever?" City girl she may be, and her life might be here in California now, but for Draven and a highland mini coo or two, she could be tempted to change that. She beamed up at him. "Thank you. I love this."

"You're welcome." He scratched the ears of a donkey who came to investigate. "Don't forget you have the treats for them, too."

"Oh, I do." She ripped open the top of the package and poured a handful of pellets onto the palm of her hand. "Don't bite me, beautiful."

CHAPTER TWENTY-NINE

Four hours later, Draven came back from the car with the picnic basket to the majestic oak tree where Indy had promised to wait for him. "Where did you go?" He placed the basket on the table and looked for her. A pop of blue topped with dark hair told him where she'd disappeared to. "I should have guessed." He wagged a finger at the squirrel who chattered at him from the branches above his head. "Don't you go raiding my picnic basket. I'll be back in a second. I'm going to make sure my lady doesn't try to stash one of your mini coo friends in her purse."

"You are so handsome…"

He could hear her crooning to the mini coos as he crossed the grass. "I'm going to get jealous if you keep talking to the coos like that and not me." Mischief flared in her eyes as she spun around toward him.

"You are so handsome, too, Drave. Such a handsome boy."

He wasn't sure what he'd expected to happen, but her reaching up and scratching under his chin and saying that wasn't it. "Brat." He scooped her up and slung her over his shoulder in a fireman's carry. "Our picnic is being eyed by a squirrel thief, baby. We need to rescue it, stat."

"Okay." She sighed and ran her hand over his lower back. "I can be persuaded to eat a little. Promise me I get to say goodbye to the coos before we leave?"

"I promise." He lowered her from his shoulder and placed her on her feet, wrapping her into a hug. "Your new friends will still be there when we've eaten."

"Best date ever." She pecked him on the lips and sat at the bench, opening the picnic basket.

"Agreed." Draven happily helped her to set out their food and dug in for one last Tupperware box. "The reviews said to bring something for the squirrels." He handed it to her. "Peanuts," he explained.

He'd eaten in too many fancy restaurants to count with women who were dressed to the nines, decked out in pearls and finery. Yet here in this little piece of paradise on a petting zoo, with the woman next to him in comfy shoes and purple Vans, his heart had found its happy place. "You know what I just figured out?"

Indy held a peanut shell in her hand and squeaked when an impatient squirrel snatched it from her fingers. She shook her head. "Nope, tell me?"

"I figured out that love isn't always fireworks and drama. Sometimes it creeps in, makes itself at home, and stays in your heart."

That sounded stupid.

Corny and stupid.

She stared at him for so long he was convinced it wasn't just him who thought that.

"I'm not sure what you are trying to tell me."

Told you it was stupid.

He had to make her understand. "Baby." He cupped her cheek with his hand, making sure he had her full attention. "I never knew love could be like this."

Her eyes widened as understanding dawned. "Love?"

He nodded. "I love you, India Fox. More than you know. There are things to figure out… but I don't care. I just know I love you, and I want to be damn sure you know it, too."

"Tell me you aren't fucking with me?"

He reared back and narrowed his eyes. "Why the hell would I do that?"

"Because, Draven, you are hella slow on the uptake." She tugged him back to her. "I've loved you almost my whole life." She hiccupped. "And you pushing me away…" She blinked away a tear. "It devastated me."

"You were sixteen, and I was an adult." He brushed the next tear away with his thumb. "If I hadn't pushed you away and joined the Navy to make sure I had to stay away from you, I'd have ended up in jail."

He'd thought what she'd felt back then was puppy love. Similar to the title of the Olivia Michaels's book he'd spied on her bedside table last night. He'd been wrong. Now he remembered that book had been called *More Than Puppy Love*, he decided he liked that title more than the other.

How appropriate. I should have known what we both felt was more than puppy love.

He knew he'd hurt her; just as he knew she was it for him. Damn, Trev had been right all along, Hallmark would be asking for the rights to their story any freaking minute. "I love you," he repeated. "I swear I'll never push you away again." He tugged her into his chest, ignoring the squirrel who sat on the picnic table watching them as it stuffed a whole peanut shell into its mouth. The damn squirrel could have the whole basket for all he cared. She needed to know it. To feel it deep in her soul. He loved her. Period.

"I'm ugly crying all over your shirt."

"As long as those ugly tears mean you believe me, then

they aren't ugly at all. They are beautiful, baby." He kissed the tears away.

"They do." Indy turned her head and captured his lips in a sweet, brief kiss. "I love you too, Drave."

Thank fuck.

Relief and happiness almost took his knees out from under him. He leaned against the picnic table with her still wrapped in his embrace and breathed a slow breath. "I love you." Now that he'd started saying it, he didn't want to stop. It may be sappy, it might be ridiculous... but did he care? Not when India had just confirmed she loved him too, he didn't.

Bring it on, world. She's mine now.

"I love you, too."

He kissed her once more and guided her back onto the picnic bench. "Food, and then you can say more sweet nothings to the coos."

"Jealous?"

"Nope." He handed her a chicken sandwich. "I get to take you home. They get to stay here."

She snuggled into his side, munching on her sandwich. "Drave?"

"Yeah, baby?"

"You rock at this dating thing. Thank you."

Thank fuck! I didn't screw it up for once.

* * *

"I THINK my feet are going to be on strike from all the walking."

Out of the corner of his eye, Draven saw her toe off her shoes and tuck one foot under her butt on the seat. Her classic 'I'm comfy and happy' pose. "I'll rub them for you later or run you a bath."

"I'm not complaining." She leaned her head against the window with her face turned toward him. "Best date ever."

"It doesn't have to be over yet." He made a snap decision. "We could go to Aces Bar and Grill for a drink before we go home?"

"I've peopled all day. Can we do a raincheck on the bar and just go home? Curling on the couch and relaxing with you sounds amazing right now."

"Does Lizz count as people?" he asked. "Because she'll probably be home when we get there."

"She isn't people," she reminded him. "But can you deal with the teasing?"

"Yup, I'll sic Momma on her if she interferes." Before she could reply to him, a phone rang from somewhere down near her feet. "That's yours. Mine's in my ass pocket."

"This better not be someone who needs something from me tonight, because I'm going to be mad if it is."

He could see a weird expression cross her face when she got the phone out of her purse and looked at the screen. "What's wrong?"

"It's my dad."

Of course, it was. "Are you going to answer it?" He whipped the truck into a parking lot and pulled the handbrake. He wanted his full attention on her and not on the road.

"I don't know." The phone stopped ringing and immediately started again.

As much as the thought pissed him off, he offered her the option anyway. "Do you want to talk to him in private? Because I can get out…"

"No." She sighed heavily. "Please stay."

CHAPTER THIRTY

Her heart sank when she saw the caller ID. Why couldn't she just have one day to bask in the glorious sunshine which was knowing Draven loved her? Was that too much to ask? Apparently so, as here was her father coming along like a dark cloud rolling across the sky.

"Do you want to talk to him in private? Because I can get out…"

"No." *Jesus, no, don't leave me right now.* "Please stay."

He tugged her across the seat as close to him as she could be without sitting on his lap. "You've got it, baby."

She glared at the phone for a heartbeat more before swiping across the screen and tapping speaker. "Hi, Daddy—"

"Don't you hi Daddy me!" her father yelled down the phone. "What did you do?"

There was no point in playing stupid. If he was calling her, he already knew what she had done. "What was right. Daddy, I did what was right."

"Stupid—"

"Don't call her that again, Deputy Director Fox," Draven

growled. "You don't want to piss me off right now, because I'm feeling really fucking protective of my fiancée."

Your what now?

She gaped at him in shock, her mouth opening and closing, but no words came out at all. He touched his fingers to his lips, asking her silently to be quiet. She had words if she could find them, but for now she trusted him, so she was happy to wait a minute to see how this would play out.

She could hear her father coughing as if something he'd been drinking went down the wrong pipe, and when he spoke it was weird, as if he still hadn't cleared the liquid from his lungs. "I sent you to protect her, not to steal her."

"She has always been mine," Draven replied. "I protect what's mine." There was a warning in his words that even she recognized. "When you are ready to tell us what the fuck is going on, call back. Until then..." Draven cut off the rest, allowing her father to fill in the blanks.

Stunned silence filtered through the phone before her father choked two words and the phone call ended. "Be happy."

They glanced at each other. She could see Draven was as confused as she was. "Did that sound weird to you?"

"Yeah." Draven pulled out his phone. "I'm going to call Nem and see if he can find out what's going on."

"I don't understand what's going on, and up until the other day I was involved." None of this made sense. Her father had always walked the narrow line between right and wrong while working for the CIA. The higher up their ladders he'd climbed, the more that line seemed to blur around him. "God, I hope he isn't involved in whatever it is that those documents were for." She knew she was clutching at straws; there was no way her father wasn't involved. She'd gone to Congo because he'd ordered her to.

"One sec." One of Draven's hands stroked up and down

her arm. The other held the phone out in front of him where she could see too.

"Go, but keep your voice down," Dalton said. "My wife and boy are sleeping."

"Sorry for interrupting family time, Boss," Draven said. "We have kinda a situation and I'd like your input."

"Lemme guess," Dalton said. "This is about your woman's father, and I know she's yours, I spoke to Gunnar two days ago, so don't deny it."

"I—uh—I'm not going to deny it. She's mine as long as she'll have me," he told Dalton. "And yes, her father."

"You haven't seen the news, have you?"

"Boss, we don't all live with the news channels running twenty-four seven like you do," Draven grumbled. "Tell us what happened. You're on speaker."

"First, you are an asshole for not following protocol and telling me that straight off," Dalton grunted. Then the sound of his voice faded, but they could barely hear him whispering, "Those were my balls, son. If you want siblings, don't kick them in your sleep, k? Good boy. Shhhhhh."

Indy covered her mouth with her hand, because despite the inkling of what was to come, there was something about a warrior like Dalton Knight being brought to his knees by a baby which touched the soft spot of her heart.

Draven with babies will be a sight to see.

I can't wait for that day.

"Okay." Dalton came back on the line. "I'm clear to talk."

"Sorry for interrupting…"

"Shut it, Draven," Dalton cut him off. "From what Gunnar tells me, India is yours."

"She is."

"That makes her family. We look after family, period," Dalton said. "India, are you there too?"

"Ye—yes."

"How are you doing, sugar?"

"Just tell me straight out, Nemesis." She didn't want him sugar coating it. Pain was pain, even if it came with a dusting of confectioners sugar over the top. "No filtering needed."

"Your father was arrested for espionage and colluding with terrorists earlier this morning." He had apparently taken her at her word. "Those papers you gave to Gunnar proved it."

Guilt slammed into her so hard she couldn't breathe. "It's my fault. It's all my fault."

"No." Draven turned her head toward him with a finger under her chin. "This is not your fault. None of it is your fault."

"But…"

"He's right, India, this is not your fault," Dalton interrupted. "You did the right thing. Despite that he is your father, you handed over the papers."

"I didn't know they'd incriminate him."

"Would you have handed them over if you did?" Dalton asked.

Somehow, she knew her answer to this question was important, but she answered without hesitation. "Of course, I would have. I'd have sulked about it for at least a year afterward, but I would have still done it," she answered honestly. How had such an awesome day gone to hell so fast? Oh, yeah, the fucking CIA.

"And that's why you are still free and have a presidential pardon for any involvement you might have unknowingly had."

The memory of a previous conversation twigged on the edges of her brain. "Shit…"

"Tell me," Draven demanded. "Tell us."

She refused to look at him. If she cost him everything,

she'd never forgive herself. "Nemesis, what about Draven's clearance if he's in a relationship with me? Does he lose it?"

"No, Ma'am," Dalton replied. "That's the first thing I verified as soon as I saw your father being hauled out the front door of his house in cuffs."

"Thank God."

"Nah, God had jack to do with that," Dalton drawled. "That was all on you. You doing what you did means you both keep your clearances."

"I resigned…"

"Awesome, less paperwork for me when you come to work for me," Dalton replied. "The CIA gets salty when I poach from Ground Branch."

"Boss…"

"Shut it, Kilkenny," Dalton ordered. "This is between me an' your lady. She decides if she wants the offer we are going to email her. You get to have her six and keep your trap shut."

Did Draven not want to work with her? She had so many emotions flipping through her right now she wasn't sure what she really felt about anything—anything but Draven. Him, she knew she loved. "I can't promise anything, Nemesis, until I see your offer and discuss it with Draven."

"Fair enough," Dalton replied. "I expect both of you at the ranch on Tuesday."

"Tomorrow Tuesday?"

"Nah, even I'm not that much of a dick," Nemesis said. "Tomorrow week, my place and we discuss terms… deal?"

She glanced at Draven. He lifted one shoulder as if to say 'it's your decision.' She nudged him with her elbow and gestured to the phone. It wasn't her decision, it was theirs. Draven blew out a breath and nodded. "Okay, Nemesis, we'll see you next Tuesday to discuss terms."

"Deal?"

She glanced at Draven again and waited for his nod to come. When it did, she replied, "Deal."

"Good." The phone screen went black.

She tapped the screen with her fingernail and it stayed dark. "Did he hang up?"

"Yeah."

"What do you think?"

"How do you feel?"

They both spoke at the same time. He squeezed her into a hug. "How are you doing, baby?"

She had no clue how she was doing. Mad, upset, worried, scared, and a whole host of other things all jumbled up together. "Honestly, I don't know. It's going to take a bit for it to sink in. My father is a spy."

"Right?"

She was the reason he was arrested. She should have known something was off from the start. "I wonder what was in the papers?" she mused. "Nemesis didn't say, right? I didn't miss it because my brain jumped on the 'what if I'd done things differently' merry-go-round."

"No, he didn't say," Draven confirmed. "You didn't look?"

He knew how these things worked. "Why would I look? It was none of my business and my orders said transport them, not read them."

Draven reached between them and snapped the seat belt open, then lifted her until she was sitting on his lap with her feet on the passenger seat. "We'll figure it out, okay?" He brushed her hair back from her face with one hand. "Don't shut me out, baby. We will figure it out, I promise."

"You shouldn't want anything to do with me." It physically hurt to say it. "You should run as fast as you can and never look back."

"You've lost your mind.

"You are mine.

"I am yours.

"The rest is bullshit we figure out how to navigate together."

"We do, huh?"

"Yup."

Bullshit we navigate together sounded pretty damn awesome. "Okay." She nodded. "Okay, I'm good with that."

"Thank God, because I fully intend on being the person you wake up with every morning for the rest of our lives." He scooted her off his lap and back into her seat, snapped the seat belt closed, and put the car back in gear. "Ready, baby?"

"Yes." She had no clue what the next few days and weeks would bring, but she knew she'd figure out a way to get through it as long as she had Draven by her side.

Draven reached for the car radio and switched it on, but immediately hit the off button again when the news reporter started speculating on the crimes Indy's father may or may not have committed. "We don't need to listen to that."

"I'd sing for you," she fell back into her habit of joking to cover up the hurt, "but I really don't want to walk all the way back to Riverton."

"I wouldn't do that to you." Draven paused a heartbeat before tagging on, "I might stick you in the trunk to muffle the sound, though."

"Just you try it." She poked him in the arm. "I know how to knock out the rear lights. You'll be the one on the news later."

"Ha."

Teasing each other back and forth made the journey home shorter, and before she knew what was happening, he slowed almost to a stop at a detour which stopped them from turning off near the store close to her apartment complex. "What's going on?" All those flashing blue lights and multiple police and emergency vehicles were not a good sign.

Draven lowered the window when a cop approached and motioned for him to do so. "Is everything okay, Officer?"

"I'm sorry, Sir, you can't come down this way," the officer said. "Which way are you headed?"

"Copper and Fifth."

"Sorry, Sir, we are dealing with a hostage situation and need to keep the area clear."

"I'm a contractor for the DOD. Do you need backup?" Draven fished a badge out of his pocket and handed it to the cop.

"We should be good, Sir." The cop scanned the badge and handed it back to him. "We have a Navy EOD on site."

Both of them tensed as understanding dawned. If they had an EOD in play, then it wasn't just a hostage situation, but there were explosives involved too.

"A dangerous situation all around, then." Draven swapped his badge for a business card. "I'm at the apartments just off Copper and Fifth. If shit gets out of hand, call that number and I'll come on the run with backup not far behind me."

"I appreciate the offer, Sir." The cop gave them a tight smile. "But I'm sure we have it under control." Just as the words were out of his mouth, gunfire rang out. The cop took cover next to their truck. Draven pushed her head down, using the engine block to provide them with cover if a stray bullet happened to come their way.

"Sounds like sniper fire," he whispered in her ear.

She agreed. It did sound like sniper fire. "More than one shooter."

"Yeah."

The cop's radio crackled outside their vehicle. They couldn't make out the words, but understood the cop's response. "Ten-four." He cautiously raised from his crouch near the car door with his hand still on his holstered weapon.

"Sir, it really would be better if you took your lady some-where safe until this is over."

"Roger that." Draven touched his fingers to his forehead. "I'm just going to do a U-turn here and get out of your way."

"Thank you, Sir." The cop watched them until he disap-peared from sight in the rearview mirror.

"This is Riverton," Draven grumbled. "It's supposed to be a safe place to live, damn it."

"It usually is." She patted his arm. "This is not normal for here. I just hope all civilians are okay and nobody is caught in the crossfire."

"Yeah."

Silence fell between them, and neither spoke again until Draven pulled into the visitor parking spot at the front of her apartment block.

"Drave?"

"Yes, baby?"

"Thank you for today. I loved every second."

His eyebrows flew upward as if in disbelief.

"Yes, every second. It was you and me together, and I got to see and love on some mini coos. Everything else is for tomorrow me to worry about. Today, it's you and me against the world."

"You're right." He parked the truck and locked it when they were both standing on the sidewalk. "Tomorrow is time enough to deal with the rest of the world." He shifted the picnic basket into the hand further from her and caught her fingers with his, linking them together. "Tonight is for us."

She freaking loved the sound of that so bad. "Yes. It is."

CHAPTER THIRTY-ONE

Draven took the keys from Indy, but before he could put them into the lock, the door opened and Lizz stuck her head around it. "Oh. Crap, I didn't know you'd be back yet. I was just leaving."

"Hell no." If she thought she was going anywhere until he knew the bomb threat was over, then his sister had lost her mind. "Get your ass back in the house, there is shit going on at the corner and I do not want either of you getting hurt."

"But…"

"Nope." He'd pick her up and carry her back in the door if he had to. "Tell her, Indy."

"You know how much I hate to admit any man is right, even this one." Indy winked at him where his sister couldn't see. "In this instance, he is right. It's dangerous in town tonight. It's safer for all of us to stay behind closed doors."

Lizz glanced from one to the other and back again before she huffed in annoyance and led them back into the apartment. "Fine. I'll be the third wheel."

"Ah, fuck." The last thing he wanted to do was make Lizz feel that way. This new dynamic between all three of them

251

BELLA STONE & ANNABELLA STONE

was going to take a little time to figure out. "You aren't the third wheel." He caught his baby sister by the arm. "I still love you just the same as before…"

"I know that, you idiot." Lizz slapped at his arm. "Why would you think that you and Indy being together doesn't thrill me to bits? I get her as my sister for realsies. That's the best gift on the planet."

"Ah, Drave," Indy called from the kitchen doorway. "You've gotta see this."

"Do not leave the apartment," he warned Lizz. "It's not safe. Please stay." He went to the kitchen, where Indy waited at the door.

"Don't be mad at her," Indy whispered. "Look what she did for us." She stepped out of the way and he scanned the kitchen, skimming over the counters and onto the breakfast nook which was set up for dinner for two. Candles and a centerpiece were in the middle of the table.

"I made stuffed pork chops, gratin potatoes, and veggies," Lizz said from behind him. "I wanted tonight to be special for you two without me in the way."

"We love you!" Draven drew his sister into his arms and hugged her. He glanced at Indy over Lizz's head, and she must have read his mind as she nodded and went to grab another chair and put it next to the table. "Family is important," he reminded Lizz. "We are your family, and you are ours. Please stay."

She nodded and sniffed. "I only made dinner for two."

"Then it's just like old times," Indy said. "When your momma made food stretch to make sure I was taken care of, too." She blew out the match in her fingers and lit a second one for the other candle. "Family."

"Family." Draven smiled when Lizz spoke in time with him. "Jinx." The old teasing from when they were kids snuck in, and everything was back on track. They added more salad and a side of veggies, then split the meat and potatoes between them. They laughed, they reminisced, and they enjoyed the simple pleasure of sharing a meal with family who mattered.

By the time he and Indy made it to her bedroom, his heart was full and it had begun to sink in that Indy was his, and he was hers.

Wow. Just wow.

Indy stood in front of him and cupped his face, her eyes shining with emotions which tugged at his heart.

"You're an extraordinary woman, Indy."

My woman! My world!

"No." She shook her head. "I don't want there to ever be a time where I forget my best friend just because I'm in love with you. Or for either of us to make her feel less because we are a part of something she isn't."

If he hadn't loved her already, that would have done it. He lowered his head to scan her face and placed a delicate kiss on her lips, kissing her slowly and tasting her. As they kissed, he could feel the urgency, the desire to lose himself in her, but he refused to allow it to take over. Tonight he wanted to savor, to devour, and to love Indy until she felt it in her soul.

He leaned down and scooped her into his arms. She buried her face into his neck as he crossed the room to the bed, where he carefully put her back on the floor.

He smiled as the moonlight from the window seemed to light her up, reminding him of an angel. His angel. His bright spot in the darkness when the world went to hell and back. He stripped off his shirt and dropped it on the floor.

"Do you have any idea how beautiful you are?" She traced the muscles of his chest with one finger, leaving a trail of goose bumps in her wake. He helped her undress and she wriggled to help him get her jeans over her hips. "God, I need to touch you so bad."

She smiled softly at him, slid her hands up his arms to his neck, and wrapped around him. Standing on her tiptoes, she pressed against him.

"Make love to me, Draven," she whispered against his lips.

He kissed her as they moved backward until her calves bumped against the bed. He laid her gently down onto the covers.

"You make me feel positively tiny, yet you fill my heart so full I think it might explode," she whispered. "I've never felt this way about anyone before."

"You're so beautiful, baby, and it blows my mind that you don't see it." He lowered himself over her, and she wrapped around him, pressing a kiss to his throat. This moment, that kiss, was the one which he knew would be etched in his memory forever. This moment mattered more than anything ever had before or would again. This was the moment he heard the sound of her heart welcoming him home.

Indy moaned without restraint as his hands explored her body. She gasped with pleasure, arching under him when he found sensitive spots.

"Your reaction to my touch drives me crazy." He pressed his erection against her, letting her feel what she did to him. She ran her nails down his back as he blew across one of her nipples.

"Please don't make me wait." She pressed kisses to the skin she could reach and shifted her hips, opening herself wider, offering herself to him. "Please, Drave, I need you inside me."

"Me too." He grasped his cock and lined it up with her opening, pushing in deep. Her gasp and smile urged him to take her hard and fast. But tonight, he wanted more, he needed the connection. Leaning on his forearms, he took her slowly while watching her eyes. It was so easy to get lost in the magic which seemed to weave around them. He took his time, building up the ecstasy, savoring every breath, every touch between them.

Indy sighed. "So good."

He smiled at her, bending down to capture her lips and kiss her passionately until both needed air. The need to say the words pushed at him, begging him to tell her. But before he could, she pushed at his side. "Roll over, babe."

Babe?

I love that she called me that.

He lay back against the pillows as she positioned herself over the head of his cock. He stayed still as she slid down until her tight pussy opening pulsed around the base of his cock. He groaned, a low animalistic sound which wracked through him.

Her hair fell over her shoulders, brushing off his chest and adding to the sensations. His hands curved around her hips, flexing and squeezing as she took him deep inside her. She placed her hands on his shoulders as she rolled her hips back and forth, making them both moan.

Draven moved one hand from her hip and ran one finger down the side of her neck. When she tilted her head to one side, he wrapped that hand around her throat.

"Yes, love it." She sped up, her pussy caressing his cock with each stroke. Jesus, he'd never felt the fire of an orgasm building like this before. She was the spark, and he was the firework waiting for her touch. "My Indy," he murmured softly.

"Yours," she agreed.

The more she rolled her hips, the closer he needed to be to her. He sat up and pressed his chest against hers, kissing her slow and deep in time with the rocking of their hips. This connection was everything and more. He leaned his forehead against hers. "I love you, baby."

"I love you, too. So much." She kissed him again, her arms

around his neck, keeping their bodies flush together. Somehow while they were kissing, they shifted positions again with Indy under him, and Draven couldn't resist the control she offered him. He moved harder and deeper, long slow strokes alternating with some faster shallow ones. He called on every ounce of discipline he'd gained over the years to get her to the point where he could feel she was right on the edge. He forced himself to keep his rhythm steady, and her moans turned to a scream as she arched under him, climaxing and taking him with her.

Drave exploded inside her, every pulse of his cock shuddering through his whole body as he emptied himself deep inside her. His forehead pressed gently against hers and her fingers stroked through the hair at the back of his neck until they rolled onto their sides and he could keep her in his arms as they reveled in the bliss of afterglow.

"I love you." He wanted her to know this wasn't just something he'd say during sex. "I love you, baby."

"Love you." Her words were sleepy as she blinked up at him. "Love you too."

"I know." He did know. The knowledge wrapped around him, soothing the harsh edges life had given him. Knowing she loved him was the bandage his heart hadn't known it needed.

"We are doing this again, right?" She winced when his cock slid free of her body.

"Yeah, baby, every time you want until forever comes."

"Forever."

She rolled away from him and he let her go, knowing she'd want to clean up. It killed him that she wouldn't let him do it for her. But if that was her line, he'd respect it. He watched the sway of her butt as she walked to the bathroom and closed the door behind her.

Forever is never going to be long enough.

CHAPTER THIRTY-TWO

Nemesis Ranch, Montana

DRAVEN WATCHED Indy walk into the conference room with Dalton and his team leaders. Today was important for her. She wasn't the type of woman to sit at home expecting her man to bring home the bacon. She needed to have something to do, and after the life she'd led to this point, working in a store with his sister wasn't going to cut it. "Good luck, baby."

He must have spoken louder than he'd thought as she turned and gave him a small smile just before Dalton shut the door behind them.

Please let this go okay.

Hopefully the position Dalton was offering her fit her. She'd been one hell of an analysist. In his opinion, if that meant she rode a desk from the safety of the compound here, then he'd be a happy camper. Having Indy safe behind the ranch gates and in the depths of Nemesis Inc. meant he could do his job without worrying if she was safe. He glanced at the door once more and turned away to go find the person he hoped was waiting for him. He stopped on the way past the war room door and knocked before sticking his head in. "Hey, Trev?"

"Hey, is your woman in her meeting?"

He liked how they called it a meeting when they all knew it was an interview with multiple parts to it. "Yeah, she just went in. Will she be about the same time it was when I came through?"

Trev flipped through his computer screens. "The boss has blocked off four hours."

"Awesome. Thanks, man."

"You're welcome," Trev called after him as he left the room again. "Hey, Kilkenny?"

He tensed. Damn, he'd been just about to give himself a mental pat on the back for escaping without *that* coming up. "Yeah?" He paused and looked over his shoulder at Trev.

"You owe me big for this." Trev folded a piece of paper into an airplane and flew it across the room to him. "Plus…" The asshole had the audacity to smirk at him. "I told you so."

Draven unfolded the paper plane and scanned the invoice. "Holy shit, that's a lot."

"I got you two of them," Trev said. "So, me and Logan doubled up on everything. It was the only way the previous owner would sell us one. Me and Winters figured two was better than one."

Indy was going to lose her mind, if she didn't murder him first. "Do I have enough in the main account for you to pay that invoice?"

"Already taken care of, bro." Trev grinned at him. "Oh… and I told you so," he repeated, and waited for Draven to look at him.

"Shut up," Draven grumbled. He'd known this was coming. He'd even given himself a silent pep talk in front of the mirror before he'd left his place with Indy this morning.

Little good that did him, as he could feel himself bristling under Trev's smirk.

"Hallmark. I'm callin' you Hallmark from now on." Trev scribbled a Post-it note. "You are no longer Bravo Three, you are Hallmark. I'll send out an intel notice."

"Fuck you, Trev. Just fuck you." He hurried his ass out of the war room, because Trev sometimes didn't pick up on social cues or remember when to stop teasing people. This was to be a good day; he didn't want to get all kinds of mad about something he couldn't change. He glanced at his watch. It was time to find Winters and put the rest of his plan in place.

* * *

SHE'D SPENT years facing down operators, generals, and a whole host of very important people. But after the last three hours, Indy figured she was safe to finally brush her palms over her pantsuit. She'd done what she could. Sent more rounds down range and climbed more ropes than she had since she'd graduated through the farm at Langley.

She kept her gaze on a smudge on the wall just past Dalton's left ear, which kept her gaze almost directly in the center of the table, and forced her body to remain still while they scrutinized her. Finally, Dalton looked at each man. She couldn't detect any movement or response from any of them.

Jeez, they don't give much away, do they?

Gimme a hint.

I'm dying here.

Dalton cleared his throat. "We're all set here." He got to his feet and offered her his hand across the table. "Welcome to Nemesis Inc., India." He finally smiled for the first time in the last three freaking hours. "We'll get you with Trev tomorrow and figure out your orientation and shit."

Kentucky Smith, Bravo team's leader, scribbled something on a piece of paper and pushed it across the table to her. "We have one more stop for you to make," he told her. "This one isn't a test as such. But you do need to report to this office before the end of the hour."

"Okay." She took the paper and glanced at the hand drawn map. Were they seriously sending her out by herself? She hoped Draven was still out there waiting so she didn't wander into a field with a bull or something equally silly.

"Just stay on the path and you'll be fine." Kristof offered her his hand, too. "If I'd known this was how things would turn out, I'd have insisted you came straight here instead of detouring to Cali."

Heck no, even with all the drama over her father and the bomb threat at the store on the way back from their first date, she wouldn't change the last week for anything. "California was awesome. I was meant to be there."

The three men came around the table and guided her to the door. "We'll bring you up and through security." Dalton held the door open for her. "Then you get to that location and you're done until seven in the morning."

"Thank you." India appreciated the job, especially one in her field, more than these men would ever know. "I won't let you down."

"We know." Kentucky scanned his badge for the lift and ushered her in before them. "You wouldn't be here if we thought that was possible."

"Agreed," Dalton said, and Kristof nodded too.

"You might be family," Dalton said, "but I don't hire people just because they are family. I'd have offered you a standing invite and a place to live if it was needed. I offered you a job as it's one I believe you are more than capable of excelling at. Clear?"

"Crystal." Relief slammed into her. She'd worried that

they were doing this as a favor for Draven rather than for her skills. She should have known better. Nemesis only hired people he wanted. Draven's desires weren't even on his radar. "Still, I appreciate it."

Once they were on the main floor and through security, she was brought outside the front door. Kristof plucked the map from her fingers, turned it around to orientate it, and handed it back. "You're going that way." He pointed toward the barns and corrals she'd passed on the way up here with Draven a while ago. "Don't get lost."

There was nothing left for her to do but get moving. If this was somewhere she was supposed to go, then she'd follow orders and go there. But if there was a pissed off bull at the other end, then she was going to beat the lot of them. She wouldn't even care that they were her bosses if that happened. She would show them no mercy at all.

That's an odd place for balloons.

She decided they were nothing to do with her, and paid little attention to them at first, the papers nailed to the fence posts along with balloons. It was only when one of the balloons hit off the barbs on the wire and popped, making her jump, that she took a closer look. She brushed the page down from where it had curled up with the wind. "U."

These people are kooky as all get out.

She moved onto the next one and peered at the letter, written in big bold purple sharpie. "M."

U.M. Um? That doesn't make sense.

She glanced at her watch. She had forty-five minutes to make it to her destination, and these papers went all the way to the corner of the barn. There were only four more posts until she reached that point. Her curiosity got the better of her, and she glanced over her shoulder and counted back the posts with balloons flying overhead. "Eleven of them." She had time. Nosey or not, she was invested now. She went back to the first post and peeled down the page. "I." The next post revealed the letter N. "In." The next three letters revealed gave her pause. "D.I.A." *Shit, it wasn't in, it's India.* "They could have told me this was part of the test. Assholes."

She dug into her purse for a pen and turned over the map Kentucky had given her, writing her name on the page before starting with the rest of the letters.

India W.I.L.L.U.M.A.R.R.Y…

India will U marry…

This cannot be happening!

This isn't real!

I refuse to believe this means what I think it means.

Fluttering around the side of the barn, she spotted one lone balloon and turned the corner. Her brain still refused to get four when she put two and two together. In front of her in massive letters built out of hay bales was the word 'him?'

Her heart pounded in her chest as she looked for him, and her eyes narrowed in confusion when she saw who, or rather what, was at the end of the hay bales. Munching to their hearts content were two itty-bitty baby Galloway coo calves. "Will I marry a highland coo? What kind of ranch is this?"

The sound of a throat clearing behind her scared the crap out of her, and she whirled around. Her purse was heavy enough to use as a weapon. She gripped it, ready to let it fly if needed, and stumbled to a stop. Spontaneous tears welled in her eyes.

From his position on one knee in front of her, Draven smiled up at her. "Not will you marry him," he said softly. "Will you marry me?"

Her mouth opened and closed. She couldn't speak around the lump in her throat. She glanced back at the word him, and the calves, then back at him again.

Answer him.

YES!

Absolutely yes!

But still no words came out of her mouth.

"The guys had this whole idea to hogtie me in place," he grumbled. "I wouldn't let them." He closed his eyes briefly and opened them again. "India, will you marry ME?" He held up the white gold solitaire ring and offered it to her. "I don't want to spend any more of my life without you. Will you keep my heart along with this ring and let me have yours forever? Be my wife. My life. My forever love?"

"Yes." It came out as a squeak as she dropped to her knees and threw herself into his arms. "Oh my God. Yes!"

"Thank fuck." Draven slipped the ring on her finger, pressed a kiss to her skin where it rested, then captured her lips for a slow, sweet kiss. When he pulled back, he dashed away a tear from his eye and brushed one away from hers with the other. "You had me worried there for a minute."

"I thought someone wanted me to marry the freaking coo." She swatted at his chest. "I was all kinds of confused."

"I figured with a new job, you might be too busy for us to get around to having the kid conversation. But these babies might make the perfect gift from me to you." He helped her to her feet. "It makes my heart happy when you coo to the coos, because it tells me you are happy."

"I am." She sat on one of the hay bales and extended her hand for the calves to sniff.

"Did she say yes?" a voice yelled from the barn.

"Yes, I did!" she yelled back, startling the calves who bounded away, kicking up their hind legs. A whoop drifted from the barn.

"I'm not dreaming, right?"

"No, baby." Draven wrapped her into his arms against his chest. "Unless it's dreaming of how our life will look like here in Montana."

She remembered the teasing Draven had received when they were overseas and grinned up at him. "'Hallmark in Montana' has a good ring to it."

His mouth dropped open. Hah, he hadn't been expecting her to say that. She giggled as she watched the emotions play across his face, then he called over his shoulder.

"Someone look after the babies."

"You got it."

She didn't have time to figure out what was happening as she was looking for the source of the voice. She squeaked as he scooped her up into his arms and took off toward Bravo House at a brisk walk as if she weighed nothing. "Is Hallmark in Montana about to move way past the PG rating?"

"Damn straight, baby. Damn straight."

The rest of the world could wait. That happy place she'd been looking for for most of her life... it turned out it was right here in Montana in this man's arms.

She laughed happily and wrapped her arms around his neck, kissing his cheek. "I love you, Draven Kilkenny."

"I love you too, India Fox. For now, and for always."

*

I hope you enjoyed Draven & Indy's story as much as I did writing it. To find out more about Gunnar McKinley and The Four X's Group, please click here My Book

BOOKS BY ANNABELLA STONE
(WRITING AS BELLA STONE)

Nemesis Inc. Bravo Team

Rexar

Kentucky

Draven

NEMESIS INC: ALPHA TEAM

Dalton

Cormack

Logan

Rory

MORE BY ANNABELLA STONE
(WRITING AS BELLA STONE)

Nemesis Inc

#0.5 Lina

Will their surprise wedding be their downfall, or will it bring them a love that lasts a lifetime?

Navy SEAL Dalton Knight only wanted a night of drinking with his team brothers. The last thing he expected was to meet the other half of his soul.

Lina Maxwell knew she should have stayed at home. Drinking and dancing is so not her jam. When her drink is spiked, a knight in shining Kevlar insists he marries her to protect her from the demons who haunt her nightmares. Will their surprise wedding be their downfall, or will it bring them a love that lasts a lifetime?

#1 DALTON

The war on terror tore them apart. Will a terrorist bring them back together?

Former Navy SEAL, Dalton *Nemesis* Knight thought he had it all. A Navy career he loved. His SEAL Team brothers, and her… his Lina. The war on terror proved him wrong. It cost him everything, including his wife. With his trust broken, he'd had to find a new way forward and a new system he could believe in. Eventually, he picked the shattered pieces of his broken heart up off the floor and built Nemesis Inc. from the ground up. Now he makes the rules, he signs the checks, and his heart is off the table for good. Nobody is ever going to get close enough to destroy him again.

For years, Lina Maxwell has watched him from the shadows. Cheering his successes and mourning his losses. He's always been hers; she's always been his. Neither anger nor distance can change that. The time has come to gather her courage and fix the wrongs of the past. In leaving him, she protected him the only way she could, Lina needs Nemesis to see that she did not betray him, that she still loves him with everything that she is. Her bosses and her mission will not allow her to make contact. Her whole life is an illusion. She no longer has an identity, no longer has a name. As far as anyone, including her husband, is concerned, she never existed at all.

Just when Lina is ready to ignore her orders and step silently out of the dark, a terrorist wages war on Eastern Europe. With Nemesis running headfirst into danger, she will use every contact and source in her network to protect him. Will showing him she's still alive destroy not only their memories but any chance they might have had of a future?

Will this mission be the bandage to fix two broken hearts, or will it finally destroy them both?

#2 CORMACK

His happy sunshine girl didn't deserve to be pulled into his world of fire and brimstone. All he could do was hope like hell he found her in time.

As a Black Ops Contractor for Nemesis Inc. Cormack *Jeep* Ford, has seen the worst humans can inflict on their fellow man—in some of the shittiest hellholes on earth. With a twenty-year military career under his belt, he's not one bit sorry when Nemesis Inc. relocates from Kabul to Montana. Maybe now his boots are firmly on US soil, he can peruse a happy ever after with woman who calls to his soul.

To Willow Black it feels like she's waited a lifetime for her soldier to come home. Who'd have thought a connection made over emails and letters would lead her to the man who makes her heart and body sing. With Cormack moving back to the US full time, she can't wait to see if the connection between them can withstand the test of time spent in the same freaking time zone. Just when she's starting to believe he may be her happy ever after, a terrorist destroys everything she trusts in— dragging her into the terrifying reality of the world's underbelly.

A man forged in fire and brimstone—a woman made for sunshine and roses—and a terrorist determined to make them pay. Can Cormack convince Willow her life's not over? Can she convince him to let her go? Or will their hearts have the final say?

#3 LOGAN

They say opposites attract, but can two such different people really find an everlasting love?

Losing his parents in the south tower of the World Trade Center on 9/11 changed the trajectory of Logan Sensei Winters' life. Once an up-and-coming MMA fighter, the rancher's kid from the Midwest crossed over the line of right and wrong in a haze of grief-fueled fury. A second twist of fate changed his world again. Nemesis Inc. gave him a soft place to land and taught him how to direct the rage living in his soul toward targets who deserve it—tangos and terrorists across the globe became his focus… until fate threw him yet another twist and cast his meticulously organized life into chaos.

Eedana Crawford is tired of the rules. She's over the 'show the world a happy family in their Sunday best' façade her family demands. There is no way on earth she's giving up the freedom she's worked so hard to earn—spending the rest of her days in her art studio, teaching classes and painting pretty pictures—following her dreams. When a request for a commissioned piece turns those dreams into a nightmare, the freedom she loves becomes impossible to keep. But trusting Mr. Tall, Dark, and Deadly who appears when she needs him would be a bad, bad idea. Right?

Eedana is his to protect—even if she doesn't know it or agree with it. But Logan will make sure she survives The Organization's attempt at a power grab. There is no way in hell he's losing another person he cares passionately about. Not on his watch.

She is his to protect. End. Of. Discussion.

#4 RORY

They say love is a losing game. But what if the only thing you lose is your heart?

Taking his mandated leave was supposed to be a fun trip for Nemesis Inc.'s Alpha Team, recon expert Rory *Mokaccino* Costa. Leave which lasts all of five minutes when a phone call from a teammate sends him to Paris to rescue Adalyn Cassidy and her son, Sam. Changing things up on the fly and living life at a hundred miles an hour is typically his jam. He'll rescue the divorced author and her kid, send them home, and get back to his vacation. A couple of days in the French capital could be fun... right?

It was supposed to be a first author signing for Adalyn's alter ego, Saffron R. Cassidy. She doesn't do people and isn't overly thrilled about crowds, but she'll figure it out as she goes, and hope she doesn't screw up too much. Passing up the opportunity to be the headline signing author in Paris, a signing which could skyrocket her publishing career, would be a stupid move... right? So how did it all go so wrong? She's been beaten, her son is missing, and she has to rely on a complete stranger to save them. A stranger who could have stepped right out of the pages of one of her books. Big, bad, and oh so very swoony, Rory Costa.

He shouldn't touch her.

She shouldn't want him.

Falling in love should not be an option... right?

But what happens when love sneaks in quietly and fills your soul when you least expect it?

More in Nemesis Inc:

Aria

ABOUT THE AUTHOR

Bella Stone is the MF Pen name for Annabella Stone, all books published under this name will be MF. While there may be character crossover to my Annabella stories, the storylines etc. will be different to the story arcs in Panthers, Tags of Honor, etc.

Newsletter/Free book: https://BookHip.com/CTQKFRD
Facebook: https://www.facebook.com/authorbellastone
Website: https://www.annabellastone.com/bella-stone

Annabella Stone and Bella Stone are the alter egos of a wife and mom, who was lucky enough to find happy ever after with her own personal hero.
Annabella loves to write Military Romance and Romantic Suspense where warriors love harder when bullets fly. She believes in love at first sight and wants everyone to have the happy ever they deserve. Even if they have to dodge bullets and fight with everything that they are to get it.
Born and raised in Ireland, Annabella has a Grá for a good story and the breakfast blaa, but funnily enough, prefers Jack Daniels to Irish whiskey. Having lived across 7 countries and 3 continents over the last thirty years, she loves to explore new places and cultures. In her world, coffee is king, and she is 100% sure it deserves it's own food group.
Annabella is owned by a pack of malamutes, whom she loves to both work and show. If you can't find her at the computer writing, chances are she and her woofers have escaped to

enjoy at day at a dog show, or they are on a mountain trail with the dryland rig or the sled, depending on the time of year.

Annabella's motto is "Live life like a malamute who found the gate open, but take the time to enjoy the sights while you're running."

Follow me on social media:

Facebook: https://www.facebook.com/authorbellastone
Instagram: https://www.instagram.com/bellastoneauthor/
BookBub: https://www.bookbub.com/authors/bella-stone
Amazon: https://www.amazon.com/Bella-Stone/e/B09FBQKBZG
Binge Books: https://bingebooks.com/author/bella-stone
Goodreads: https://www.goodreads.com/author/show/17126278.Bella_Stone

There are many more books in this fan fiction world than listed here, for an up-to-date list go to www.AcesPress.com

You can also visit our Amazon page at:
http://www.amazon.com/author/operationalpha

JM Madden: Rescuing Olivia
A.M. Mahler: Griffin
Ellie Masters: Sybil's Protector
Trish McCallan: Hero Under Fire
Naomi McKay: Twist
Rachel McNeely: The SEAL's Surprise Baby
KD Michaels: Saving Laura
Olivia Michaels: Protecting Harper
Annie Miller: Securing Willow
MJ Nightingale: Protecting Beauty
C.K. O'Connor: Delaney's Bodyguard
Melinda Owens: Betraying Katie
Victoria Paige: Reclaiming Izabel
Danielle Pays: Defending Sarina
Lainey Reese: Protecting New York
KeKe Renée: Protecting Bria
Taryn Rivers: Savage Cove
TL Reeve and Michele Ryan: Extracting Mateo
Ariana Rose: Chasing Paige
Deanna L. Rowley: Saving Veronica
Angela Rush: Charlotte
E.M. Shue: Discovering Tyler
Rose Smith: Saving Satin
Tyler Anne Snell: Cowboy Heat
Dee Stewart: Fighting for Brielle
Lynne St. James: SEAL's Spitfire
Bella Stone: Rexar
Jen Talty: Protecting Ainsley
Reina Torres, Rescuing Hi'ilani
LJ Vickery: Circus Comes to Town
R. C. Wynne: Shadows Renewed

Delta Team Three Series
Lori Ryan: Nori's Delta

Becca Jameson: Destiny's Delta
Lynne St James, Gwen's Delta
Elle James: Ivy's Delta
Riley Edwards: Hope's Delta

Police and Fire: Operation Alpha World
Freya Barker: Burning for Autumn
B.P. Beth: Scott
Jane Blythe: Salvaging Marigold
Julia Bright, Justice for Amber
Gia Cobie: Saved from Revenge
Hadley Finn: Exton
Emily Gray: Shelter for Allegra
Danielle M. Haas: Crossroads of Betrayal
Deanndra Hall: Shelter for Sharla
Jenna Harte: Dead But Not Forgotten
Amber Kuhlman: Protecting Paisley
Reina Torres: Justice for Sloane
Aubree Valentine, Justice for Danielle
Maddie Wade: Finding English

Tarpley VFD Series
Silver James, Fighting for Elena
Deanndra Hall, Fighting for Carly
Haven Rose, Fighting for Calliope
MJ Nightingale, Fighting for Jemma
TL Reeve, Fighting for Brittney
Nicole Flockton, Fighting for Nadia

As you know, this book included at least one character from Susan Stoker's books. To check out more, see below.

SEAL Team Hawaii Series
Finding Elodie
Finding Lexie
Finding Kenna
Finding Monica
Finding Carly
Finding Ashlyn
Finding Jodelle

Eagle Point Search & Rescue
Searching for Lilly
Searching for Elsie
Searching for Bristol
Searching for Caryn
Searching for Finley
Searching for Heather
Searching for Khloe (May 2024)

The Refuge Series
Deserving Alaska
Deserving Henley
Deserving Reese
Deserving Cora
Deserving Lara (Feb 2024)
Deserving Maisy (Oct 2024)
Deserving Ryleigh (TBA)

SEAL of Protection: Alliance Series
Protecting Remi (July 2024)
Protecting Wren (Nov 2024)

Protecting Josie (TBA)
Protecting Maggie (TBA)
Protecting Addison (TBA)
Protecting Kelli (TBA)
Protecting Bree (TBA)

Delta Team Two Series
Shielding Gillian
Shielding Kinley
Shielding Aspen
Shielding Jayme (novella)
Shielding Riley
Shielding Devyn
Shielding Ember
Shielding Sierra

SEAL of Protection: Legacy Series
Securing Caite (FREE!)
Securing Brenae (novella)
Securing Sidney
Securing Piper
Securing Zoey
Securing Avery
Securing Kalee
Securing Jane

Delta Force Heroes Series
Rescuing Rayne (FREE!)
Rescuing Aimee (novella)
Rescuing Emily
Rescuing Harley
Marrying Emily (novella)
Rescuing Kassie
Rescuing Bryn

Rescuing Casey
Rescuing Sadie (novella)
Rescuing Wendy
Rescuing Mary
Rescuing Macie (novella)
Rescuing Annie

Badge of Honor: Texas Heroes Series
Justice for Mackenzie (FREE!)
Justice for Mickie
Justice for Corrie
Justice for Laine (novella)
Shelter for Elizabeth
Justice for Boone
Shelter for Adeline
Shelter for Sophie
Justice for Erin
Justice for Milena
Shelter for Blythe
Justice for Hope
Shelter for Quinn
Shelter for Koren
Shelter for Penelope

SEAL of Protection Series
Protecting Caroline (FREE!)
Protecting Alabama
Protecting Fiona
Marrying Caroline (novella)
Protecting Summer
Protecting Cheyenne
Protecting Jessyka
Protecting Julie (novella)
Protecting Melody

Protecting the Future
Protecting Kiera (novella)
Protecting Alabama's Kids (novella)
Protecting Dakota

New York Times, *USA Today* and *Wall Street Journal* Bestselling Author Susan Stoker has a heart as big as the state of Tennessee where she lives, but this all American girl has also spent the last fourteen years living in Missouri, California, Colorado, Indiana, and Texas. She's married to a retired Army man who now gets to follow *her* around the country.

www.stokeraces.com
www.AcesPress.com
susan@stokeraces.com

Made in the USA
Columbia, SC
13 June 2025

59386607R00161